MAZE OF MADNESS

Dr. Jennifer Westwood had to keep telling herself she was sane—for no one else would believe it.

The doctors she worked with at Montrose Clinic called her growing suspicions about what was being done to patients there the product of a hypersensitive, perhaps unbalanced imagination.

The law and the press would have turned a deaf ear if she went to them for help.

The only one who would even listen was one of her own patients, a police detective himself on the verge of a breakdown even as both of them trembled on the edge of a love affair.

But Jennifer knew she was far from alone as she followed the twisting trail toward the fearful truth. Watching her every move . . . waiting for her first unguarded moment . . . were those who were bent on making her, too, a victim of—

THE MEDUSA SYNDROME

Exciting Fiction from SIGNET

(0451)

- [ ] **THE DEVIL TO PAY** by Earl Thompson. (119096—$3.95)*
- [ ] **RED SUNSET** by John Stockwell. (119126—$3.50)*
- [ ] **HEADING WEST** by Doris Betts. (119134—$3.50)*
- [ ] **DEATH BY GASLIGHT** by Michael Kurland. (119150—$3.50)*
- [ ] **HEART CHANGE** by Lynn Freed. (119169—$3.50)*
- [ ] **FEVER** by Robin Cook. (119932—$3.95)*
- [ ] **NIGHT CALL FROM A DISTANT TIME ZONE** by Herbert Lieberman. (119940—$3.50)*
- [ ] **SHAWNEE DAWN (The Indian Heritage Series #2)** by Paul Joseph Lederer. (120000—$2.95)*
- [ ] **WINTER LORD** by Jean Brooks-Janowiak. (120027—$2.95)*
- [ ] **FALLBACK** by Peter Niesewand. (120531—$3.95)*
- [ ] **NIGHT SANCTUARY** by Monique Van Vooren. (120558—$3.95)*
- [ ] **WATCHDOG** by Faith Sullivan. (120566—$2.95)*
- [ ] **THE MEDUSA SYNDROME** by Ron Cutler. (120574—$2.95)*
- [ ] **WINTER OF THE WHITE SEAL** by Marie Herbert. (120612—$3.50)†
- [ ] **THE NIGHT CHASERS** by Jamey Cohen. (120604—$3.50)*

*Prices slightly higher in Canada
†Not available in Canada

Buy them at your local bookstore or use this convenient coupon for ordering.

THE NEW AMERICAN LIBRARY, INC.,
P.O. Box 999, Bergenfield, New Jersey 07621

Please send me the books I have checked above. I am enclosing $_____
(please add $1.00 to this order to cover postage and handling). Send check or money order—no cash or C.O.D.'s. Prices and numbers are subject to change without notice.

Name_____

Address_____

City _____ State _____ Zip Code _____

The
Medusa
Syndrome

By Ron Cutler

A SIGNET BOOK
NEW AMERICAN LIBRARY
TIMES MIRROR

This book is dedicated to my daughter, Morgan
Jennifer, with all my love and affection.

PUBLISHER'S NOTE

This novel is a work of fiction. Names, characters, places,
and incidents are either the product of the author's imagination or are used fictitiously, and any resemblance to actual per-
sons, living or dead, events, or locales is entirely coincidental.

NAL BOOKS ARE AVAILABLE AT QUANTITY DISCOUNTS
WHEN USED TO PROMOTE PRODUCTS OR SERVICES. FOR
INFORMATION PLEASE WRITE TO PREMIUM MARKETING
DIVISION, THE NEW AMERICAN LIBRARY, INC., 1633
BROADWAY, NEW YORK, NEW YORK 10019.

SIGNET, SIGNET CLASSICS, MENTOR, PLUME, MERIDIAN AND NAL
BOOKS *are published by The New American Library, Inc.,*
1633 Broadway, New York, New York 10019

FIRST PRINTING, FEBRUARY, 1983

    1   2   3   4   5   6   7   8   9

PRINTED IN THE UNITED STATES OF AMERICA

PROLOGUE

No one on the subway platform noticed the young woman in the black cashmere coat. There was nothing special about her to arouse anyone's interest. Not at first anyway. Not until she started to jump.

Mary Ann was more smartly dressed than most. She carried a handsome brown leather pouch over her shoulder and a model's zippered portfolio in one of her gloved hands. Her hair had been cut in the breezy style being shown just then in some of the more exclusive Madison Avenue salons. But most of the people around her would not have known that. They did not shop on Madison or frequent its fashionable hairstylists. Most were overweight office workers returning to their homes in the outer boroughs. They stared straight ahead with pupils as animated as the electric eye of a supermarket door. None of them would have remembered Mary Ann's face, which had stared out at them from so many magazine and subway ads. Standing there now she was just another face in the mass of passengers lining the platform of the midtown IND station.

Mary Ann's features were scrubbed clean of makeup. Without it, she was no longer striking enough to break through the boredom and disinterest around her. No one took particular notice of the peculiar way her eyes glittered or the unnatural way she folded her elbows against her sides, as if

1

she were afraid of touching those around her. In seconds'
time, the thundering monster of steel and glass would come
crashing along the tracks and the young woman would be
pressed against the others, inhaling the sour smells of the
crowded car. But the train was late. Eyes darted back along
the darkened tunnel or glanced impatiently at their watches,
then looked upward in exasperation.

Mary Ann was edged closer to the platform's edge. Her
eyes read but did not record the name of the station. She had
been swept down with the crowd from the street above and
was unaware of her location. Her eyes drifted to the trickle
of dirty water running between the rails, then traced the
scrawls of graffiti on the tile walls. The furtive darting of two
gray mice made no impression on her, nor did the moldering
swill between the tracks. Mary Ann saw nothing but the vel-
vet darkness of the tunnel with its glimmer of yellow lights
disappearing into nowhere and the silver shimmer on the
curving rails. She felt hypnotized by the silence, until she
sensed the powerful force hurtling toward her out of the
darkness. Mary Ann felt its power, like the beckoning hand
of a spirit, irresistible and final. Promising an end to her agony, to the round of rejections in a failed career. Mary Ann
felt the bodies around her surge forward as if they partook of
her knowledge and were about to share this journey with her.

"Hey, watch out! She's gonna jump!"

With a voiceless cry, Mary Ann threw herself off the edge
into the thundering darkness speeding toward her with the de-
vouring force of a demon.

Mary Ann Spreull . . .
Mary Ann heard the voice clearly through the din of
voices around her. Someone was calling her name. She raised
her head and glanced around at the other faces in the hospital waiting area. The lobby was crowded. People sat or
sprawled on leather benches waiting to be taken into the
series of small rooms that opened along the paneled corridor
on either side. Each time one of the doors opened, Mary Ann
saw one of the doctors seated behind his desk in a long white
coat.

At the far end of the area, women moved back and forth
between an office and a counter that was continually mobbed

with people. Some of the women wore long white coats with plastic name tags pinned to their lapels. Mary Ann wished she were one of them. Anything was better than being seated beside her mother with everyone staring at the wide gauze bandage that circled her head. She felt like an exhibit in a museum.

"Mary Ann, we can go in now," she heard her mother say in a patient voice. Her mother looked out of place as usual. She was a short woman with mousy gray hair, dressed in a badly fitting fall coat and cheap shoes. Mary Ann always felt sorry for her mother. Now she was saddled with the burden of her daughter as she had once been saddled with a husband who drank too much and earned too little and had died leaving not enough insurance to cover the cheap frame house in the dingy Long Island development where Mary Ann had grown up.

Mary Ann rose when her mother did. Together they walked toward an attractive woman in her late thirties wearing a dark woolen dress beneath her starched white coat. Her name tag read, Dr. Benjamin. Mary Ann noticed her stylishly cut hair just as she noticed Dr. Benjamin's expensive shoes and fine gold jewelry. She reminded Mary Ann of the sharp-eyed woman who ran her modeling agency. But the woman's name was just out of reach, lying in a heap of letters beyond the edge of the huge plate of gleaming china her mind had become

Dr. Benjamin stood beside an open door holding a folder in her hand. She smiled warmly at Mary Ann but said something to her mother that caused the older woman to back away with a resigned expression. "You'll have to go in alone, dear," her mother said. Mary Ann was pleased. Her mother always made her feel embarrassed.

Mary Ann entered the room and glanced around. It was not a large room. Bookshelves lined one wall opposite a window made of an intersecting metal grid separating the panes. Mary Ann could see the books were never read. There were only three chairs. One was already occupied by a dark, heavyset man Mary Ann's roommates would have called cute but chubby. He looked about forty-five and had thinning hair and a badly shaven face showing red and irritated blotches above his blue collar and knit tie. His vest rolled over waves of fat beneath his wrinkled white coat. His name tag read Dr. Boise. He looked at Mary Ann with the solemn expression of a minister who's just learned you've had an abortion.

Dr. Benjamin closed the door and told Mary Ann to sit down. Then she seated herself and began speaking in a soft tone. "Mary Ann, my name is Dr. Benjamin. I'm an admitting psychiatrist. This is Dr. Boise. He's one of our supervisors here at Montrose. His job is to find a suitable doctor should you want to stay here and be treated."

Mary Ann felt the china plate in her head tilt first to one side then the other. There were words on the plate but Mary Ann could not get them to roll into a pattern. She watched Dr. Benjamin's wide mouth begin to move like a soundless motor.

"Can you tell us why you want to be admitted to Montrose?"

Mary Ann stared at Dr. Benjamin, wondering how to answer. She felt so far away from everything, seated somewhere in the middle of her plate. Answering took as much effort as posing in front of a camera.

"Is it hard to answer my question, Mary Ann?"

Mary Ann shook her head firmly. "No. I can answer. It's because I tried to kill myself."

"Why did you feel you wanted to do that?"

Mary Ann felt the doctor knew the answer to the question. She was like the people in her modeling agency, always asking questions that were really little traps. You could never be right, no matter how you answered. Mary Ann wanted to laugh. Instead, she said, "I didn't feel very good about myself. I didn't feel anyone really cared about me."

"How long have you been feeling this way?"

"I don't know. For a long time, I guess."

Dr. Benjamin nodded in an understanding way. "What do you think we can do to help you?"

"I think you could help me feel better."

"Do you want to feel better?"

"I think so," Mary Ann answered. The truth was she did not feel anything. She was in a wonderful place where nothing could hurt her. Answering Dr. Benjamin's question was like being back at school telling a teacher what she wanted to hear.

"If you stay here, you will have to agree to follow all the rules set by your doctor and nurses. Do you think you will be able to do that?"

Mary Ann nodded. Then she watched Dr. Benjamin slip a printed sheet out of her folder. Mary Ann was handed a pen and was told to sign at the bottom, after which Dr. Benjamin informed her she was being admitted as a voluntary patient. Mary Ann found herself staring at another printed sheet outlining her rights. But when she tried to read the lines blurred together like subway tracks.

Dr. Benjamin rose and went to the door. "All right, Mary Ann someone will take you up to your room now. We're glad you're here with us." Her words almost sounded recorded.

"Can my mother come with me?"

"Yes. But only for a little while."

Mary Ann rose and went to the door. A young man in jeans and a sweat shirt stood outside. Dr. Benjamin introduced him as Mark. He would take Mary Ann upstairs. To her mother, Dr. Benjamin said, "We're glad Mary Ann has decided to remain with us for treatment. We think this is the right place for her. She'll be going up to her room now. You can go along with her for a short time. We'd like you to see Mary Ann's social worker and Dr. Freedman, her treating psychiatrist."

Mary Ann watched her mother absorb the words. Then Dr. Benjamin excused herself to take a call and Mark picked up Mary Ann's suitcase and led the way to the elevator. Inside, there was a mirror and Mary Ann stared at her reflection. Without makeup her face looked as pale as a negative. Nothing like the images in her portfolio. Which was her real face, she wondered; this one in the glass or the other in the glossies. She began to feel a sense of panic. What was she doing here? She had rounds to make. Appointments to keep. She felt trapped in fibers of spun glass. *Help me, someone help me, someone help me. . . .*

The elevator doors opened.

Mary Ann faced a long corridor half paneled in dark wood. Her first impression was of the hotel for women she had first stayed at on the Upper East Side. It too was a relic of another era. The doors they passed were as wide as the hotel's, as were the rooms beyond. The carpeting was worn and some of the walls needed painting. They were a tint of pale green like dying grass.

Mark stopped in front of the nurse's station. Through the large plate-glass window Mary Ann could see the nurses inside. None of them was dressed like a nurse. Like Mark they wore informal clothing. Glancing around, Mary Ann saw two telephones in closed booths and a dining room behind a closed glass door. Opposite she saw was an open lounge filled with shabby furniture.

Several nurses came out to be introduced to Mary Ann. Their names did not register but formed a little pile of letters on her plate. They all smiled and remarked how pretty her hair was. Mary Ann watched her own hand rise to touch her hair. When it contacted the bandage she winced in pain.

Mark disappeared and a blond nurse picked up her bag and led them around a turning. Mary Ann heard a TV and noticed a room at the end of the corridor with people sitting around a color set. Her own room was two doors away. It was softly lit and furnished with a walnut dresser and desk. A single bed was covered in flowered chintz like her room at home. On it was an assortment of folded night clothing. There was a spacious tiled bathroom with an old-fashioned tub on legs. The bathroom door had a large glass window. The room door also had a window. Another window offered a view of the Manhattan skyline across the East River. Mary Ann remembered the hospital was on an island. She remembered crossing a bridge to get here but the other details of the cab ride were too difficult to recall.

Mary Ann watched her clothes being put away. The nurse removed her razor, an injector-blade pack, a small cuticle scissors, and her eyebrow pencils. Then the nurse told her to change into the clothes on the bed. Mary Ann would have to wear them for the next forty-eight hours. After that she could wear her own clothes. Then the nurse left, saying she would be back in ten minutes.

Mary Ann allowed her mother to help her undress and get into the pajamas and robe. Turning, Mary Ann caught a glimpse of her naked breasts above the grooves of her rib cage. How stupid she had been to jump. She was already a skeleton.

When her mother tried to comb her hair, she hurt the

wound in her head but Mary Ann did not cry out. The pain was too distant to bother about.

The nurse returned and led Mary Ann along the corridor to the lounge. She explained that Mary Ann was to remain on center lounge restriction for the next twenty-four hours, except for sleep and meals and when she was called for various examinations.

The nurse had a pretty face and smiled reassuringly before she left, but Mary Ann did not return the expression. Other people sat around her in the lounge. Some stared at her bandage, others were indifferent and looked through her as if she weren't there. A teenage girl passed back and forth speaking in a loud voice, but what she said made no sense. An old woman stared out a window listlessly. A very tall young man with a long neck went back and forth to a small refrigerator, looking for something he never found. Mary Ann was not concerned. She remained where she was, staring at the schedule she had been given.

Breakfast was at seven-thirty, after which there was something called "RT." Visiting hours were from two to three, followed by a forty-minute session with Dr. Freedman. More RT followed. There was also dance therapy and group therapy. Visitors were again allowed from seven to nine. Before Mary Ann could memorize the schedule as she had been told to do, a nurse arrived with a bottle for a urine specimen. Mary Ann was led to a bathroom. Then she had some blood drawn. She watched it flow into the hypo, dark and purplish like dye from an orchid. Mary Ann watched the nurse put a small Band-Aid over the wound; then she was escorted along a corridor and through a door at the end of the TV lounge to Dr. Freedman's office.

Dr. Freedman wore a white coat and a name tag over a blue button-down shirt and rep tie. He was much younger than Mary Ann expected. His hair was light brown and combed in a low sweep over his forehead. He was not really handsome but his features were regular and he was pleasant to look at. He reminded Mary Ann of the young men who tried to pick her up at singles' bars.

"You're a lucky young woman," he said when the nurse had left and Mary Ann was seated in a chair beside his desk. "That was quite a fall you took. Do you have any pain?"

"My head hurts a little. And my elbow and hip."

"Do you feel any dizziness?"

"Only once in a while."

Dr. Freedman asked Mary Ann to stand and hold her arms straight out, then touch her nose. Then he asked her to count backward from one hundred. Then to subtract by nines. Mary Ann did everything she was told though it was painful to concentrate.

"Can you tell me the names of the presidents, starting now and going back in time?"

Mary Ann felt silly doing so, but she had always been good at history and rattled off the names until he stopped her at Truman.

"Very good. Now I'm going to give you a physical examination. Will you please undress."

Mary Ann felt awkward. She did not want to show him her body. "Wouldn't you rather see my portfolio?" she asked.

"No. I want to see the real thing," he said with a smile.

Mary Ann slipped off her robe and unbuttoned her pajamas while Dr. Freedman questioned her about a whole list of diseases. Then he drew a stool close to her. "You're a very pretty young woman," he said placing the stethoscope against her chest. Mary Ann winced from the feel of cold metal. "You're a model aren't you?"

"Part of me was."

"And the rest of you. What was it doing while you were modeling?"

Mary Ann focused on that for a moment. "I don't know."

She followed the doctor's instructions to breathe in and out. He surprised her by putting his hands on her breasts and kneading them very slowly. He did not really look down at her breasts, which were small but very firm. Mary Ann had always been ashamed of them until she became a model and their smallness became an asset. She wondered if the doctor wanted to have sex with her. It would not be any more of an imposition than the needle they had jabbed into her arm.

Dr. Freedman took her blood pressure and tested her reflexes with a triangular hammer. Then he gently felt her groin. He probed her ears with a light and then her eyes. He examined the bruises on her body and removed the gauze bandage from her head. She endured the sting when the padding came away.

"That's a pretty nasty gash. We're going to have to take some pictures of it. Okay?"

Mary Ann nodded. She felt tired and wished she could sleep. But he was not finished with her. After he told her to get dressed he moved her to a table against the window. She saw trees and the outline of buildings farther away down the island. She noticed for the first time that while there was regular glass in the windows, the panes were so crisscrossed with metal strips that no human being could slip out of one.

Mary Ann was asked to draw a picture of herself. Then to draw her mother and her father. Dr. Freedman asked her a long list of words and she had to say the first thing that came into her head. Then he showed her inkblots and asked what she saw in them. After that he asked her a series of questions that reminded her of the SATs but were not as difficult.

When he was done, he said, "That's fine, Mary Ann. That's enough for one day. I know you're tired. Why don't you go back to your room and take it easy before dinner. Do you want me to send for the nurse or can you find your own way?"

"I can go by myself."

"Good. Then we'll see you tomorrow. Come when it says on the schedule, okay?"

Mary Ann nodded and waited for Dr. Freedman to open the door. Then she went out.

When she was gone, Dr. Freedman returned to his desk. The doctor was thirty-four and a resident in psychiatry with a degree from a prestigious eastern university. He had been employed at Montrose for a little over a year. Mary Ann Spreull had a type of affective disorder he was very familiar with. It was too early to make a firm diagnosis but all the evidence pointed to a form of depression. Most of his patients fitted into that category. The pressures of mid-twentieth-century existence made the ordinary individual as susceptible to depressive syndromes as a coal miner was to black lung disease.

Mary Ann was fortunate. She was young and physically healthy. No evidence of mental illness appeared in her background, so far. Dr. Freedman was confident he would have Mary Ann out of Montrose and into an outpatient program within the fabled thirty days. Montrose was famous for its thirty-day rehab. That was the period of coverage most medical insurance policies allotted for a mental condition. With hospital costs climbing past the ten-thousand-dollar-a-month point, it became necessary to limit the average patient stay to no longer than one month. Naturally, no patient was ever discharged if his case took more time to resolve. But Montrose was not a long-term-care facility, which would, moreover, entail emergency Medicare funds and "Time es moolah, *kinder*," Dr. Freedman liked to joke, with a thick, mock-Viennese accent.

Much of the treatment at Montrose consisted of controlling a patient's symptoms with an arsenal of antidepressant drugs, ranging from the more traditional tricylics to the newest mode of tetracyclics. These newer medications were almost miraculous in their ability to alleviate the more oppressive symptoms of gloom and detachment. They did this without the arrhythmias and rapid blood pressure changes that were side effects of the earlier medications. Once the symptoms were controlled, the patient was referred to an appropriate therapeutic modality as an outpatient.

At the moment, Dr. Freedman was as concerned with the trauma to Mary Ann's skull as he was with her depression. She had been fortunate that her fall on the tracks produced only a few minor lacerations, except for the deep gash in the side of her head. She had been taken to the emergency room at Bellevue—the best of its kind in the country. They had cleaned and sutured the lesion but her X rays showed a hairline fracture. Getting hold of these X rays, however, constituted a bureaucratic hurdle he preferred not to leap. He would have a new set made and get the resident neurologist to examine them. In the meantime, Mary Ann would be given an EEG to determine if there were any irregularities in her brain-wave pattern. Should these appear, Dr. Freedman would have to order a CAT scan of her brain.

Dr. Freedman glanced at the pictures Mary Ann had drawn. They showed a negative personality pattern. Then he picked up the Rorschach test. Normally, the inkblot and other tests would have been administered by Dr. Brady, the clinical psychologist. But Brady had not reported for work that day, which dumped things squarely into Dr. Freedman's lap. He held off notifying Dr. Boise of Brady's absence, but he was sure someone else would. It took little guesswork to figure out who would actually report him. Dr. Boise had his little spy on the staff. But that was not Dr. Freedman's concern. It was four o'clock. He still had one more patient to see and a slew of medication forms to write. Shit! He hoped Brady got his ass roasted.

Mary Ann felt uncomfortable about being rolled along the corridor in a wheelchair. Earlier, an overweight technician in a badly fitted toupee had attached electrodes to her head in a small room filled with electronic equipment, none of which she had ever seen before. Now her wound throbbed with pain. A salve, which had been applied beneath the electrodes, gave Mary Ann the feeling that her hair was saturated with Vaseline. It made her skin crawl.

Mary Ann had been asked to lie flat on a table during the procedure. Beside her stood a machine with a needle that danced across a sheet of graph paper that unrolled like an endless tongue. The technician had asked her various questions, telling her to think the responses rather than say them. After a while, Mary Ann felt dizzy and told the technician, who then stopped the machine and removed the electrodes.

Mary Ann was led back into her room, but no sooner had she fallen asleep than a nurse arrived with the chair to take her upstairs for what she called a CAT scan. The nurse explained that this was a picture of her brain, promised it would not hurt, and asked Mary Ann if she was allergic to shellfish because the latter was an ingredient in the dye they would use to color her brain so it would record on film. Mary Ann had no recollection of any such allergy and said so. But the image of tiny helpless shrimp being ground up and injected into her body sickened her more than the Vaseline had. She also had to sign a permission form, which she agreed to do after the nurse explained Dr. Freedman's concern about her skull injury.

Mary Ann was wheeled into a room with one glass wall behind which she could see a light-skinned black man busy with a series of dials. On one side was a wall made entirely of metal. A hemisphere had been inserted in the center; Mary Ann assumed this was where her head would go during the filming. The nurse instructed her not to move while she adjusted the table and injected the dye. Mary Ann winced when the needle was inserted and pretended to listen to the nurse explain how the scan actually worked.

The machine on the wall behind her was a huge camera that would move around her head while she lay still. Mary Ann's mind digested this information, but the rest of what she was told blurred into the background noise. Mary Ann was a model. Being photographed was almost second nature to her. Only this time they were interested in the inside of her head not the outside. Mary Ann wondered how that would look on the cover of *Vogue*.

The nurse left the room and closed the door. Mary Ann lay still, keeping her eyes open. She heard the whir of a motor and began to feel a little uneasy. Over the intercom she heard the nurse's voice telling her to relax and begin counting backward from one hundred. Mary Ann began to count as she had done before. Her eyelids began to feel very heavy, even though she remembered someone telling her she would be awake during the scan. She tried to resist but her lids felt like closing shutters. She was being drawn into a deep and powerful slumber.

Images circulated in her mind, combined with a sense of movement. She felt as if she was traveling on a slow-motion roller coaster, going in and out of darkness. Every few moments she felt the movement and heard the sound of wheels rolling over linoleum. She was in the subway tunnel again. Only now she was moving instead of the train. Light flickered beneath her lids but she could not raise them to see. The glare of a distant station shot toward her out of the blackness then was swallowed up again as she moved by. She caught glimpses of people staring down at her. They were people she knew. But their faces were elongated like grimaces in a funhouse mirror.

She saw the lonely figure of her mother on the platform above her, staring down with a mournful expression. A red-faced policeman leaned over her and whispered that everything was going to be all right. Dr. Benjamin's face loomed out of the darkness, her mouth twisted in a grotesque smile. There was another man beside her, who looked like a benign grandfather wearing a helmet of silver. Then she awoke.

She was enclosed in a gleaming circle of light. Faces stared at her, distorted faces pressed against glass with flattened noses and lips like fish in an aquarium. Mary Ann felt as if she were drowning among these twisted masks. She heard voices but they sounded distant, as though she was hearing them underwater. Something was being fitted around her head. It touched her wound and she shuddered with pain. But this time the pain would not stop. It felt like a thousand needles drilling into her head.

Mary Ann felt her brain turning into fire. She forced her eyes open. She was no longer dreaming. The terrible faces around her were real. She saw eyes staring down above green masks that shrouded their mouths. *Then she saw the snakes.*

They were alive, slithering and twisting above her head. Their mouths were enormous, and were filled with gleaming fangs.

She heard her own scream fill her head but no sound emerged. *Please, no . . . don't let them . . .* But her lips would not form the words. She twisted her body, trying to raise her arms, but her hands would not obey her commands. They felt paralyzed, part of the table itself.

Mary Ann surged against the restraints, opening her mouth to scream, feeling the terror deep in her throat, but she was not able to cry out. Her eyes bulged, rolling backward as the black shapes slithered and coiled around her face, hissing and stabbing with their wet tongues. *Oh God, please help me . . . don't let them . . . please don't let them touch me. . . .*

The plate in her head began to crack. She felt her mind beginning to divide like jagged splinters of porcelain. She tried to keep it from coming apart but she was too frightened. *God help me. . . .*

But God would not help her. No one could help her. The shapes hissing and twisting around her head were not part of a dream. They were alive and they were growing out of the top of her own head. They were being born in her own mind.

The scream, when it finally came, rose in a single terrifying wail. Then the plate shattered into a hundred pieces.

Dr. Freedman stared at the report on the desk in front of him with a sickening feeling. The sensation was even worse because the report was his own. It documented the clinical history of a patient admitted only three days before with no recognizable history of mental disorders, who was suffering from what apparently was a treatable condition of affective psychosis yet who had been suddenly drawn into the bottomless horror of paranoid schizophrenia.

Around him was all the data. Psychological tests, lab tests, medical history, neurological analysis, EEG, Cat scan. No matter how many times he went over the results they still remained a mystery. All the scientific data modern medicine could muster and they still failed to yield a single clue.

Dr. Freedman had graduated second in his class in med school. At Montrose he had compiled an enviable record of success. Something like the report before him both irritated and depressed him. Schizophrenia is to psychiatric medicine what cancer is to biological medicine: it defied all attempts to find a cure, a cause, even an acceptable definition. *But why was this happening to him?* Freedman felt as if he had received a visitation from hell, a personal plague of locusts, or something equally unfathomable.

It was true that schizoid symptoms manifested themselves with alarming suddenness in young women of Mary Ann Spreull's age. Still, something usually preceded it. Here there was nothing. To have seen a beautiful girl turn into an uncontrollably violent lunatic was more than unnerving. It bit into the very core of his self-confidence.

For the umpteenth time, Dr. Freedman picked up the drawing Dr. Brady, the clinical psychologist, had given him an hour earlier. There were a dozen more of the same stacked in the file. All were variations on the same theme. They showed the outline of a woman's head, her face horribly distorted as if she was suffering some great agony. But the most distinctive aspect of the drawings made him shudder. Growing out of the top of the woman's skull was a thicket of twisting lines that looked like . . . *like what?*

Dr. Freedman stared at it for another moment before he put it down. The paper floated to the top of the file and then it struck him. *A nest of living vipers.* That's what it looked like. A Medusa head of growing serpents. *Snakes . . .*

He felt a sudden tremor of recognition. He had seen something like this before. But where? He wracked his brain for several moments but nothing came. *C'mon you schmuck, remember . . .* "My God!" he said aloud. "Of course!" And suddenly he knew.

In a moment he was on his feet, searching rapidly through his files. Suddenly he stopped. The file he was searching for was missing. But that was impossible. Dr. Freedman's forehead wrinkled, his eyes narrowed. Something was wrong, very wrong. *This could not be happening. . . .*

ONE

Dr. Jennifer Westwood could not resist unfolding the telegram she carried in her brown leather bag and rereading it for the tenth time since its arrival yesterday morning. The words had not changed, but the message was still unbelievable. It simply read: CONGRATULATIONS. RESIDENCY CONFIMED. BE PREPARED TO ASSUME DUTIES, 10-18. Simple, but they had changed her whole life.

The content seemed much too mundane to produce such incredible excitement inside her. But the words had set off a propulsion of activity that transported Jennifer over the short period of twenty-four hours from the quiet residential Washington, D.C., suburb where her parents lived to the frenzy of the arrivals building at LaGuardia Airport in New York. Seated now in the backseat of a battered yellow cab, she listened to Latin rhythms from the driver's radio while he negotiated his way through the congestion of Manhattan's East Side Drive.

The entire process seemed miraculous and Jennifer glanced around her with wide and glistening eyes. She felt like a child being taken to see her first department-store Santa. It was very unlike her normally unflappable demeanor and in a very definite way she was enjoying the contrast. She was also enjoying the sequence of events that was not only moving her from one geographical location to another but altering her mental state as well.

Exactly five days before Jennifer had been in the lowest

17

depths of a stomach-grinding depression. She had celebrated
the weekend of her twenty-seventh birthday trying to pull her
self out of the gloom produced by her rejection as a candi-
date for residency at one of California's finest psychiatric
hospitals. Jennifer knew she was more than qualified, even
with the competition as fierce as it was. She had graduated
within the top five percent of her medical-school class and
had received glowing recommendations from both her professors and supervisors at the Baltimore University Hospital
where she had interned.

Jennifer could have understood a rejection if it had been
based on merit. But the real reason produced such an ungov-
ernable frustration it made her feel as if she had been shoved
through a meat grinder. Pure and simple, Jennifer had been
the victim of reverse discrimination. Her application had
been subject to the quota system meant to prevent the
discrimination against her sex that had existed for so long in
medicine. Unfortunately, the hospital already had a large per-
centage of women doctors on its staff, including those on the
admissions committee. That was where the problem lay. To
add insult to injury, there were already too many female applicants as well as other, equally deserving minorities to play
affirmative action with.

Jennifer's reaction had been even more acute since this was
the first real obstacle she had encountered in her young life
that she had not been able to overcome. It was even more
ironic since she had gone through several career changes before deciding on medicine. In a way the choice had also been
her family's, although she had come to fall in love with "the
bridegroom" after the marriage, as she sometimes liked to
picture it. Jennifer had first chosen law, then social work,
then acting. She had been well suited for all three but most
of all for the last. Her college drama teachers had actively
encouraged her to pursue a career in theater or films. Not
only was she talented but she had been gifted with the most
elusive of qualities an actor can have—charisma.

The special presence she possessed was ascertainable the
moment she entered a room. Along with a willowy figure and
long dancer's legs, full hips and breasts, Jennifer had also
been graced with facial beauty. She had striking black eyes,
dark vibrant hair, and a straight, almost Grecian nose set between cheekbones that were both high and slanted. But what

impressed the directors of her college plays most was the quality of expression she brought to a role. Jennifer had that rare ability of being able to project her thoughts on her countenance, which proved something less than an asset in certain of her academic classrooms. Not only had her good looks bred a certain suspicion that her mind had to be less than first-rate, but her charismatic presence created even more discomfort, especially among certain professors who might have excused it had they been able to sleep with her. Many of them tried. Jennifer had gone through several teaching assistantships only to discover she had only been appointed to give one or another professor a chance to get her in the sack.

Jennifer was not entirely unaware of the ache she inspired in certain males, nor was she immune to aching herself now and then. It was just that Jennifer's background bred a certain degree of competitiveness and drive that made anything but academic excellence a cause for deep existential *angst*. Perhaps it was to combat these feelings that Jennifer was first led to psychiatry. In any case, it was a field she seemed to have a natural bent for. The ability to gain insight into others showed itself early. Jennifer might have been isolated because of her beauty. Instead, her almost intuitive understanding of the feelings of others made her a favorite confidant among her girl friends. As she progressed through high school and college those who confided in her came to include males as well. Spilling out their souls to Jennifer became a regular practice and sometimes even interfered with her studies.

This insight aided her in acting as well, and was one of the reasons her drama teachers had been so encouraging. But sometime in her sophomore year, Jennifer experienced a sense of mission, a need for something deeper and more important than a career in show business. Only medicine seemed to offer the means of answering the questions she asked of life. But it came with a price. Jennifer found that the beauty, which had been such an asset as a dramatics major, now became a liability. By her second year in med school she had learned to camouflage her appearance behind a drab matter-of-fact exterior. She wore no makeup and concealed her figure beneath a shapeless hospital coat. While not actually erasing the effect of her looks completely, it diminished their obvious impact and made her life a lot more tolerable.

The drive to excel, however, still kept Jennifer at the head of her class, even earning recognition from a group of professors who were free of the taint of male prejudice. That was why the rejection of her application came as such a shock. Jennifer could not really accept the idea that she might have been refused merely on the basis of her sex. Luckily, she had not been allowed to lick her wounds for very long. The rejection letter arrived on a Friday. Jennifer had spent the weekend of her birthday at her parents' home. Monday arrived with a nine-o'clock phone call. When her father handed her the telephone, Jennifer was surprised to hear the voice of Doug Andrews, one of her favorite professors at med school. He had been the one who encouraged her to apply to the California hospital and Jennifer had contacted him immediately after her rejection. He had hung up saying he'd see what he could do. But Jennifer did not expect the words that poured from his excited lips when he called back. Nor did she truly believe what she was hearing.

A vacancy had suddenly opened at the Montrose Clinic in New York, one of the country's premier psychiatric centers. One of the residents, a doctor named Freedman, had met with a freak accident. Andrews had been surprised by the news over the weekend, hearing it from none other than Dr. Kessler himself, the clinic's director. Kessler had contacted Andrews in the hope that he might be able to recommend someone to fill the position until the end of Dr. Freedman's contract, eight months hence. Kessler would prefer a woman and Doug immediately mentioned Jennifer. "You're just the kind of person Kessler is looking for." Jennifer did not quite understand what Doug meant by that and she was much to frightened to ask for an explanation.

The explosion behind the words came seconds after Jennifer matter-of-factly agreed to fly up to New York the following morning for an interview. Jennifer was dazed. She had only been able to mumble her thanks to her professor and barely answered her parents' excited questions. What Andrews had done was the equivalent of a journalist receiving a Pulitzer Prize. Montrose was tops. One did not simply apply for a residency. One was *invited* to apply. So difficult was it to get accepted that Jennifer had not even considered attempting an application. Besides it was one of the few all-male preserves still left in psychiatric medicine.

Dr. Kessler was one of the country's—if not the world's—

leading specialists. He had recently made a breakthrough in the field of psychopharmacology with a drug named Nitholin. The drug was still in the experimental stage but it had already been cited as creating a remarkable susceptibility to suggestion in certain patients, almost akin to hypnosis, that produced incredible behavioral changes. It was the threshold of a whole new concept. The changing of personality through the use of drug therapy.

Jennifer did not delude herself into thinking that she would be working side by side with Dr. Kessler. But just being in the same clinical environment was like being invited to work at the Center for Advanced Studies when Einstein was in residence. Jennifer found herself spinning through a whole series of moods, from absolute euphoria to ice-cold fear. Only when she was actually seated in the shuttle and flying to New York did any sense of reality penetrate.

She opened the copy of the New York newspaper she bought before boarding and stared at the single-column headline noting the accidental death of Dr. Freedman. The article went on to describe the details, stating that Dr. Freedman had been cycling in the early hours of the morning when he had been hit by a car on a roadway in Central Park. It had not been a case of hit-and-run. Both the driver and two witnesses described the doctor's apparent carelessness in operating his bicycle in a misty drizzle.

Jennifer knew she should have felt something but in truth she felt no more than the bettor on a horse race feels when the jockey of the favorite takes a tumble, allowing his own horse to win. Jennifer was bothered by her lack of emotion. But after all the doctor was a stranger. She did not even know what he looked like and could hardly be expected to grieve over an abstraction. Jennifer felt a sense of loss less for the dead man himself than for the waste it represented. All those years of study and accumulation of knowledge beneficial to humankind ended by a careless peddle around the park. She even felt a tiny sensation of resentment against Dr. Freedman for his carelessness.

These feelings evaporated quickly when the plane landed and Jennifer was immediately caught up by an intense feeling of excitement she could not control. The streets seemed to rush by in a blur. Her knowledge of New York's geography was limited but she knew that the clinic was located on

Roosevelt Island, part of a group of islands situated in the East River between Manhattan and the Borough of Queens. The cab had conveyed Jennifer from the airport, which was located in Queens, along a series of unattractive boulevards bordered by industrial buildings and low-income housing. She scanned sullen faces and a blend of dirt and poverty before being whisked across a newly painted bridge onto the island itself.

Here, the landscape immediately changed. The cab drove around a ramp from which Jennifer could see a new housing development that resembled the Montreal Habitat but was less attractive. She saw trees, grassy quads, cobblestone streets and wide esplanades alongside the river. Joggers loped, mother's wheeled carriages, children played in modern playgrounds against the panorama of the Manhattan skyline across the glistening band of river.

The cab turned north toward a wooded area which effectively sheltered the hospital from the residential area. As far as Jennifer could determine, Montrose occupied the entire northern tip of the island. But she did not have time to dwell on the geographic details. She glimpsed a cluster of functional-looking modern buildings before she entered the lobby and was directed to the administrative wing.

Two years as an intern had prepared Jennifer for the bureaucratic side of hospital life, and Montrose was no exception. Jennifer was kept waiting by a bored secretary while Dr. Murchison, the head of psychiatric staff, was paged. She was glad of the delay, hoping her nervousness would decrease by the time the doctor arrived. But exactly the opposite occurred. She was more nervous at that moment than at any other time in her life. Even her palms were sweating.

Dr. Murchison turned out to be a pleasant-looking man in his late fifties who got right down to business. After a rather grueling hour of cross-examination during which Jennifer was questioned on everything from her academic life to the kind of future she saw for herself in medicine, Murchison escorted her on a tour of several offices. Jennifer met a series of administrators whose faces all blended into one. The only significant contact was with Dr. Kessler himself, and this occurred by chance when the director emerged from an elevator and was halted by Dr. Murchison.

Jennifer got a measured appraisal from what she felt were

friendly eyes. In that instant, all of her nervousness vanished. Jennifer did not feel that she was standing in the presence of a world-renowned scientist but of a benign grandfather. She recalled little of what he said, except for his smile and his words of compliment.

"She is as pretty as Andrews said, Murchison. I must send him a thank-you card." There was laughter and then he became serious. "I hope you're up to a bit of pioneering."

Jennifer smiled and nodded.

"Good. It's about time we opened some windows around here. In this stodgy bastion of male prerogatives."

When Kessler walked away, Dr. Murchison explained that hiring more female staff was just one of the changes Dr. Kessler was attempting to bring about since he had become director. The others concerned turning Montrose into the finest psychiatric research center in the world.

It was nearly midnight when Jennifer arrived back at her parents' home. The next two days were torture. Every time the phone rang she was paralyzed with fear that it would bring another rejection. She barely ate or slept. On the third morning the telegram arrived.

Now, seated in the cab, Jennifer suddenly became aware that she was far enough south on the Drive for her to actually see the island. Just before they swerved out of lane toward the exit on Seventy-third Street, she caught a glimpse of green and the shape of a dome between the trees. Then they drove down York Avenue. Before Jennifer realized it the cab had passed the enormous Gothic complex of New York Hospital and was turning into a narrow side street full of double-parked cars. They pulled up in front of a converted five-story brownstone, and with a start, Jennifer realized she was home, at least for the next eight months.

"Here we are, lady," the driver said.

Studying the building, Jennifer felt a disturbing chill. She would not only be filling Dr. Freedman's unexpired term at Montrose, but also the unexpired term of his lease on the brownstone. Dr. Freedman's apartment had been rented by the hospital at an incredibly low cost. Jennifer could not very well have refused to take it, considering how high current rents were in Manhattan.

The apartment was located in prime territory, within walking distance of the overhead tram that would carry her back and forth to work each day. It was also only a few blocks from some of the finest restaurants, shops and cinemas in the city. Not to mention its proximity to the Metropolitan Museum, one of her favorite places in Manhattan. All these facts had been relayed to Jennifer when she called the hospital after receiving her telegram. She had visited the city on infrequent shopping trips after her parents had moved to the East Coast from San Francisco. Jennifer's mother had grown up in New York, which made Jennifer feel a certain closeness with the city which in truth she did not really know. She was familiar with the major points of interest but she was far from considering herself a Manhattanite. The situation was more than a little frightening, she admitted to herself.

"Moving in?" a male voice called.

Jennifer looked up from her position beside the open door of the cab as she waited for the driver to unload her bags from the trunk. She found herself staring at a redhead with a freckled face and horn-rimmed glasses and a body clothed in hospital whites. A stethoscope was jammed in his jacket pocket.

"Yes," she answered. "I'm moving into four-G."

"Four-G? Isn't that Dr. Freedman's place?"

"That's right." Jennifer said as she placed a bill in the cabbie's hand and told him to keep the change.

"I'll give you a hand," the redhead reached for one valise.

"No, please," she protested, but he lifted the bag anyway.

"I'm going upstairs," he said with a smile. "Might as well use me."

Jennifer picked up the remaining bags and followed him inside.

"You're not from New York." he said, as they started up the stairs.

"Can you tell that easily?"

"Not really. It's just that most of us are from other places. I'm Phillip Rosen by the way. My wife and I live above you."

"Jennifer Westwood."

"Are you in the business?"

"I'm a psychiatrist, if that's what you mean."

"That's what I mean," he said, pausing on the second landing. Jennifer realized she was already a little out of breath.

"You'll get used to the climb. I'm an internist over at New

York Hospital. Most of the people in the building are medical. Two nurses in three-E. Two more in five-J. A couple of foreign residents. One Indian. One Indonesian. Two more from Peru, down in one-A. Sooner or later you'll meet everybody."

"I thought most New Yorkers kept to themselves."

"Most do. But we're not New Yorkers so we tend to party a lot with the rest of the outlanders."

Rosen continued on up and Jennifer trailed after him. He dropped her bag in front of 4G and waited. Jennifer realized there were only two apartments on each landing. The staircase bisected the building like a spine.

"Who lives across the way?" she asked.

"Peter Marchetti. The one exception to the rule. He's a lawyer for some big corporation. You won't see him much. He travels a lot."

"Well, thanks," Jennifer said digging out the key that had been rushed to her by express mail along with a thick wad of forms.

"No problem. Where are you working by the way?"

"Montrose. I'm taking Dr. Freedman's place."

The internist's eyebrows went up. "Oh I see. Well anything you need, just come up and knock. And good luck."

Jennifer waited for her neighbor to continue up the stairs before she opened the two locks and went inside.

She half expected the apartment to be filled with the doctor's belongings and was glad to find it empty except for the furniture the hospital had rented for her. The three tiny rooms contained a convertible sofa covered in blue corduroy and two walnut end tables supporting atrocious-looking ceramic lamps, a glass-topped coffee table, and an upholstered chair. There was also a set of chairs and a small circular table in what passed for the dining area, since the kitchen was too small to actually eat in. The bedroom contained a double bed and dresser which just about filled it. There were white venetian blinds on the windows which overlooked an airshaft and part of a rooftop if you craned your neck far enough.

Jennifer was surprised to find gates on all the windows but there was no key to open them. She made a note to call the administration office. "All the comforts," she said aloud. Luckily there was a phone which offered a dial tone when she picked it up. Jennifer used it to call her mother and spent a hysterical half hour describing the apartment and listening to her mother relate stories about her own experiences with New York apartments. Jennifer found herself not wanting the conversation to end. She did not want to face the empty apartment.

"I just hope it's not haunted," she whispered when she put down the receiver. "Silly . . . silly . . . silly," she commented as she opened the refrigerator. It was empty and smelled of disinfectant.

Jennifer looked around. It was actually the first time she had actually lived alone. She had always had roommates. "Get to it," she said and spent the next few hours unpacking her suitcases, hanging her clothes in the two narrow closets, and filling the dresser drawers with her things. She made a start at filling the refrigerator and cupboards with two bags of purchases from a market she found on First Avenue. She was not hungry enough to go out for dinner and munched on a roll instead, trying to go over the notes she had brought with her. But her mind was too agitated to concentrate. Tomorrow was her first day at the clinic and she faced it with all the uncertainty of a surgeon before his first operation.

TWO

Jennifer woke well before the alarm, with an ache in her limbs from a restless night in a strange bed. After staring at the ceiling for what seemed like an eternity the night before, she had finally drifted off, but it must have been after two by the time she did. She was well into her morning ritual in the cramped bathroom when the alarm finally went off at six. Jennifer was due at Montrose at seven-thirty for a morning briefing with her psychiatric social worker, someone named Anne Bridgeman. That was to be followed by the weekly floor meeting attended by all the patients and the entire staff. But first she was supposed to have a quick meeting with Dr. Boise, her immediate supervisor. Dr. Murchison had mentioned him but time had been too short to arrange an official meeting. Dr. Murchison had said nothing else about him. All of these events to come filled Jennifer with trepidations she had not experienced since her first day at med school.

Waking up in the bare-walled apartment provided her with a strange feeling of loneliness. The previous evening had been spent listening to the sounds of the building. Jennifer's most powerful impression was of the continuous wail of police, fire-truck, and ambulance sirens that punctuated the night, which turned everything she had ever heard about New York into a frightening reality. The building itself provided a sound track of its own. The stairs were metal and resounded every time anyone went up or down. The greatest activity occurred after six when she supposed most of the tenants returned

27

from work. The air came alive with the sound of stereos and TV newscasts. She could even hear the voices of people on the telephone.

Just before eleven, Jennifer made the acquaintance of the city's oldest inhabitants when a small troop of cockroaches paraded across the kitchen wall. The sight filled her with revulsion and she had put down bug spray on what was becoming a very long shopping list, which included everything from shelving paper to a full length mirror.

Before she left, Jennifer had to face the problem of what to wear. She had spent her internship in a white jacket and pants. Doctors at Montrose were expected to wear shirts and ties. She despised uniforms of any kind, but had decided to conform to the dress code. She chose a navy-blue one-piece jersey dress from her small collection of formal wear, as she termed anything other than jeans. She realized she would need a whole new wardrobe for her new position. But she was not pleased about having to shop for it. Shopping was the one chore she most despised, even for clothes.

The early fall weather was pleasant enough to go without a jacket but Jennifer took one anyway, carrying it over her arm. She had no idea how late she was expected to stay. Before she left she glanced in the small bathroom mirror. The dress hugged her breasts and hips without being overly provocative. A single gold chain provided the only adornment. Her bag and shoes were a conservative black while she wore her long hair in a severe upswept style.

Breakfast began with a glass of orange juice at a crowded luncheonette on the corner. Jennifer was not really hungry but she felt she should have something to eat. She tried to down scrambled eggs and bacon and absorbed her first real experience of the fabled New York pace. People leaned over her, taking their outgoing orders or plucking napkins from a holder beside her. She was nudged by truck drivers and executives, all infected by the same driving demon.

The movement became even more intense when she left the restaurant and walked toward the tram. Jennifer had never really experienced the rush hour in its fullest dimension. Certainly she had never been part of it. But now, like the millions around her, she faced the horror of struggling to be on time in a city whose transportation system was in rapid decay.

Jennifer found herself drawn into the rushing stream along the sidewalk, realizing only after she had been bumped several times and received a dozen dirty looks that there was a definite pattern. The right side swam upstream, the left, down. Crossing was less an ordinary action than a major achievement. The crowds coagulated on the corners only to surge across before the lights even changed, swarming around the still moving cars and dancing between them like matadors.

Jennifer went a block out of her way before she realized she had passed the tram. For a confused instant she was almost swept down a subway entrance. Only when she climbed the stairs to the tram and sailed over the teeming streets did she realize just how lucky she was to be going against traffic, leaving Manhattan when everyone else was pouring into it.

The tram was sparsely filled with people Jennifer imagined were bound for the same destination. Many wore white shoes or other telltale pieces of medical attire. They made lively conversation as the car rose along the cable past the windows of Sutton Place co-ops. Below was a grid of traffic and the unceasing movement on the sidewalks. It seemed completely unreal, though she had been a part of it only moments before, and Jennifer felt a sense of exhilaration. She was taking a magic-carpet ride to her first important job and it all felt so marvelously special, even though her stomach was wound as tight as the cable of the car she rode.

A bus waited outside the tram stop on the island side. As it rumbled north Jennifer realized what a contrast this island presented to the other island she had just left. This was a reserve of peace and almost suburban tranquillity.

Few people got off at the stops along the attractive road that wound through the housing development. Nervous as she was, Jennifer was still able to observe that certain landmarks had been preserved when the complex had been constructed. She saw several old churches before the bus pulled into an open stretch and passed the bridge that first brought Jennifer to the island. Then the noisy vehicle swung around through the stand of trees and the hospital appeared with almost alarming suddenness.

Jennifer waited for the other passengers to disembark before she got off with a fleeting smile at the driver. He was a friendly-looking black man with a massive paunch who said,

"Have a good day," as she stepped down. Jennifer prayed she would.

She followed the others into the lobby and headed toward the elevator in her wing when she was stopped by a security guard. "Can I help you, miss?" he asked politely.

"I'm sorry." Jennifer faltered. "I'm new here. My name is Jennifer Westwood." She realized her face had turned red.

"Doctor Westwood?" the guard said checking a clipboard.

"That's right," Jennifer answered, realizing that she had to add the title now. Calling herself doctor was never easy.

"I'm sorry, doctor," the guard continued, "but you have to wear your ID. It's a hospital rule."

"Yes, I know. But it's my first day. I haven't been issued one yet."

The guard nodded patronizingly. He had a narrow Dober-man-pinscher face that Jennifer mistrusted. "It makes it easier for all of us, doctor," he said, stepping aside.

Jennifer felt her cheeks flame. She had been scolded by service personnel before. She remembered how shocked she had been the first time she heard a veteran nurse chewing out a resident like an irate teacher. Hospitals often treated their RNs better than their doctors. And after all, they were harder to come by.

The elevator brought Jennifer to the second floor and opened only a few feet from the nurses' station. It was a large rectangular chamber with a glass window fronting the corridor and rows of cabinets and desks along three walls. A door in the fourth led to the pharmacy. Jennifer saw a schedule and was surprised to see her name on it.

Inside, several nurses and orderlies were going through the motions of starting their shift, reading the last shift's nota-tions and preparing medication trays. Except for an occa-sional stethoscope it would have been difficult to tell the nurses and aides apart. No one wore traditional whites, mak-ing it even more ridiculous in Jennifer's mind for the doctors to conform to a dress code. It looked more like the teachers' lounge in some progressive school than the ward of a psychi-atric hospital. But this was done deliberately, to make the floor seem as little like a hospital as possible.

"Can I help you?"

Jennifer turned to face an attractive woman of thirty or so, with curly blond hair and bright blue eyes. She wore jeans and a pink sweater that revealed a trim figure.

"I'm Dr. Westwood," Jennifer said.

"Oh, yes, we're expecting you. I'm Rita Kahn, the head nurse on your service. You're supposed to be meeting with Dr. Boise. He told me to send you in when you got here."

"Am I late?" Jennifer asked.

"I don't think so. Dr. Boise is in Anne Bridgeman's office. She's your social worker. Why don't you wait here and I'll tell them you've arrived."

Jennifer watched the young woman walk toward a door down the corridor. When she disappeared inside, Jennifer turned to survey her surroundings.

The floor would be her home for the next eight months. It had none of the utilitarian atmosphere of most psychiatric hospitals she had been in. The walls were paneled and the entire setup resembled a hotel more than a hospital. Even the lighting was subdued, giving the pleasant feeling of being in daylight.

The corridor occupied the center of the floor and disappeared around corners in both directions. Jennifer imagined that she was standing in the center of a large U-shaped wing. On one side was a lounge furnished with well-worn furniture. Games and books were jammed in a bookcase beside a small refrigerator. Across from the lounge was a dining room with round tables set for eight. Jennifer could see uniformed cafeteria personnel behind a counter. Breakfast was only a few minutes away according to the schedule, but none of the patients was visible. Remembering her own experience with hospital food she knew they would not be overly eager to come down on time.

Two phone booths with folding doors stood between the lounge and the nurses' station. A bulletin board informed the patients of their rights as well as containing typed schedules for psychiatric visits. Again Jennifer saw her name listed and was filled with a mixed sense of fear and belonging. There would be no breaking-in period, she had been told. Part of the price of accepting the residency was having to jump into an ongoing program feet first. She had been warned by Doug Andrews not to expect too much in the way of assistance. The staff was probably overworked as it was.

"Dr. Westwood."

Jennifer wheeled around at the mention of her name. Rita Kahn was signaling from the open door. Jennifer went toward it quickly. "Dr. Boise is inside waiting for you," Rita said. Then her voice dropped and she whispered, "Good luck."

Beyond the door was a narrow vestibule containing three doors. One of them opened on a cramped office. A plaque on the door was lettered ANNE BRIDGEMAN, SOCIAL WORKER. Two people were inside. Both wore hospital coats and were bending over a desk examining a folder. Jennifer stood in the doorway waiting.

An instant later, the woman smiled and said, "Oh, hello. You must be Dr. Westwood."

Jennifer returned the smile but she felt something artificial in the other woman's expression.

"I'm Anne Bridgeman. This is Dr. Boise."

Jennifer and the woman shook hands. Anne was a short, extremely well groomed woman with reddish-tinted close-cropped hair, almost like a crew cut, which accented her well-modeled head. She was not really pretty but was making the most of what she had, Jennifer could almost hear her mother say. She wore a smart tweed skirt and a silk blouse with a high neck. A beautiful cameo was pinned to the collar—all of which earned her an "A" for taste. Anne's features were thin, and when she smiled lines appeared around her mouth and eyes as if her skin had little resiliency.

With a precise movement, she shut the folder and placed it under her arm. "I'll be outside when you've finished with Dr. Boise. Don't forget we have our floor meeting at eight."

"Yes, I know," Jennifer responded, moving aside so Anne could leave.

"Please, sit down," Dr. Boise said, taking the seat behind the desk and leaving the one beside it for Jennifer. She cast a quick glance around her as she sat. The office contained a sink and a small bathroom. Several abstract prints hung on the walls, expensively framed and matted. They probably belonged to Anne. Like its occupant the room was small and neat.

"I wanted to give you a quick briefing." Dr. Boise began leaning back in the swivel chair and fixing Jennifer with a scrutinizing look. "This is kind of short notice, I know. But we'll try to do whatever we can to get you adjusted."

"Thank you," Jennifer said, returning Dr. Boise's frank stare. Jennifer had an almost automatic defense against the X-ray gazes fixed on her by all too many males in her profession. No matter what their position, she generally managed to stare them down. But Dr. Boise continued his probing glance.

Boise was a young man who was doing his best to look like an old man. Beneath his starched coat was a body already turning to fat and clothed in the shapeless ivy-league fashions of another era. Dr. Boise was preppy to his core. He even wore cuffs on his tweed trousers, expensive cordovans, and argyle socks. His vest sported a gold chain and a pocket watch along with an elk's tooth and a Phi Beta Kappa key. His tie was pure Brooks Brothers silk rep and his shirt a blue broadcloth button-down. Spidery strands of blond hair were combed across his dome lengthwise, to conceal his obvious baldness while his jaw dissolved into the fat of his neck. He was handsome actually but sexless. It was the sort of face Jennifer pictured on a eunuch.

"Anne will fill you in on your patient roster and give you all the particulars of your schedule. We've left you as many of Dr. Freedman's notes as we could find. That should be a help. Of course, I'll be there to help as much as I can. But you'll soon discover we all earn our way around here."

Jennifer was not sure if he meant that as a joke but smiled anyway. She was beginning to detect an irritation behind his words along with an unmistakable coolness and wondered if Dr. Boise was one of the staff who Dr. Kessler thought needed to breathe a little fresh air. It was going to be just charming having a supervisor who was actively hostile. Jennifer stifled the notion. She was being unfair and she knew it. Like most men in his position, Dr. Boise was overworked. The prospect of having to break in a new resident could hold little joy for him.

Boise leaned forward, adjusting his bulk in the chair. "What I want to impress upon you this morning, and which I think is of foremost importance to your position here and our working relationship, is an understanding of the Montrose approach."

Jennifer felt suddenly very attentive.

"What we are not," Boise continued, "is a mental hospital in the fullest sense of the word. We do not institutionalize patients on any kind of long-term basis. We are what we say we are, a clinic for the treatment of psychotic disorders. We deal in the short-term management of psychotic symptoms. Our object is to get our patients back into their normal existence as quickly and painlessly as possible. To accomplish this we use a battery of approaches, some you may be familiar with, others not. Many will be new to you, especially the tetracyclics. My main function will be to guide you in the use of these rehabilitative techniques. Do you have any questions?"

Jennifer fumbled for a response. She had a thousand and she had none. How could she ask a question without having been exposed to her patients or knowing anything about the routine. Still, she said, "How long is the average patient stay?"

"Thirty days."

Jennifer raised her eyebrows in surprise. "That's a very short time for any kind of competent analysis."

"Analysis?" Dr. Boise repeated with a tolerant smile. "You'll have a forty-minute session with your patients each day. During that time you'll be expected to concentrate on their feeling profiles above everything else, to determine the effect of your medication. I don't think you'll have the time to waste on analysis."

The word "waste" struck a basic response in Jennifer. "You don't sound as if you think analysis is worth the effort."

Dr. Boise readjusted his legs, crossing one over the other. "At Montrose we place more faith in medication and try to keep the voodoo to a minimum."

"The voodoo?" Jennifer stared at him with surprise. "You can't be serious?"

"I'm sorry, doctor. We're not running a course in psychiatric theory," Dr. Boise said sharply. "Remember what I told you. We deal with symptomatology. We don't seek cures. Analysis is a long-term enterprise beyond our scope. Part of your function here will be the setting up of proper outpatient therapy. You'll find Anne will be quite helpful to you there. She is one of the best there is."

Jennifer wanted to say more, but Dr. Boise glanced down at his watch. "I suggest you get together with Anne now. She'll get you started. Good luck."

He rose and extended his hand. Jennifer's palm was surrounded by soft wet flesh. The sensation was not pleasant.

She left the office with a feeling of apprehension. Dr.

Boise's words hinted at the controversy raging within her branch of medicine between those who believed mental illness was biologically related, and therefore treatable with the right chemical combination—or as Professor Andrews had put it, with an antibiotic for the mind—and those who believed that though drugs may alleviate symptoms, mental disorders stem from a combination of causes and are treatable by a battery of techniques both pharmacological and psychological.

Jennifer saw her own role as more than an impersonal prescriber of chemicals. She did not believe that any combination of drugs, no matter how effectively they might treat the symptoms could be the whole answer.

Anne Bridgeman was waiting inside the nurses' station when Jennifer came out of Dr. Boise's office. Several patients had already finished breakfast and were congregating in the lounge waiting for the floor meeting to begin. Anne explained that new admissions were required to remain in their hospital pajamas and robes for the first forty-eight hours as part of the effort to keep from attempting to return to the outside. After that they could dress in their own clothing. From the staff clothing to interior decoration, every attempt was made to free the patient of the feeling of being confined to a hospital. Even the main exit doors were unlocked. Only the staff psychiatrists were required to wear white coats. It was a small hypocrisy Jennifer could not help smiling at, knowing the tendency of her profession to maintain the barrier of authority between doctor and patient.

Anne quickly introduced her to the nurses, orderlies, and therapists who were gathering for the meeting which was to be held in the patient dining room. Jennifer could see that Anne's brisk businesslike manner did not conceal a certain coolness between herself and the others, most of whom treated each other with casual friendliness.

The weekly floor meeting was a general gripe session in which patients could air their grievances and discuss hospital policy. It was supposed to give the patients the feeling of participation in their care. But it seemed to have the opposite effect. Jennifer noticed how closely Anne controlled the meeting, shifting focus whenever a patient expressed anything too critical or became angry at not being informed of the side effects of a drug or some other matter. Anne had a way of

turning aside the thrust by asking the other patients how they
felt about the same problem. Only once was a question actually answered, when a patient asked why the rug in the
lounge was so worn. With a professional smile, Anne informed him that the requisition for new carpeting had been
in the administrative logjam for nearly a year.

After the meeting broke up, Anne introduced Jennifer to
those therapists who were working directly with her own patients. They all had the same brisk efficiency and sense of
dedication Jennifer had missed in the other hospitals she had
seen as an intern. It had been impossible for her to get a fix
on which patients were hers during the meeting, so the therapists' comments were in a sense wasted, though Jennifer tried
to remember as many as she could. All the patients on the
floor were suffering from some form of affective psychosis
commonly classified as depression. Each of them was undergoing some form of drug therapy and some were undergoing
electroconvulsive shock. They exhibited a wide range of be-
haviors. Some were sullen; others were more manic. Those
nearing the end of their stay were generally normal in their
outward actions.

"If you like, I could show you to your office now," Anne
said when the others went off to their various duties.

"I'd appreciate that, thank you," Jennifer replied and followed Anne along the corridor and around the turning until
they came to an opaque glass door at the end of a large room
used as a TV lounge. Jennifer was concerned about the location until she entered the office and realized it was completely
soundproof.

It was a pleasant office, Jennifer realized, with two large
windows that offered views of the East River facing north
toward the bridges connecting the three boroughs of Manhattan, Queens and the Bronx. It was also far more spacious
than Anne's and included a small white-tiled bathroom, a
wall of bookcases behind glass doors, and several filing cabinets. There were also several comfortable chairs, one of
which had been drawn up in front of her desk for patient
sessions.

Anne opened one of the drawers in the filing cabinet and
withdrew a batch of files. "Homework," she said with a smile.
"You're going to have quite a bit of catching-up to do.

These are Dr. Freedman's patient records. I've rescheduled your day so you'll have a few hours to go over them. Your first patient session is at one."

Jennifer stared at her incredulously. That only gave her three hours to absorb the eight files. But she kept herself from making a comment. She would do what she could and try to catch up in the fifteen-minute space between each session.

"Will I be able to take the records home, tonight?" she asked.

"I'm afraid not. That's strictly against hospital policy."

Jennifer glanced up at Anne, half expecting a confidential wink that would signal her willingness to bend the rules a little, but there was none.

"How did your session with Dr. Boise go?"

Jennifer was about to blurt how she really felt about Dr. Boise's unfriendly manner but something in Anne's expression held her back. There was just a little bit too much eagerness. Holding back was not Jennifer's style. In the past she had been much too outspoken about her feelings, especially when they related to her superiors. All too often her acerbic comments had come back to haunt her. Jennifer had a biting wit that often left a scar. She had paid for her indiscretions with some scars of her own.

"It went very well," she answered casually. "Dr. Boise seems very helpful."

"He's an extremely competent supervisor," Anne commented. "His record of patient release within the thirty-day period is the finest in the hospital."

"I'm sure it is," Jennifer remarked. "Did he and Dr. Freedman get along well?"

"Did someone say they didn't?" Anne asked.

The way she said it made Jennifer immediately glad she had not confided her true feelings. "No," she replied. "I've hardly had a chance to speak to anyone. I was just wondering, that's all."

"Dr. Boise's record has caused a great deal of envy. You'll be surprised just how much of that there is in our profession."

"I'm not surprised. I saw quite a bit of it when I was an intern."

"You'll see even more here. Montrose is a prestige institution. Reputations can be both made and broken here. That's
why cooperation is so important."

Jennifer realized the way Anne spoke was meant to convey
more than idle comments. Still, she had not actually answered
the question of whether Dr. Freedman and Dr. Boise got
along.

But before Jennifer could pursue it further, Anne glanced
at her watch. "Well, I'll let you get started. Remember we
have a meeting at five."

"So I see," Jennifer said, glancing at her schedule. When
she looked up Anne was already out the door. That was
when she noticed the clock on the bookcase against the wall.
It had been marked with a thin red line for the forty-five-
minute hour. It was such a paltry amount of time to unravel
the problems of a lifetime, she realized. But those were the
realities under which she would have to operate. She had already learned that the practice of medicine is quite different
from its theory.

She started to open the first folder when she was struck
with an uneasy feeling. She had been at Montrose less than
two hours and already she was being manipulated. But pursu-
ing Anne's motives was a luxury Jennifer could not afford.
The stack of folders faced her like a mountain she had to
climb.

Time was holding a whip over her head. She had barely
enough to give each folder a cursory going-over, noting each
patient's diagnosis, prognosis for recovery, and current medication, before she had to go on to the next. She scribbled
notes to herself on a pad she found in the top drawer. Dr.
Freedman's desk, she realized, had been cleaned as effectivly
as his apartment. She would need a whole battery of office
supplies besides the scanty pad and two pencils she found in
the desolate drawers.

Jennifer had barely gotten past the halfway point when the
phone on the desk beside her began to ring. Someone from
the administrative office was on the other end asking for her
social security number and informing her of the battery of
forms awaiting her in the administrative office, all marked
top priority. Jennifer had already learned one of the facts of
hospital life. Neglect of administration bookkeeping could

bring greater difficulty than a malpractice action. She agreed to stop and pick up the forms during her lunch break. She hung up wondering if she was even allowed to have one.

The administration office was located on the first floor of the adjoining wing in the area where she had first met Dr. Murchison. Jennifer reached it by following a three-colored band of painted lines on the hospital floor which branched off in various directions when they reached the main lobby. Montrose was not as large as the Baltimore hospital where she had interned, but it was just as bewildering. Jennifer could see that the clinic had once consisted of a central core, which had been added to until it was an architectural mishmash of different styles—the result, she supposed, of spiraling construction costs. The original white-brick structure was locked within a series of glass and steel rectangles sprouting off in all directions. The names of the various wings revealed either private or public financing. The names revived Jennifer's excitement at being appointed to Montrose where so many recent breakthroughs in psychiatric medicine had originated.

Jennifer was surprised when she entered the administration office. Instead of the usual indifference and delay she expected, she was ushered into a glass-walled cubicle by a smiling black woman who spoke in a West Indian accent and aided her in filling out a series of printed forms that covered everything from tax status to her insurance liability. She was handed a plastic envelope containing her name tag and booklets explaining her benefits as an employee as well as various hospital regulations. Jennifer was told she could return the other forms she had received when she had the opportunity. Then she was smiled out as painlessly as she had been smiled in.

The experience reinforced the feeling of competency Jennifer felt around her. In the hour before she left for the administration office, Jennifer had received several calls from the nurses' station informing her of the progress of her various patients. The idea of being told pleased her and made her feel part of things. Dr. Freedman's extensive notes reinforced the feeling. They indicated a thoroughness and precision she had not encountered before. Record keeping in the Baltimore hospital had often been so sloppy it bordered on negligence. Even the feeling profiles of the patients' daily changes of mood were kept with enormous detail. It gave Jennifer a strange feeling of connection with the dead man that was more than a little disturbing.

Dr. Freedman's diagnoses, ranged from uni- and bipolar depression through various forms of compulsive behavior and such nonpsychotic disorders as alcoholism. But the bulk of his patients were suffering neurotic dysfunctions such as anxiety and hysteria. One of his diagnoses especially interested her. It was the case of Jeffrey Cox, a patient suffering what Dr. Freedman had diagnosed as an endogenous depression which was considered biochemical in origin. It was a tricky dysfunction to analyze. Jeffrey was a twenty-six-year-old playwright and actor admitted with an affective disorder that featured both suicidal tendencies and writer's block.

Along with Jeffrey, Jennifer found herself most interested in two other cases. One was an especially attractive young woman of her own age, Jennifer had noticed at the floor meeting. Her name was Laura Archer and she was apparently suffering from a career-related breakdown. Perhaps it was the similarity in their ages or an awareness of the stresses in her own career, but whatever the cause, Jennifer found herself feeling a special interest in Laura's situation.

The other patient who arrested her attention was Brae Haskill, a thirty-four-year-old New York police detective with no previous history of mental illness. His disturbance had apparently struck with peculiar suddenness. Dr. Freedman noted that the patient was especially difficult to reach. He kept to himself, exhibited sullen tendencies, and skipped his various therapy sessions. He was also resistant to medication.

For Jennifer, noting this was like waving a red flag before a bull. She felt an undercurrent of excitement, knowing that all three of these patients had been scheduled for visits that afternoon. Her other patients fell into categories she had experienced before. One was a twenty-four-year-old mother suffering postpartum depression after the birth of her infant son. A seventeen-year-old hysteric with a long history of institutionalization. Two menopausal syndromes, one female one male. And a manic-depressive taxi driver, although how he could be otherwise, considering the traffic in New York streets, was a mystery Jennifer would have to decipher.

After leaving the administration office Jennifer followed the yellow line that would take her to the cafeteria, which was located in the basement, past a wall of lockers. The cafeteria was noisy and badly lit, dominated on one side by the usual depressing hot table dispensing the usual institutional fare. Jennifer smelled the familiar aroma of macaroni and cheese and cringed. Here she was in the culinary capital of the world and she was fated to eat the same overcooked green beans, pulverized pasta, and indigestible bacon served by the same fleshy women in spotted uniforms as any school kid back in her hometown.

Jennifer passed up the special and settled for an American-cheese sandwich on white, coffee floating an oil slick that reminded her of the river outside, and a cellophane-packaged cruller. She paid the bored-looking cashier and glanced around for a place to sit down. She had brought along Dr. Freedman's medication orders and intended to study them while she ate but she realized that the poor lighting made that impossible.

When three orderlies vacated a nearby table, Jennifer headed for it. She was halfway through the sandwich when she heard a male voice say, "Mind if I join you?"

Jennifer looked up. The doctor standing before her with a tray in his hands wore a name tag that read Mark Tobey. He was smiling so expectantly, so confident he would not be refused, that Jennifer almost said she minded. Instead, she shook her head and he took the place opposite her.

"You're new around here," he commented with a satisfied smile.

"That's right. First day." Jennifer responded, swallowing hard,

"Which wing. No let me guess. Tobler, right?"

"That's right."

"I'm over in McKeon."

Jennifer nodded, remembering McKeon was one of the more modern sections of grotesque grafting. She had passed it on the way over from administration.

"Welcome to the Inferno," Mark said with a toothy smile. Jennifer realized that Mark possessed almost male-model-like perfection. His face even had a slight tan along with its various clefts and dimples.

"The Inferno?" Jennifer questioned, wondering which part of the hospital he meant.

"This is the Inferno," Mark said, gesturing around him. "The food's hell and the staff treat you worse than the devil."

Jennifer forced a smile at his little joke. She had the feeling he repeated it more often than it was worth.

"You know there was a pretty serious incident over in your neighborhood recently," he said, suddenly growing serious.

"If you mean Dr. Freedman, I'm his replacement."

"No kidding." Mark raised his eyebrows. "They move pretty fast around here."

"So I notice."

He grinned at her remark and took a large bite of his sandwich. He had an easygoing quality Jennifer wished she possessed and found herself resenting. Like many doctors she had encountered, he had an insular quality of innocence when it came to things of the outer world.

Although Jennifer wanted to rush back upstairs and use the hour before her first patient to go over Dr. Freedman's medication reports, she was held by the same magnetism she felt each time she entered a new institution. The desire to fill in all the unknowns.

"So what's it like working here?" she asked.

"Pretty damn marvelous if you enjoy twenty-four-hour days. Kessler's a genius of course. Have you met him yet?"

"For a few minutes, when I came up for the interview."

"You're lucky. Not everybody does. He's usually locked away in his inner sanctum."

"What do you mean?" Jennifer questioned. "What inner sanctum?"

Mark stared at her incredulously. "You mean you've been at Montrose for one entire day and you don't know about Kessler's inner sanctum?"

Jennifer felt at a sudden loss, not knowing if he was kidding or not.

"C'mon, I'll show you." Jennifer started to protest but Mark was already on his feet, tossing away the unfinished half of his food. "It's okay," he said. "You'll stay healthier if you don't eat it."

They dumped their trays at the station and continued back along the yellow-brick road, as Jennifer was beginning to think of the thickly painted line.

"Where do you live, by the way?" Mark asked as they approached the elevator.

"I have an apartment in the east seventies between York and First."

"Oh-oh, watch out for all the horny interns."

"You sound like you speak from experience."

"I've graduated. Now I'm a horny resident," Mark said, allowing her to precede him into the elevator. "I live on Second and Eighty-third, so we're practically neighbors."

The elevator brought them to the first floor. Mark guided her across the lobby to the rear of the building. They emerged through double glass doors into a pleasant area shaded by trees. Hospital personnel sat on benches, sunning themselves in the pleasant autumn weather.

"It's just past here," Mark said. "So get set."

They turned a corner and stopped. Ahead was a futuristic two-story building surmounted by a steel-ribbed dome. The building looked more like sculpture than architecture but it was impressive, though not as ominous-looking as Mark made it sound. Only when she looked again did Jennifer become aware that the entire structure was surrounded by a double wall of cyclone fencing topped by barbed wire. Signs bolted along the mesh every few feet warned of electronic protection and that all visitors had to report to the main gate for a pass. The building was actually set within its own landscaped grounds and connected to the rest of Montrose by a catwalk shaped like a tube of reflecting glass.

"So that's Dr. Kessler's inner sanctum," Jennifer remarked.

"Actually, it's called the Center for Special Psychiatric Research. It's where Kessler does his work on schizophrenia."

"Why is it so carefully guarded. Is it some kind of government project?"

"You *are* new, aren't you?" Mark grinned, shaking his head and continuing along the path that gradually curved around the building. "Actually with all the cutbacks in grants, the government couldn't afford anything like this anymore."

"Then who is paying for it?"

"IPC International."

"IPC? You mean the pharmaceutical concern?"

"Conglomerate is more like it. Doctor, if you're going to make it in this profession, you better know the names of your largest conglomerates, the definition of putts and calls, and your leading money-market analyst."

"Very funny. But just why is Kessler associated with them?"

"Because they have the exclusive rights to market whatever Kessler produces. The same way they've been marketing Nitholin."

"Okay, fine. But this place is guarded like an atomic reactor."

"My dear, I can see you are obviously ignorant of the current state of competition among international drug concerns. Look, new drugs are allowed to be patented for only seventeen years. Half of that time is spent in testing and development. Do you realize how much is invested before they can submit a safety profile to the FDA? That's the Food and Drug Administration in case you were wondering."

"Thank you," Jennifer said curtly. She felt a sense of irritation that Mark should possess knowledge about an aspect of her own field of which she was almost totally ignorant. Jennifer had never concerned herself about the business side of medication, only its uses and application. What Mark was saying gave her a perspective on a different aspect of pharmaceuticals.

"What exactly is a safety profile?" She asked as the path brought them around the far side of the center toward the old stone retaining wall bordering on the river.

"Well," Mark said patiently, "before any company can get an INP—that's not a new subway; it stands for Investigational Drug Permit—they first have to present a compilation of investigations, animal studies, chemical and biological reactions, high-dosage studies, and reliability data showing the drug can be produced safely."

"And once they get their INP, then what?"

"Ah, that's where our venerable genius, Dr. Kessler, enters the picture. Once the company gets the INP they have to choose a reputable clinical investigator."

"And the more prestigious the investigator, the better the chances of getting approval."

"You catch on quick, senorita," Mark said, taking a seat on the stone wall. "Once the research methodology is resubmitted to the FDA, they have a one-month veto. If a university does the investigating and it's funded by federal funds, then the institutional review board connected with the college gives the official approval, saving the FDA the bother."

"All of this is fascinating," Jennifer said sarcastically. "But it still doesn't explain the security."

"Okay. Look; psychiatry is entering a major period of change, from the analytical to the biological. Old Sigmund Freud may be turning over in his grave, but that's the way it is. All over the world doctors, institutions, and universities are experimenting with pharmacology. They're tossing out the couch and bringing in the pills. Not that we didn't have medications before. Only now its like an avalanche. We're talking billions of dollars in new products. IPC is headquartered in Taiwan. They finance Kessler's center and market his drugs. They don't want his research stolen or sabotaged or even copied before they have a chance to market it exclusively."

"Sabotage? You're joking."

"I wish I were."

Jennifer could see that Mark was serious.

"When you go past the main gate, take a look inside. You'll see why I call it the inner sanctum. Everyone working there—and I mean everyone—from the chemists and researchers to the nursing and psychiatric staff down to the porters and security men, has been brought in from Taiwan. Kessler is the only guy in there who isn't Oriental. Except for the patients of course."

"You're not serious. You mean no one from the rest of the hospital works there?"

"Works there? Listen, señorita. They're not even allowed *in* there. It's strictly off limits for peons like us."

Jennifer stared at Mark, then she looked over at the center. She had never experienced anything like this before. The information startled her. Security was common enough in medical facilities to prevent drug pilferage, among other things. But what Mark had just told her belonged to the dimension of the CIA or the Pentagon. Besides James Bond, those were the only similarities she could think of. Only this was not fiction but something very real.

Jennifer checked her watch and realized she had better start back to her office. "Thank you for the guided tour," she said, extending her hand. "It's been nice meeting you."

Mark took her hand but did not release it. "You don't think my lecture on current trends in pharmaceutical research comes gratis do you?"

"What do you mean?"

"I mean what are you doing for dinner tonight?"

THREE

All the way back to her office Jennifer felt amused by Mark's offer and the effect of her refusal. A crushed-little-boy look had crossed his handsome features that almost made her laugh. She could see that an eligible young doctor like Mark was not often turned down. But the new world she had entered was much too awesome for her to even start thinking of a social life. Her schedule called for her being on duty over part of the weekend anyway, and even though no patient sessions were set she would need the time for study and review. Jennifer realized she had quite a bit of background to catch up on. She felt like someone trying to race up a down escalator.

Rita Kahn, the head nurse, greeted her when she stepped off the elevator. "Find your way around okay?" she questioned, heading in the same direction.

"I just followed the yellow-brick road." Jennifer replied.

Rita laughed. "If you've survived the cafeteria then the rest is a snap."

"Is that the only place we can go?"

"Besides the coffee shop which is just as dismal. Unless you bring something from home you're stuck. Of course you could try one of the places in the housing complex, if you have the time. Usually, no one does."

Rita turned the corner, passing a powerfully built man who was shuffling toward the lounge in his robe and pajamas. Jen-

47

nifer recognized the cadence usually produced by some antipsychotic drug.

"You'll be seeing your first patients this afternoon?"

"That's right. Anne gave me a pretty good briefing."

"I'll bet she did," Rita said coyly.

Jennifer glanced at her. There was something behind the remark but she had trouble locating it. "Has Anne been here long?"

"About three years. She and Dr. Boise are very chummy, I suppose you noticed," Rita said with a different kind of smile, one whose meaning was pretty obvious. "And I don't mean they're having an affair."

"Thanks for the tip. I'll remember that."

Rita smiled and disappeared into one of the patient's rooms. Jennifer continued on to her office. Her internship had taught her some valuable lessons about hospital rivalries. The Hippocratic oath did not extend to backbiting, intrigue, or professional jealousies—even among those cleansed by the detergent of psychoanalysis. If Anne reported back to Dr. Boise, then Rita had presented Jennifer with the first important tool of hospital survival: having the nurses on your side.

Jeffrey Cox was on time for his session, which did not really surprise Jennifer. She recognized his face from the floor meeting that morning. He was a dark-haired young man with theatrical good looks. His eyebrows were dark lightning streaks across his forehead. More striking was his expressive mouth, set like a slash of red paint against his pale complexion. His eyes were also extraordinarily animated, darting from one side of the room to the other but rarely settling on her.

Dr. Freedman, she recalled, had diagnosed Jeffrey's illness as an endogenous depression based on biological factors. This theory supposed that his condition was caused by disturbances in the nerve impulse transmission to the various portions of his brain. The exact workings of the problem were not fully known but it was believed the fault lay in the way the chemical transmitter substances were released and absorbed across the synapses between two nerve cells. Dr. Freedman believed that this dysfunction caused Jeffrey's extreme changes in mood. He had prescribed several different kinds of antidepressant drugs, including two of the newest types of tetracyclics. Neither had caused any of the discomforting side effects common to the older generation of drugs, like high blood pressure, dry mouth, or the horrendous feeling of having to urinate but not being able to.

Though these drugs promised so much, Jennifer felt a certain skepticism about their efficacy. She remembered the old saw—that if a drug was strong enough to have an effect, it was strong enough to have a side effect. Being a natural-born disbeliever, as her father used to say, she knew that in their enthusiasm for a super cure doctors often overlooked what they did not want to see. But she wanted to keep an open mind and make her own judgments.

Jeffrey's case was difficult. In spite of the new medications his feeling profile did not show any significant change; in fact it indicated exactly the reverse: an exacerbation of his symptoms. Jeffrey had been admitted with feelings of serious bodily changes. He complained of insomnia and altered levels of energy. He had a loss of appetite and sexual feelings, as well as a general loss of interest in life. He could no longer concentrate on his writing and was unable to express such emotions as grief or sadness. He lay awake nights contemplating suicide.

Jennifer had to admit that such symptoms would tend to support Dr. Freedman's diagnosis and that the use of drugs was indicated. But Dr. Freedman had only seen part of the reaction before he was killed. After the doctor's death Jeffrey's mood swung wildly. He went from elation to gloom within the space of an hour. Manic exuberance was followed by listless passivity and a desire to sleep, which Jennifer could only interpret as a desire for death. She was bothered by the pattern, but whoever was treating Jeffrey now had continued the medication. She noticed that all the medication orders were signed by Dr. Boise after Dr. Freedman's death. He had actually increased the dosages when all of her instincts told her to stop them altogether.

"I'm glad to see you, Jeffrey," Jennifer said when he seated himself before her desk. "You know I'm going to be seeing you from now on, every day at this time."

Jeffrey nodded, but his eyes continued their furtive wanderings.

"Does Dr. Freedman's not being here bother you?"

Jeffrey's restless gaze settled on the filing cabinets on the side wall. But he said nothing.

Jennifer studied him with a critical eye. She had been trained to observe every nuance of behavior and appearance, no matter how slight. She was also aware of just how tricky the first few moments in a doctor-patient relationship could be. Should the patient perceive the doctor as hostile or critical or even demanding, he might become unwilling to unburden himself. If, however, he feels the therapist is helpful or tolerant, the chance of a true rapport is increased. Thus Jennifer's main task was to relieve him of any anxiety he might feel about the session. She looked for learned patterns of behavior in the patient's important relationships. In the process of transference, the patient would project his own expectations of how others regard him onto the physician, and her observation of this process in any given patient gave Jennifer a keen insight into his personality structure. Dependent personalities usually sought some kind of magical reassurance, expecting the doctor to be a sorcerer. Certain neurotics showed suspicion, hostility, or became actively seductive. Still others attempted to bribe the doctor for special attention or openly attacked him. Jennifer had already been subjected to a whole gamut of responses from sarcasm to tears.

"Tell me Jeffrey, did you like Dr. Freedman?"

Jeffrey shrugged and continued his fidgeting.

"How did you feel when you heard about his death?"

Jeffrey suddenly snapped around to face her. "I felt he was lucky, okay. It ended."

"What ended?"

"Life in the shit hole. The sewer. The sooner it's over the better."

"I see. So you find nothing good about it?"

"You tell me, doctor?" he snapped.

"I could tell you a lot of things I feel personally. But we're here to help you deal with your feelings not mine."

"You want to help me, doctor. Get me fucked, okay. I want to suck a beautiful big dick. Can you find me one?" he asked aggressively.

Jennifer's expression did not change. She knew he was doing everything he could to try and shock her. "Is that what you really want?"

"Yes. That's what I really want. To get fucked up the ass."

"Then what's stopping you? Why don't you go outside and

find someone? You're good-looking enough. It shouldn't be very much trouble."

He stared at her for a moment, then he said, "You know I can't."

"Why not?"

"I'm in here, aren't I? I can't just take a walk outside."

"You know the doors are unlocked. You're a voluntary patient."

"And you'd call the fucking security guards."

"Try me."

Jeffrey's eyes were no longer moving. They were fastened on Jennifer as if debating something. "No. It's a trick. You know what happens when I start to suck."

"No, Jeffrey I don't. What happens?"

"They start to shrivel up and die. They turn into turds in my mouth."

"Do they die just because you suck them?"

"No," he said, shaking his head. "They're already dead. I see them smile and I see the skull beneath their skin. They walk and I can see their skeletons. I see them turn into dry little apples, all withered and shriveled. That's what I see. Life is only death postponed."

"I'd like to read one of your plays, Jeffrey."

"I don't write plays anymore."

"Why not?"

"They would fail like everything I do. I tried to kill myself. Did Dr. Freedman tell you that?"

Jennifer shook her head.

"I tried to drink lye but they took me to the hospital."

"How long have you been wanting to do that?"

"Since I blew out my first birthday candle."

"Do you remember who bought that cake for you?"

"Why, is that important? My parents, I guess."

Jennifer nodded slowly. "You told Dr. Freedman you were an orphan but your parents are actually living."

"I'm an orphan with parents. It's common enough, isn't it?"

"Still, I'd like to know something about them."

"There was a poppa bear and a momma bear and a little baby bear who liked to suck boys' dicks."

"Do you ever see your parents anymore?"

"My daddy doesn't like having a faggot for a son. He tells people I got killed in Vietnam, isn't that a gas?"

"How does that make you feel?"

"Like dancing, doctor. How would it make you feel? I hate his bloated guts. I always have. He's a fucking lump of shit and I wish he were dead."

What happened next surprised Jennifer by its abruptness. Jeffrey sat forward and his hands, which had been listless before, began to move expressively. He needed no further prompting but continued in an expressionless voice to recount the number of ways his father had tried to prevent his son from seeking homosexual experiences, from physical beatings and putting the barrel of a loaded gun against his temple to putting his penis in a fire. "Do you understand, doctor? My daddy took my cock in his hand, and when it got good and hard, he tried to stick it in the stove."

"Jennifer blanched but kept control, trying not to reveal her repugnance. "What was your mother's reaction?"

"You mean Mommy Dearest, who suckled me at the breast? She had big ones too. She just told him to make sure he put it in all the way. She wanted to see my dicky nice and charbroiled. She always overcooked meat anyway," he added with a snicker. "Maybe I should get them an anniversary present, doctor. Could you suggest something appropriate? How about arsenic?"

Jennifer noticed that forty-five minutes had passed and was forced to tell him that she would see him tomorrow at the same hour.

When Jeffrey left, she barely had time to make a recording of her impressions for his feeling profile. She realized she had done the exact opposite of what Dr. Boise wanted her to do. Instead of noting his reactions to the medication level of the previous twenty-four hours, she had begun an in-depth analysis. Jennifer continued writing until the hour struck. Then it was Laura Archer's turn.

Laura was a twenty-eight-year-old personnel recruiter for a large investment banking house. She was experiencing feelings of worthlessness and deepening gloom. This was her first hospitalization. Dr. Freedman indicated that she had been experiencing feelings of anxiety and self-doubt for some time, which had culminated in her inability to function in her job.

As soon as Laura entered her office Jennifer could not help feeling a certain closeness to the young woman. They were near enough in age and family background to be almost mirror images. Laura had been admitted only a few days before Dr. Freedman's death. She was being treated with tetracyclic antidepressants.

The young woman facing her was very pretty, Jennifer realized. There was a certain doll-like elegance in the way she held herself and her chinalike complexion made Jennifer envious. Her eyes were large and startlingly blue. She had lost a great deal of weight, which was obvious from the way her clothes hung on her. Her fingers played with each other nervously while her mouth formed a tight line of concentration.

Jennifer began with a series of questions relating to her feelings, which Laura responded to in a toneless, almost inaudible voice. At times she lapsed into a whisper, so that Jennifer was forced to ask her to speak louder. Laura confessed to having no appetite and to sleeping only a few hours in spite of her sedatives. She felt too weak to function properly in her RT sessions.

Jennifer had only moments to scan the notes Anne had made during an interview with Laura's parents. The social worker had noted an overprotective mother and dominant father whose only son had died of a drug overdose. Dr. Freedman had noted that Laura's anxieties stemmed from the father's transference of his expectations from his son to his daughter, who, believing she could not fulfill them, had begun a reactive withdrawal.

Reading this conclusion, Jennifer realized just how closely Laura's case paralleled her own family situation. Having one of their sons become a doctor had been one of her parents' fondest dreams but neither son had wanted it. Jennifer never thought of her parents as exerting any active pressure until she herself had entered analysis. Then she began to understand her own deeply rooted anxieties about fulfilling their expectations. Until then, she had thought of her decision to enter medicine as solely her own. Yet learning the contrary did not change her mind in any way. It only gave her a deeper insight into the complexities of her own psyche.

Jennifer paused when she had completed the feeling profile. She stared at Laura for a moment, then said, "I know your parents came to visit you yesterday. Do you want to tell me how you felt about seeing them?"

Laura hesitated. She seemed almost afraid to answer.

"You don't have to tell me if you don't want to."

Laura's eyes dropped into her lap.

"Are you ashamed of something you've done to them?"

Laura nodded. "I failed my father."

"Why do you think that?"

"Because I'm here."

"Don't you think he wants you to get better?"

Laura looked up at Jennifer. "He wants me to get better only so I can go back to work."

"Did he tell you that?"

"No. But I know he does." Laura looked at Jennifer boldly. "Dr. Freedman wanted me to go back to work also."

"He never said that, did he?"

"No. But he did. I know he did."

"Do you think I want you to?"

"I don't know."

"I only want you to do what you really want. I think Dr. Freedman wanted that too."

Laura stared at Jennifer as if unsure whether to believe her.

Jennifer knew she could only begin helping Laura when that question was truly resolved in the young woman's mind. She realized that she wanted Laura's trust very much—perhaps too much. But helping Laura would be possible only when Laura truly wanted her help. Until then she could do nothing.

Looking up after Laura left, Jennifer realized she had only one more patient that day, Brae Haskill. As the clock edged past the hour she wondered if he would come.

Jennifer knew she would have to wait out the entire hour. She had begun her review of the first two sessions when the door opened and Brae entered the office. He was a tall man with what she imagined was a powerful body. He had crisp sandy hair that was combed to reveal a widow's peak above a crinkled forehead. His face was drawn into a pattern of lines and wrinkles around his eyes. Jennifer would have described him as more rugged than handsome but he was compelling to look at. His dark gray eyes seemed to be measuring her as he sat in a defiant slouch, arms crossed over his chest. It almost resembled a boxer's pose.

Jennifer saw from his record that he had not attended any of the sessions with Dr. Boise after Dr. Freedman's death. Nor had he attended the floor meeting that morning. He had also skipped group therapy.

"You weren't at the floor meeting this morning. Can I ask why?" Jennifer began without any preliminaries.

"It's a waste of time, isn't it?"

"You know it's required that you attend. Those are our rules."

"If we did everything that was required, doctor, a cop like me would be out of a job."

"You also didn't attend any of Dr. Boise's sessions. Why?"

"Boise is an asshole, that's why."

"Just exactly why are you here?"

"These shrink games get to be annoying after a while. Every goddamn thing is a question. Don't you know how to talk like other people?"

"I'm not here to talk. I'm here to help you. What I'd like to know is why exactly you're here?"

"It's a way to get away from my job for a few weeks."

"There are nicer places."

"Not at full pay."

"Couldn't you have found a doctor to say you were physically ill? Then you could have gone anywhere you wanted."

"I came here because I heard you give the right kind of pills for the way I was feeling."

"And how is that?"

"Isn't it all there in Dr. Freedman's notes?"

"Dr. Freedman indicated you were extremely unwilling to cooperate."

"I cooperate fine with the pills, doc. Which is more than I can say for your questions, which are depressing to say the least."

"You don't want to be here, this afternoon, do you?"

"Not especially. But if I have to sit around until I get the pills, this is as good a place as any."

"You can leave if you'd like."

Brae stared at Jennifer, who met his eyes with a steady gaze. Not critical or angry, merely open and receptive. It was well acted. Inside she felt like striking him. Brae rose and left the room without closing the door behind him.

Jennifer crossed the room and closed the door, feeling beads of sweat on her forehead. Her heart was pounding fiercely. She had experienced her share of hostile patients before. But Brae's antagonism had thrown her. She had engineered his leaving she realized more as a defense for herself than as a therapeutic act for him. Aloud she said, "Damn it, Westwood. You've still got a hell of a long way to go."

It took Jennifer a full half hour to completely calm down after Brae had gone. He was only responsible for a small part of her tide of feeling. The excitement of the first day and the concentration she had brought to her first patient sessions were also involved. Brae's behavior only increased the pressure she felt to devise an appropriate strategy to involve him in therapy, in spite of Dr. Boise's warning against it. His behavior was only a way of denying the fact that he was actually ill and in need of help. To accept this conclusion would mean he had lost the control of his emotional equilibrium and result in his loss of self esteem.

Jennifer wrote her conclusions down, then put a pencil line through them. They seemed so pat. What she sensed was a human being in desperate pain, doing everything he could to deny that the pain even existed. Jennifer knew that unless he made that admission to himself it would be impossible to reach him. All the pills in the world would do nothing but mask the real problem. They might make Brae appear to function but it would always be with a flaw. Pain was part of therapy. Without it the patient would never experience any gains in self-understanding. That was where she and Dr. Boise went different ways. Pain was a part of living. No amount of drugs could pretend it did not exist.

With a nervous hand Jennifer headed for the pad of medication orders. For the patients she had not yet seen she continued the indicated dosages. But when it came to writing the order for Jeffrey, she hesitated. Compressing her lips, she reduced the dosage by half.

She had just slipped the orders into a folder when the door opened and Dr. Boise entered her office. Jennifer could see how poorly his smile fitted his mouth.

"So, how was your first day? Thoroughly confused?"

"Not really. Everyone has been especially helpful."

"I'm glad we're all making you feel right at home."

Jennifer could almost taste the lie behind his words. But she answered with a polite smile.

"Are those your medication orders?" he said, looking down at the file. Before Jennifer could answer, he turned the file around and began thumbing through the pink forms. He stopped at Jeffrey's. "Why have you reduced this patient's medication?"

Jennifer paused a moment, then said, "His behavioral swings were so great I thought it would be advisable to reduce the dosage until he becomes more stabilized."

"Please continue the same dosage," Dr. Boise said in a cold tone. "The swings will disappear."

"And what if they don't?"

Dr. Boise's eyes grew harsh. "A great deal of experience and consultation went into this program, Dr. Westwood. Don't you think it somewhat presumptuous to change it after one session with the patient, especially without consulting me?"

Jennifer felt her face color. "It's just that I was under the impression that these patients were my responsibility."

"As your supervisor I am ultimately responsible for your performance, doctor. Considering your inexperience, I think it advisable to allow me to examine your medication charges before you submit them."

Jennifer felt her gorge begin to rise but she controlled her tongue. It had gotten her into far too much trouble in the past. She was walking a professional tightrope at Montrose and she knew it, both as a new resident and as a woman. She suddenly felt a sense of responsibility toward Dr. Kessler for his decision to add women to the staff. That responsibility decreed that she take extreme care with every move she made. In a choked voice, Jennifer said, "Certainly, Dr. Boise."

"Fine. I'm glad we understand each other."

Withdrawing a felt-tipped pen from the plastic holder he kept in his breast pocket, Boise revised the dosage. "So then. Any other problems?"

Mr. Haskill has exhibited a good deal of defensive denial."

"Yes," Dr. Boise murmured, jutting out his lower lip.

"Haskill is a difficult case. But I'm sure you'll get him to respond. I'll be curious to hear the rest of your reactions at our staff conference tomorrow, after you've had a chance to see the rest of your patients." He snapped his smile back into place and left the office.

Jennifer's hands were trembling over her little excursion into self-control. But she mastered her feelings quickly. The thought of another conference brought more weight to her already overburdened shoulders. While other branches of medicine placed great emphasis on consultations between colleagues, none made it as much a part of its life as psychiatry. Staff conferences, clinical-staff conferences—the list went on and on, with endless cups of coffee and filled ashtrays. Bored faces and a round robin of opinions from the nursing staff, the social workers, and therapists. It was a never-ending process that Jennifer, with her quick mind and restless energy, found almost impossible to take. Yet she had chosen this part of the profession and she would have to learn the patience that went along with her choice.

She spent the next four hours in a round of meetings with all six therapists and Anne Bridgeman, with whom she shuffled and reshuffled and scheduled visits of family members, whose observations and opinions could be critical in the treatment of her patients. Drug therapy might be all the rage at the moment, Jennifer realized, but the hospital still went through all the traditional steps of documenting a patient's background and history.

Unfortunately, both Jeffrey Cox and Brae Haskill had listed no family. There were no spouses or close relatives other than a mandatory person to contact. Jeffrey had listed several names under the family heading on his admission form but none of them were actually related to him. Still, it might be a beginning, she thought. A place for her to start the process of mining his past. Brae Haskill listed only his partner, an officer named Frank Richie. Jennifer copied down as much of the pertinent information as she had time for. Then she left Anne's office and went into the nurses' station where she handed Rita Kahn her medication orders.

When Rita scanned Jeffrey's, she stopped. "Who changed this back?" she asked knowingly. "Was it Dr. Boise?"

"As a matter of fact, it was," Jennifer answered.

"Dr. Freedman was going to reduce the dosage too. He thought the swing was too wide."

"I thought he considered Jeffrey endogenous."

"I think he was having his doubts."

"Did Dr. Boise know that?"

Rita started to answer, then abruptly bent and opened a drawer in her desk. Jennifer turned and saw Anne enter the office. She approached Jennifer with a brisk stride.

"I've got that detective's work number," she said, handing Jennifer a slip of paper. "But I can't find anything on Jeffrey's parents. They're either not listed or they've moved. But I'll keep trying."

"Thanks," Jennifer said, waiting for Anne to leave before she turned back to Rita. "Did Dr. Boise contradict Dr. Freedman's recommendations about reducing Jeffrey's medication?"

Hesitantly, Rita said, "Look, Dr. Westwood. Dr. Boise has the most successful service in the hospital in terms of a win-loss record if you want to put it crudely. These new drugs are knocking them out, but let's face it, they don't work for everyone and that gets Dr. Boise fidgety. He doesn't like failures."

"What about difficult patients. He must get those."

"He transfers them out as fast as he can. He's looking for a directorship."

"I see."

"I hope you do," Rita said, and went into the pharmacy, leaving Jennifer to return to her office with a troubled expression. This was her first day and she already felt compromised. Caught between what Dr. Kessler had hired her to represent and her own beliefs as a therapist. Locking herself inside, she buried herself in her stack of patient records in preparation for the following day. Yet the feeling of agitation would not go away. "Dammit!" she said aloud. "Think of yourself for once, Westwood. Stop trying to save the world all by yourself."

But as soon as she said it, the opposite feeling washed over her. She would be damned if she allowed Dr. Boise's desire for a successful box score to overrule everything she believed. All through her training she had been badgered by people who told her to shut up and compromise. The same spirit that led her to defy certain of her professors, when, in the name of medical expediency, they sloughed over what she believed to be a doctor's first duty, rose to the surface now. *You're just the kind of person Dr. Kessler is looking for.* Jennifer remembered Doug Andrews' words. Well if that was the case, and Kessler expected Jennifer to put a shoulder against his staff's ingrained resistance, then he would also have to take a little of her own.

Jumping up she felt a rush of exhilaration. She opened one of the file drawers and slipped the records inside, then she said, "Screw you, Dr. Boise," and slammed it shut. Only the drawer rolled back out again. Jennifer pushed it back in and it repeated the same performance. Annoyed, she remembered she had to lock the drawer with the set of keys Anne had given her, but when she pushed the drawer closed she met with resistance. Something was blocking the rollers.

Jennifer pulled the drawer all the way out and stuck her hand as far in as she could, feeling for the obstacle. After a moment, her hand contacted something and she tugged it loose. It turned out to be a crumpled piece of paper. It had most likely been caught when Dr. Freedman's drawers had been cleaned out. Jennifer was about to toss it into the wastebasket when she changed her mind and began to flatten it out.

It turned out to be a drawing, like the ones psychologists asked patients to draw in a personality test. It was drawn in green crayon and was obviously meant to portray a woman's head. But instead of hair, a series of grotesque lines twisted out of the top of her head, like a nest of snakes. Jennifer stared at it, remembering her mythology. This resembled a Medusa head. The serpents were supposed to turn anyone looking at her into stone.

The drawing must have been made by one of Dr. Freedman's patients. Jennifer started to throw it away but the look in the woman's face arrested her. The expression was contorted with agony. The drawing was startlingly vivid, in spite of the crude way it was drawn. Whoever made it must have been in the throes of some terrible anguish. Jennifer smoothed out the paper and stood looking down at it for several seconds. She had often been impressed by the originality and expressive power of drawings executed by the insane. She had even saved some of the most striking. The one

on the desk in front of her certainly ranked with the best she
had collected. Its power was extremely compelling.

Instead of throwing it away, Jennifer slipped it inside a
bottom drawer and locked the cabinet. She picked up her bag
and jacket and glanced once around the office, *her* office,
then stepped outside and locked the door behind her.

Several patients were in the TV lounge, absorbed in
watching a show. Jennifer smiled as she passed them but no
one looked up. She headed toward the elevator. Visiting
hours had just begun and most patients were inside their
rooms with family and friends. But when she passed Jeffrey's
room she noticed he was sitting on his bed alone. She felt an
urge to step inside but fought against it. That was decidedly
unprofessional.

Downstairs she passed the security desk but this time instead of a scolding she received a good-night from the guard
on duty. Outside it was already dark. There was no bus waiting and she decided to walk to the tram. She started off at a
brisk pace. The sense of excitement that had churned through
her all day needed some form of release and she felt like running. But when she was halfway down the curving path that
led through the copse of trees and skirted the housing complex, she began to feel something else. There was a sense of
desolation around her that suddenly made her feel uncomfortable. It had grown colder and she slipped on her jacket.
Turning, she could no longer see the lights of the hospital
through the dark wall of trees. The housing complex rose
above her, separated from the path by an embankment.
Despite the distance, she noticed light in some of the windows. The river flowed along with glints of reflected light,
cold and mysterious. In the pattern of the waves she thought
she glimpsed a face.

It was the image of the woman in the drawing.

Jennifer felt a chill. She was suddenly filled with a sense of
foreboding. What demons created such a fear? she wondered.
There was so much misery locked away behind the walls of
the institution she had left. So much pain even their wonder
drugs could not alleviate.

A dark shape shot toward her out of the bushes. Jennifer
almost jumped, but it was only a squirrel. Looking around,
she became aware of just how alone she was. The esplanade
was deserted. She could see it stretching toward the distant

lights of the tram, a silent ribbon of concrete. Ahead was a screen of trees and the slowly moving shape of a jogger. She had been feeling so euphoric after her first day that she had completely forgotten that the island was still a part of New York, unpredictable and dangerous. She remembered the warnings she had been given not to venture out alone, especially in park areas. And that was exactly where she was now.

As the path curved closer to the tram Jennifer realized she would have to pass through a sparsely wooded area. During the day it seemed a welcome spot of green among all the concrete and brick. But at night it took on the special menace of a place where no one would hear her if she screamed.

A shout made her wheel around.

Someone was running along the path behind her. Other voices answered. In a moment a group of teenagers appeared at the top of a knoll, all of them rushing toward the tram. Jennifer increased her speed, relieved to have this company. They all arrived together and she spent a breathless minute amid the laughing crowd that was heading toward Manhattan.

The tram ride calmed her nerves and made her feel a little foolish for all her fears. She stood in front of the swaying car watching the myriad of lights approaching as the car rushed forward to be embraced by the station. Jennifer returned to the same market-deli she had visited yesterday and bought a few things before she turned the corner toward home, appreciating how busy her own street was with its double-parked cars and the neighborhood saloon almost directly across the street from her house. But as she walked Jennifer discovered a fundamental fact about New York. As noisy and crowded as the city appeared, the distance between one avenue and another, even between the entrance of one apartment house and another, could be enormous—if it was dark and you were alone.

Upstairs, the apartment looked even bleaker and more dismal than it had the night before. Jennifer was glad of her exhaustion. She put on the radio and stripped. She showered and was glad of the hot water, which she knew in certain apartment buildings was hardly bountiful. She had just gotten into her floor-length terry-cloth robe when the doorbell rang.

"Who is it?" she asked trying to peer through the tiny

peephole and finding it useless. All she saw was a tiny yellow blur.

"It's Phillip Rosen from upstairs."

"Oh sure, just a second."

Jennifer fumbled to unlock the three bolts and opened the door. Rosen was dressed in a two-piece running suit and held a bicycle wheel in his hands.

"Sorry to bother you, but I heard your radio so I knew you were up."

"No bother really," Jennifer said, almost glad of the company.

"My wife and I were wondering how you were getting along."

"Fine. This was my first day at the clinic. I haven't even started on the apartment."

"It takes time to get adjusted. Look, we usually have some friends up over the weekend. If you're interested come on up for a drink."

"Sure, if I'm not on duty."

"We're always on duty," Rosen said with a disparaging shake of his head. "I even take a bath with my beeper on." Jennifer laughed and nodded understandingly. Then Rosen said, "Actually I came down to give you this. Hank left it with us."

Rosen offered her the wheel. It took a second before Jennifer understood. "Oh, you mean, Dr. Freedman. Was this his?"

"Yeah. I have a friend who fixes them. I didn't know what to do with it and I was at the hospital when they packed up the place. You know what the space situation is like."

"Oh sure! No problem really. I'll have it sent on to his family."

"Well then, good night," Rosen said with a wave.

Jennifer returned the gesture and closed the door, feeling a warm sense of contact. It would be nice to have friends in the building. She stared down at the object in her hand. What the hell was she supposed to do with it?

She opened the hall closet and placed the wheel inside, then went to the sink and washed her hands, out of some irrational feeling that the wheel might have in some way be injected with death. Good God, and you're a doctor, she thought. Next you'll be bleeding your patients and putting

leeches on their skin. Yet she could not help the feeling, just
as she could not prevent the wheel from reinforcing the sensation that she was being fitted into a stranger's skin.

Jennifer busied herself preparing a light bite of cereal and
toast. She had no real appetite for dinner. Afterward, she
washed the plates, slipped into bed, and in spite of her exhaustion came instantly awake. Threads of sound wove themselves through her consciousness. A stereo was playing a
Mozart symphony. Traffic rumbled by on a distant avenue.
Occasionally, a raised voice punctuated the silence. Someone
clattered down the metal stairs. She heard the lid of a garbage can clang, then the downstairs door slammed and the
same feet pounded their way back upstairs. She listened to
the refrigerator change pitch.

Images of the day passed through her mind. Jennifer pictured Laura's distraught face and heard the troubled words
Jeffrey had spoken. Tomorrow she would meet her other patients. A mother whose child was crying for her and a disturbed teenage girl. What lay before her seemed vast and
unattainable. She wanted to nurse them all back to health
like the dolls she cared for when she was a child. She knew it
was impossible, but also knew she would try in spite of Dr.
Boise and his chemical panaceas, which cured patients, as it
were, by pushing a button. Jennifer's whole being rebelled
against his kind of medicine. Relieving symptoms would
never be enough. There was a cause for each illness . . . a
cause. And perhaps even a cure.

She turned over on her side and closed her eyes. But as
soon as she did so the image of the drawing she had found in
the file drawer returned to haunt her with its vividness and its
strange, almost mythic horror. It took an effort of will to
fully banish it from her mind. She fell asleep and dreamed of
bicycle wheels spinning in a dark cavernous void where she
was pursued by a menacing figure in white robes who
resembled Dr. Boise but who turned into a creature with hol-
lowed eyes and a face that was as stark and frightening as an
African mask.

FOUR

━━━━━━━━◆◆━━◆◆◆━━◆◆━━━━━━━━

The next three days flew past with hurricane force. Each night when she returned from the clinic Jennifer fell into an exhausted sleep. Getting out of bed each morning felt like a page being torn from a book. Jennifer threw off the covers before six each morning, emerging from the warmth of her bed into the chill New York dawn. She had been told the landlord was required to supply heat whenever the temperature fell below fifty-five. Those were the rules. But the radiators might as well have been sculpture for all the heat they provided. Washing with ice-cold water was another delight. Coffee was gulped down as she struggled into her clothes. Luckily, the market sold panty hose in all sizes from a circular rack that was always filled. Jennifer seemed to be going through a pair a day. Only now did she actually realize how small her wardrobe really was. When she confided this to her mother in a late-night phone call, she heard panic setting in on the other end of the line. Jennifer calmed her mother down, assuring her that she did not have to make a trip to New York. A couple of department stores were open all day Sunday and Jennifer promised she would buy several new outfits then.

Making the apartment more livable was another problem. There was just no time for her to shop for anything. The hospital savaged her days like a piranha. After the usual sessions with her patients there were endless staff meetings and medication reports along with family sessions and hasty conferences with Anne concerning outpatient programs for patients about to be discharged. And sandwiched in between everything else were the reams of paper: detailing, recording, analyzing. The list of duties seemed endless and always growing longer: EEGs, CAT scans, angiograms, and the batteries of psychological tests.

The floor was sorting itself out into good people and bad. Jennifer was learning where the pitfalls lay with amazing speed. Rita Kahn was a shining beacon. The head nurse always had a smile on her attractive face and a wisecrack to go along with some piece of valuable information she slipped to Jennifer with all the casualness of an old friend. Jennifer knew how much she had to depend on Anne. Her own effectiveness would be evaluated in large part on how they operated as a team, yet Anne continued to be an enigma. Her incredible efficiency was counterbalanced by the knowledge that Anne reported Jennifer's every move to Dr. Boise.

Dealing with Dr. Boise was another tightrope Jennifer had to cross several times a day. Dr. Boise's visits could never be predicted in advance. Sometimes he visited the nurses' station and examined the medication reports. At other times he appeared in Jennifer's office between patient sessions to question her about a particular case. These visits were over and above the regular conference scheduled at the end of each day when each patient's progress was discussed and evaluated. The sessions ran smoothly except when they mentioned Jeffrey or Brae.

In the four sessions she had with him, Jeffrey had swung from outright euphoria to withdrawal and back again. The day following their first session Jeffrey had surprised her by excitedly revealing the outline of an ambitious new play. With glowing eyes he had continued an almost nonstop monologue describing characters and situations that left Jennifer awestruck. He had to be reminded three times that they had run out of time.

An hour later a nurse passed Jeffrey's room and sounded an alarm that had the orderlies running. Jeffrey was standing in front of his sink, burning his notes. Somehow he had gotten hold of matches and set his outline on fire. He was ordered on center lounge restriction for twenty-four hours and denied smoking privileges. In their next session Jennifer found him almost morose. He barely responded to her questions and kept staring moodily out of the window.

Dr. Boise's lips twitched soundlessly when he was told of these changes. His response was to continue the present level of medication and await developments. Jennifer seethed but she said nothing, cursing herself for a coward.

The only real progress she made was with Laura. A session with Laura's parents confirmed the father's exaggerated expectations that Dr. Freedman had noted. But Jennifer detected something else. Seeing each parent separately revealed that the father's own position was actually threatened by his daughter's success, just as it had been when his son had attempted anything. The revelation gave her a valuable insight into the family dynamics surrounding her patient.

Brae continued to be difficult. The symptoms of his depression were easing but his record of attendence at RT continued to be spotty. His contact with the other patients was also minimal. Jennifer had decided to transfer him to a room with another male patient. But this did not end his self-imposed isolation. He continued to keep to himself although he did not complain about the move. He would seat himself in a corner of the lounge, and when it got crowded he walked to one of the recreational areas at the end of both sides of the corridor.

In their sessions together Brae continued to be hostile. If he answered her questions at all, it was with one-word answers. Jennifer restricted her questions to his feeling profile. Any reference to his past was quickly diverted.

"Your record indicates you received several citations for bravery. Do you enjoy your job?" she had ventured on their third outing

"Do you know what a cop does, doctor? He takes pleasure away from other people. Would you want a job like that?"

"I might if I thought there was a greater good involved. A murderer may get pleasure from killing people. But the man who stops him is giving a greater pleasure to society, isn't he?"

"He might. Unless he thought that society deserved it."

"Do you think it does?"

"Does what?" he challenged.

"Deserve to be punished."

Brae stared at her for a moment, then turned his head

away. He said little else for the rest of the session but Jennifer knew she had struck a chord.

Jennifer was not orthodox enough in her approach to merely wait for a patient to reveal another layer of himself. Time pressured her into using as many approaches as she could, relying on both questions and free association, interpretation, suggestion, and even provocation. Like a railroad crew tunneling through a mountain she bored holes, set charges. Then she consolidated the gains, trying to devise strategies to counter the various ways the ego used to defend itself against exposing its secrets.

In the cases of both Jeffrey and Brae, she had only used a pick. She needed an explosive charge to tunnel into their psyches, but she was not sure where to get one. Brae refused to provide any opportunity she could use. The reduction of his symptoms through medication made reaching him even more difficult. Jeffrey was much the same but in a different way. His swings prevented the stable state she required in order to begin effective therapy. She needed to reduce both men's medication buffers but that would involve a confrontaion with Dr. Boise. Jennifer knew that confrontation was inevitable. It came much sooner than she expected.

Frank Richie looked completely ill at ease in the hospital coffee shop. He had refused to accept Jennifer's invitation to meet in her office, telling her Brae might regard their appointment as an act of disloyalty. Jennifer knew policemen had their own peculiar codes of conduct but she had never experienced them before.

Richie was a slender man in his middle forties with sharp features and a street-wise expression. He played with a book of matches while he eyed Jennifer with a mistrustful expression. Richie already had a cup of coffee in front of him when Jennifer entered the half-filled room with its orange plastic chairs and walls lined with vending machines. The detective had taken a corner table away from the other customers.

They shook hands and Jennifer accepted his offer of coffee, which he insisted on purchasing for her and carried back to their table with the ease of a man used to organizing such minor details. "How's my partner doing?" was Richie's first question.

"He's not cooperating at all." Jennifer answered, stirring in a pink packet of artificial sweetener.

Frank laughed knowingly. "Yeah, that Brae is all knuckles when he wants to be."

"He's also very ill. But he won't admit it. Not even to himself."

"He doesn't look too bad," Frank said, cocking a suspicious eye at her. He drew a pack of unfiltered cigarettes out of his pocket. Jennifer caught the dark glint of metal at his waist and realized he was carrying a gun. "You're kind of young for this job, aren't you, doc?"

"Would my being any older make Brae any better?" Jennifer shot back angrily.

Frank smiled crookedly. "No."

"But you'd trust my qualifications better?"

"Something like that."

"Do you want to see my diploma?"

"Doc, a long time ago I learned never to ask a doctor for his diploma. What I'd really like to see are his report cards."

Jennifer stared at him for a moment, then burst into laughter. Frank could not restrain his own smile and the two of them looked at each other with a newfound respect.

"Look, I wanted to see you because Brae won't tell me anything about himself. You seem to be the one closest to him. I know his parents are dead and his brothers and sisters live halfway across the country. You're the only one I can ask."

"I guess I am," Frank said, lighting up.

"I don't blame you for wanting to protect him. But you've got to understand, unless what's at the core of his problem is brought into the open, it's going to fester and get progressively worse."

"Why is he feeling better then, doc?"

"I know he seems better. He's on special medication that can relieve the symptoms but can't reach the basic cause."

Frank pursed his lips thoughtfully. Jennifer could almost feel his resistance. He exhaled a cloud of acrid smoke, then said, "What do you think is bothering him?"

"I don't know," Jennifer said candidly. "Sometimes a person is struck by this kind of depression without any prior warning. Sometimes there doesn't even seem to be a real cause and we find that its nature is some chemical imbalance.

But most result from a single incident or a series of incidents in the patient's environment. We know almost nothing about Brae's background."

"What happens if Brae just keeps on taking the pills?" Frank said, tapping his ash into a glass ashtray.

"Most likely he'll feel better for a time. Then the condition could get worse or it could disappear as suddenly as it came on. There's no guarantee what the medication will do over a long period of time. Not by itself, without any other kind of therapy. I'm not even sure just exactly how much it's actually helping him now."

"So what you're saying is, Brae might be acting better but he's just kidding himself. He'd be a junkie to those pills."

"In a way, yes. The medication would have to be almost permanent, unless we were able to begin treating the cause."

The detective inhaled deeply. Jennifer watched his eyes trail off into space as he mulled over what she had just said. Finally he turned to her. "I don't want Brae hooked on anything. Even if it's good for him."

"I can understand that," Jennifer said. "That's why I need more information. So I can reach him without drugs."

Frank considered for a moment, then he exhaled a thin stream of blue smoke. "You know Brae is one of the sharpest guys I've ever worked with," he said with a shrug. "Maybe the smartest. He went all the way through college and half-way through law school before he quit to become a cop."

"Exactly why did he do that?" Jennifer asked pointedly.

"Commitment," Frank said with a wry smile. "The word is overused, almost a cliché. But in Brae's case it fits. I think the closer he got to becoming a lawyer the more he realized how deep the swamp really was. Not that the department is any kind of convent. We've got our own kind of corruption to deal with. But I think Brae felt he could really make a dif-ference out on the streets, where the enemy is visible. Sure you got judges who'll turn 'em loose as fast as you haul 'em in, but that's changin' too. Brae wanted to be where the ac-tion was. Where what he did was clean and meant something. Not lost somewhere in legal mazes. Am I making myself clear enough?"

"Very," Jennifer stated. "But what I'm looking for is some-thing immediate, related to his present condition. That's where I really need your help."

Frank sighed, and his eyes narrowed. Jennifer could see the small war being waged inside him. Then his jaw tensed as if he were about to impart something important. "There was a girl Brae was involved with. She was a Dominican. Not a nun. You know from the island. They've been pouring into New York like the PRs once did in the fifties. Anyway she was a pretty kid but a little screwed up. She was running with some schmuck who thought he was going to make a big-time drug score. Brae busted them, but the girl was clean. No previous record or anything. She was being used as a courier, that's all. She was a nurse, actually. Her boyfriend was an X-ray technician in a city hospital. We got on the case because the hospital suspected pilferage. It was a lot more than that. This guy was actually manufacturing heroin in his own laboratory, right there in the hospital.

"Anyway Brae gets interested in the girl, which is just like him. He's always helping out the people he busts. Anyway, this girl, her name is Mercedes, she's all broken up over the bust, really hysterical. Brae calms her down. He fixes it so she's not even on the arrest sheet. Then he and the girl start gettin' tight. She breaks off with the schmuck, and they start seeing a lot of each other. Before you know it she's beggin' Brae to let her move in with him. But Brae isn't buying so fast. I mean, Brae's not the type to open himself up to anyone until he feels he can really trust them. So he stalls her, but I can see he really feels something for the girl."

"You really believe he did?" Jennifer interrupted.

"Oh sure. My wife even spotted it. She can spot things like that faster than me." He smiled shyly.

Jennifer nodded, hoping Frank would complete the story before her lunch break ended. It had already been shortened when her teenage patient had begun destroying the furniture in her room and had to be sedated. Jennifer must have telegraphed her desire, because Frank said, "Okay, doc. I know you have to get back, so I'll make it short. One night the girl doesn't show. Brae starts looking all over for her. A couple of days pass and it's like she disappeared. Brae is beside himself worrying about her. He thinks maybe she cut out with another guy."

"But she didn't?"

"Uh-uh. They find her a week later in a basement on 110th Street. She was gang-raped and strangled. We still don't have a clue to who did it. After that Brae started to dysfunction."

"Why didn't someone come forward and tell us about it?"

Frank shook his head at her naiveté. "Let me tell you about bein' a cop, doctor. The department has a prejudice against officers who crack up. There're even a system of kangaroo courts that'll take a man apart over how he treats his old lady. We're trying to keep this as low-key as possible. Brae's in here because of overwork and strain. It's like a rest, that's all. We don't want his record tagged with some fancy psychological diagnosis that will bend his career from now on. Can you understand that?"

"Yes. I understand. My only concern is in seeing him released as quickly as possible in as good shape as I can get him in."

"Then we both want the exact same thing, doc," Frank said, stubbing out his cigarette.

"I want to thank you for coming today and telling me what you did. It could be crucial to his recovery."

"Let's hope so. Because doctor, with all due respect, from where I sit, you're pretty enough to be a centerfold instead of in here dealing with nut cases."

The detective rose and stalked out, leaving Jennifer with flaming cheeks.

When Jennifer walked off the elevator after her meeting with Frank Richie, Rita Kahn confronted her with a tight-lipped expression.

"Dr. Westwood, it's Jeffrey again." Jennifer followed the head nurse around the turning toward Jeffrey's room. "He began acting up about a half hour ago," Rita said over her shoulder. "This time he got hold of a razor blade."

Jennifer felt her stomach tense. Razor blades and other sharp implements were collected by the nurses on the first day of admission and returned only as a patient's recovery warranted. Jeffrey must have slipped into one of the other patient's rooms when no one was inside and gotten hold of a blade.

Jennifer stopped beside Rita at the door of Jeffrey's room. Two male orderlies were inside holding Jeffrey on his bed, while a nurse readied a gauze bandage from a tray of medical supplies. Blood oozed from several places on his arms. More was splattered across his clothing and on the sheets.

"It's all right, doctor," Jeffrey said, looking up at Jennifer with an exaggerated smile. "I'm fine now. No more block. I've begun writing again. See."

Jennifer caught Rita's look and glanced over at the far wall. Her eyes widened with shock. The wall was covered with a fine scrawl but the words were already beginning to blur. They had been written in Jeffrey's own blood.

"Don't you want to read what I've written doctor?" Jeffrey said as the nurse began swabbing his arms. "I dedicated it to you."

"We can discuss it later, Jeffrey. In our session together," Jennifer said, stepping out of the room. Rita followed her.

"Has he been given anything?" Jennifer said, trying to control the trembling in her hands. The sight of blood no longer affected her as it had at the beginning of her medical training. She had witnessed too many corpses and operations. The trembling was caused by anger.

"I was waiting for you, doctor." Rita said.

Jennifer dictated a drug and dosage that caused Rita to raise her eyebrows. "That's a fairly high dosage, isn't it, doctor, considering how it might react with his usual medication?"

"He's no longer going to be given his usual medication," Jennifer said sharply. She turned and strode back to her office with her mind made up. She was taking Jeffrey off medication completely.

It did not take long for the chain reaction to begin. After Jennifer had written out her drug charges, she delivered them to the nurses' station, placing them on Rita's desk in plain view, with Jeffrey's on top where she knew Anne would be able to see them. No sooner had the last patient stepped out of her office when the phone rang. Jennifer picked it up after letting it ring half a dozen times. As she expected, Dr. Boise was on the line.

"Dr. Westwood I've just been informed that you've taken Jeffrey Cox off medication completely."

"That's correct, doctor," Jennifer said coolly.

"You realize of course that such an action is entirely against my instructions."

"Yes. I do realize that."

"And you did it anyway?"

"That's correct."

"Even if I tell you the risk to the patient is too great."

"That risk is already too great, which is why I took him off medication. I assume you've been told of his latest action."

"We have to expect occasional outbursts and acting out. When they occur our strategy is to vary the dosages."

"These are not occasional outbursts, Dr. Boise. They are clearly part of a pattern. I want to take Jeffrey off medication for the time being."

"For what purpose?"

"The patient has indicated certain insights into his own behavior. I think he needs time to integrate them free of the swing state induced by the drugs."

"You mean psychotherapy, exclusively?"

"For the next few days, yes."

"I'm sorry. I do not agree," Dr. Boise stated firmly.

"Jeffrey is my patient, Dr. Boise. The responsibility is mine."

Dr. Boise began in a patient tone. "Dr. Westwood. Consider your position. You are an inexperienced resident under my supervision."

"I may be under your supervision but the responsibility for Jeffrey still belongs to me."

"Then you are prepared to contradict my direct orders?"

Jennifer hesitated. Voices began shrieking warnings about her career, voices she had heard since entering med school. She silenced them with a single word. "Yes. I'm afraid that's what I'll have to do."

There was a pause at the other end. In a controlled voice Dr. Boise said, "I'm sorry. I cannot permit you to do that."

"Then I intend going to Dr. Kessler with my resignation."

The words escaped her almost by reflex. Both of them were aware of the importance Dr. Kessler had placed on his commitment to integrate the staff. For Jennifer to be dismissed or to resign would be a blow to that effort. Jennifer could hear Boise breathing. The moment prolonged itself suspensefully. Whatever insight Jennifer had ever gained into the administrative personality was operating now. She could almost visualize Boise balancing Jennifer's insubordination with what would be seen from his superior's point of view as his inability to handle a situation of maximum importance. Sacrificing one patient was less important than incurring disfavor.

"All right, Doctor Westwood," Boise said through clenched teeth. "I'll let you go ahead and we'll see what happens. But I want to warn you that since you are acting against my orders, the entire responsibility for what happens is your own."

Boise hung up and Jennifer replaced the receiver in a state of shock. She had actually won. She stared straight ahead for a moment, feeling a slight numbness as the feeling of victory swept over her. Today was Friday. The sedative would be out of Jeffrey's system by Saturday night or even sooner, along with the last of the medication. With a sudden motion she reached across the desk. She tore off a pink medication slip and scribbled another drug order. "In for a penny, in for a pound," she said aloud and cut Brae's medication in half.

FIVE

Jennifer slept through the alarm and stared at the clock in horror. As she realized she had overslept, panic pulsed through her. Then she realized it was Saturday. It was already after ten, which meant she had garnered almost fourteen hours of needed sleep. She got up, showered and dressed, and made herself scrambled eggs and coffee. Then, outfitted in Levi's, a turtleneck, and a short leather jacket, she made her way cross town beneath a bright fall sun.

As she headed toward the department stores on Third to do the shopping she so desperately needed she felt herself relax. She was actually enjoying being among the crowds on the teeming sidewalks. For the first time she felt a sense of belonging. In the two and a half hours she spent in Bloomingdale's she purchased two woolen dresses and a tweed skirt, along with several silk blouses to supplement her working wardrobe. Then she continued uptown along Third, spending a small fortune on a full-length mirror, two framed lithographs, and several other items to make the apartment more livable.

She was too loaded down with packages to continue her shopping spree, so she hailed a cab and went back home. She spent two hours rearranging the apartment before she began to feel hungry and treated herself to dinner at a Chinese restaurant she had noticed in the area. It was turning out to be her favorite kind of food. She was seated by herself at a table next to the window where she could see the never-ending flow of movement in the street outside. The idea of being away from the hospital filled her with a strange sense of freedom, but it felt like time she had stolen, not actually earned. For her patients, she knew the weekend was a long and boring ordeal, relieved by a few sessions of RT and the twice-a-day visiting hours. But for those without visitors it could be a painfully lonely time.

The thought of being alone herself had not occurred to Jennifer until then. In all the excitement of accepting the position at Montrose, it barely occurred to her that she actually knew no one in town. Her mother had supplied her with the names of two single girls, both daughters of members of her bridge set, which automatically prejudiced Jennifer against calling them. The image of Mark Tobey began to loom more and more favorably in her mind. He was certainly an attractive enough diversion, and for a moment she regretted turning down his offer of a date. The words of one of her former roommates rang in her ears. "Better find someone honey, and fast. It's gonna be a long, hard winter."

Jennifer consumed her meal with distinct pleasure. The food was marvelous. Afterward she took a long walk, filled with a sense of well-being and fueled as much by her victory over Dr. Boise as her achievement in getting Brae's partner to talk. Progress had been recorded on several fronts. Her teen-ager's behavior had leveled off, Mrs. Carey, her postpartum depression, had expressed a desire to see her baby, and she had finally made a breakthrough with Laura.

It had come in a remarkable interchange on the afternoon of the previous day. Jennifer had been so absorbed with Jeffrey she wished the clock would race through her next few sessions. Instead, just the opposite happened. The session with Laura seemed never ending until Laura suddenly looked up and said, "My father doesn't want me to succeed, does he?"

"What do you think, Laura?"

Laura shook her head. "I don't think he really does."

"Do you want to?"

Laura raised her eyes. In a whisper she said, "Yes. Very much."

"Then that's all that counts, isn't it?"

Laura nodded slowly. The comments revealed a break-through in Laura's relationship to her parents. It might even provide a lever in separating her from her dependency on them. More importantly, it had begun the process of transference which was so basic to her own relationship with Laura. For Laura the ultimate adventure of self-discovery was about to begin, leading to emotional maturity and the ability to lead an independent existence. The satisfaction Jennifer felt at being midwife to the process filled her with a sensation of infinite pleasure.

It was after dark when Jennifer returned home. Instead of going upstairs she decided to take in a movie but she was put off by the idea of standing in a line of mostly couples. She passed several singles' bars crowded with young men who ogled her. Jennifer wondered if these were the kinds of places Mark went to find women. It was not really her style and she continued past them toward home.

The phone began ringing when she let herself into the building and continued as she rushed upstairs and struggled with three locks. She charged into the apartment and picked up the receiver breathlessly. "Hello."

"Dr. Westwood. It's Rita Kahn. Am I disturbing you?"

"No. It's okay. What's wrong?"

"I thought you should know. Jeffrey has gone AWOL."

Jennifer's pulse stopped. "When?"

"We think it happened during evening visiting hours."

"What do we do now?"

"There isn't much we can do. We've notified the police of course. The local precinct often finds our people wandering around before they can reach the bridge to Manhattan."

"Do you think he'd try to do that?"

"Anything is possible."

"Did he have any money?"

"We think he might have gotten hold of some. One of the nurses' wallets is missing. We'll call you if there's any word. I just wanted to let you know."

"Please do that. And Rita. Thanks."

"No problem, doctor."

Jennifer hung up in a state of panic, her heart pounding, her mind flooded with possibilities. Jeffrey had tried to kill himself several times before. He could easily try again. She began to realize just how stupid she had been. She had made herself responsible for him no matter what happened, a responsibility rendered all the more onerous by the hospital's open-door policy.

Jennifer was, however, less concerned with her own fate than with the immediate danger to her patient. She paced back and forth in a frenzy, wondering what she could do. Rita had told her how hopeless it would be to find Jeffrey once he made it to the bridge and crossed into Manhattan. Her anxiety increased even more when she realized how little she actually knew of Jeffrey's mental state. She thought of calling Rita back but restrained the impulse. What could she add that Rita did not already know? Then Jennifer remembered she had brought home xerox copies of Jeffrey's file.

Flicking through the pages, Jennifer found his personal record. He had listed several names and addresses of people to contact in case of an emergency. All of them were in Manhattan. Jennifer picked up the phone and dialed the first number. It was busy, as were the second and third when she tried them. She waited a few minutes and tried again but the numbers were still busy. Fifteen minutes later, after trying again and again, she received the same busy signals. It was possible that Jeffrey had gone to one of the people on the list and this person was now contacting the others. Jennifer scribbled the names on a pad and charged out of the apartment. She hailed a cab on the corner of York Avenue and gave the driver the first address, which turned out to be in the Village.

As the cab traveled downtown Jennifer felt suffocated by tension. The streets were filled with cars. Her agitation increased every time they slowed down for traffic. The avenues were filled with weekend pleasure seekers and exuded a holiday atmosphere. Jennifer was uncertain what Jeffrey might feel at the sight of so many people obviously enjoying themselves when he felt so much pain. The contrast could trigger some desperate action, provided he was still alive.

The West Village streets were filled with a Mardi-Gras-like exuberance as the gay world paraded by in all its colorful variations. The cab nosed through the narrow streets until it pulled up in front of a bar. Jennifer paid the driver and stood in front, realizing that Jeffrey had given the name of the bar. Confused, she thought she had the wrong address until she double-checked.

Edging her way through a crowd of leather-clad males, packed together as closely as a rush-hour subway car, she managed to get inside and eventually got the bartender's attention. She asked for the name Jeffrey had written down.

"Are you kidding, sweetheart?" the bartender said, staring at her in surprise. "That's the name of this place. There ain't no such person." Jennifer repeated the phone number, but the bartender shook his head with irritation. "That's our number. But we're too busy to bother answering. We just take it off the hook."

He started to walk away but Jennifer held him a moment longer while she described Jeffrey.

This time he shrugged. "Lady, I'm just here on weekends. Besides this crowd changes faster than a movie line."

Jennifer elbowed her way outside. She felt a sense of bewilderment, but after checking the next address and asking directions several times she found it on a narrow twisting side street a few blocks away. It also turned out to be a bar, pulsating with disco music and gyrating male bodies. This time hostile eyes darted toward her as she entered. Jennifer realized she was the only woman in the place. She got the bartender's attention and asked the same questions she had asked before. She got the same responses. The person Jeffrey listed did not exist. It was only the name of the bar. And when she described Jeffrey, the bartender merely shook his head and laughed.

Jennifer knew before she even reached the third address that it would yield the same result, but she tried it anyway. It turned out to be a carbon copy of the other two, swarming with young men all wearing identical skin-tight Levi's. Leaving in despair, she found a cab on Hudson Street and gave the address of the hospital. The ride uptown was a different kind of torture. Jennifer tried to fathom the desperation that prompted Jeffrey to list three gay bars as his closest living relations. She recalled a magazine story she had recently read about an obviously deranged young man who had been stripped naked and chased onto the subway tracks by a howling mob; there he had fallen on the third rail and been electrocuted. The story haunted her. The city's brutality was a factor that could not be ignored. The open-door policy she had once thought so progressive also came back to torment her.

The cab pulled up in front of the clinic before Jennifer realized it. They had come the long way, along the East Side

Drive and over the Fifty-ninth Street Bridge, then across the smaller bridge from Queens. It was the same route Jeffrey had taken. Jennifer tipped the driver and headed inside the silent and almost deserted lobby.

Upstairs, the floor was quiet. Most of the patients were already sleeping and the few that were still up had only minutes before the orderlies made their rounds and turned out the lights. The nurses' station was lit but no one was inside. Jennifer hesitated. Being there was not entirely professional. She should have waited for word at home but she was haunted by Dr. Boise's pronouncement. She was responsible for whatever happened to Jeffrey. Her decision to take him off medication would be viewed as the immediate cause of his escape. It was an error of judgment that might possibly destroy her career even before it got off the ground.

Impulsively, Jennifer went past the nurses' station and headed for Jeffrey's room. When she turned the corner of the corridor she was surprised to find one of the orderlies, a muscular black man dressed in a sweat shirt and seated in an armchair before Jeffrey's room, reading a magazine beneath the subdued light of a floor lamp.

"It's okay, doctor. Jeffrey returned an hour ago by himself."

Jennifer wheeled around. The speaker was Rita Kahn. She stood behind Jennifer with a reassuring smile. "Is he all right?"

Rita nodded. "You can see him if you'd like."

"Just for a minute."

Both women walked toward the room. The orderly looked up with an expression that signaled the fact that everything was all right. With a wildly beating heart, Jennifer stepped toward her patient's door.

Jeffrey lay on his bed with his arms shielding his eyes. Sensing Jennifer's presence, he rose on his elbows. His face was masked by shadow, but even in the reflected light from the hall, Jennifer could see his wildly expressive eyes.

"I'm sorry, doctor," he said softly. "I had to be by myself."

"We can talk about it on Monday," Jennifer said. "I'm just glad you're all right." But instead of leaving, she took another step into the room. "Are you feeling any calmer?"

Jeffrey nodded. "Yes. I'm okay."

She looked at him for another moment, then turned and started to leave.

"Dr. Westwood."

Jennifer turned around. Jeffrey was sitting up with his feet off the bed. "I discovered something outside," he said forcefully. "I can't write because I can't love." He hesitated, as if unsure of what he wanted to say next. "Can you help me learn how . . . to love someone?" He whispered.

Jennifer stared into his tortured eyes. "First you have to learn to love yourself, Jeffrey. I can help you learn how."

As she left the room she turned away so the orderly would not see the emotion in her face. The corridor was dark enough so no one could see how wet her eyes really were.

By the time she had turned the corner and reached the nurses' station she had regained her composure. She stepped inside to find Rita and thank her but a different nurse was seated at Rita's desk.

"Has Rita gone home?" Jennifer asked.

"No. She's down the hall in isolation."

"Has there been an emergency?"

"You could say that, doctor. It's been one hell of a weekend. First Jeffrey and now, Laura."

"Laura?" Jennifer repeated, not sure she had heard correctly.

"That's right."

"I'm Dr. Westwood. Laura is my patient."

"Oh. I'm sorry, doctor. I thought you knew. Laura went berserk a little while after I came on duty. She attacked a patient with a scissors. We had to put her in restraints."

The shock of seeing Laura in a straightjacket brought a different kind of horror to Jennifer's mind. Laura sat in a corner of the isolation chamber with her back against the wall. Her legs were spread wide, a trickle of urine running between them and onto the floor. Jennifer had only been in the isolation chamber once before, when she had been shown around the floor on her first day. It was entered through a double door, a wooden door on the outside and a metal one inside, with a handle only on one side and a small wire-mesh window. It was the fabled padded cell. Only at Montrose there was no padding except for two gym mats on the linoleum floor.

Laura was in a frenzy. She had been given a sedative but it would be some time before it took effect. Her face was twisted into an unrecognizable mask. Her bulging eyes were focused on something only she could see. Her lips moved rapidly, uttering phrases too garbled to understand, rising and falling erratically.

Her body was equally active. She tossed herself back and forth violently, trying to smash her head against the plaster wall. Jennifer bent and tried to move Laura away from the wall but she grew rigid, trying to tear herself out of Jennifer's grip. Jennifer knelt closer, trying to hear what Laura was saying.

"Don't let them . . . stop them . . . No! God, don't let them touch me."

"Who is touching you, Laura?" Jennifer whispered. "What is it? Tell me."

Laura's anguished eyes rolled around toward her. "They're crawling. Stop them . . . don't let them bite me!" Her eyes darted away and her head twisted sideways, as if the vision tormenting her came from somewhere above.

Jennifer felt snared in her own nightmare. How had this happened? It didn't seem possible. Not from someone as passive as Laura. Not unless . . . Jennifer refused to think of the word that shot into her mind. *Please God, not that. Don't let it be that.*

"Should we increase the sedation, doctor?"

Jennifer rose to face the nurse who had entered and offered her the medication chart. Jennifer glanced at it. "No. Not yet."

The nurse walked out and Jennifer slowly backed away, leaving Laura to the horror she could not escape. There was no more she could do. Laura was as unreachable as some distant star.

SIX

Jennifer arrived back at the hospital early Sunday morning after a night of fitful sleep. The bus ran on a weekend schedule. Instead of waiting, she walked the distance from the tram. The island wore its weekend vestments. People in casual dress carried thick armfuls of the *Sunday Times*. Joggers ran in packs. Teenagers played football on the grassy quads while mothers wheeled newborns in carriages. A brisk wind blew the river into sharp ridges of silvery foam. But Jennifer was too absorbed in what lay before her to enjoy the magnificent October day.

The hospital was cloaked in its own weekend silence. Many of the patients had been taken down to the garden to enjoy the sunshine. When she arrived on the floor the nurses' station was empty except for a single orderly who waved a hello.

Laura was still in isolation but the drug had taken effect. Through the window Jennifer could see her curled in a fetal position on the mat, her legs drawn up against her chest. Her eyes were open and her lips twitched but her feverish activity had come to a stop.

In her office, Jennifer spread Laura's record across her desk. With a growing sense of anxiety, she began to trace several erratic patterns in Laura's EEG she had not noticed before. It was strange that she had not seen them earlier. The only reason she could give herself for the error was the disorienting effects of her first few days. A CAT scan had been ordered by Dr. Boise, but the results appeared normal. The neurologist, a doctor named Kraft, noted no signs of actual injury to the brain nor any evidence of a tumor or lesion in any of the lobes. There was a note in Dr. Boise's handwriting, which Jennifer now had no trouble recognizing, to retest Laura. But a thorough search of her file indicated that no new test had been administered.

Laura's sudden psychotic episode became even more chilling when Jennifer realized that no prior traces of mental disturbance existed in her history—or at least none that had been reported. The thought occurred to her that Laura's parents might be concealing facts about her previous history, but she dismissed the idea as nonsense. Jennifer was aware of the recent trends in depression research that tried to isolate symptoms into special subgroups. The results were impressive and offered the promise of treatment for certain types of depression that had been linked to hereditary factors. Only none of these depressions was remotely present here. Laura's condition appeared to have struck as suddenly and unexpectedly as a tornado. Jennifer felt completely unable to explain it.

Before she left the hospital, she wrote orders for a new series of tests to be done on Laura. She ordered an EEG to study her brain-wave patterns and repackaged the CAT scan in an envelope with a note to Dr. Kraft to recheck his findings in the light of Laura's present condition. She also ordered a new series of psychological tests. For the first time since coming to Montrose, Jennifer felt desperately alone, almost isolated. In the normal hospital setting, she would have confided her fears to her chief resident, but under the present circumstances she could not approach Dr. Boise. Nor did she have any contacts among the staff, aside from a brief conversation with Mark Tobey. The thought of calling Professor Andrews crossed her mind, but she would have to explain why she had not spoken to her supervisor. The whole incident with Dr. Boise was too embarrassing to repeat in light of the effort Professor Andrews had made in getting her appointed. Jennifer already had more of the reputation for being a maverick than she needed. She did not want to be labeled as impossible to get along with.

She decided to await the test results and pray for the best.

On Monday morning Jennifer arrived to find that Laura

had already been taken down for her EEG. The nurses' report indicated that her condition had stabilized. But Jennifer knew this was the effect of the Thorazine she had been given. She was still delusional.

Rita Kahn ducked her head in while Jennifer was reading the report to inform her that Dr. Boise had approved all the tests. The two women exchanged sympathetic glances, then Jennifer headed for her conference with Anne to set up the week's schedule. The pressure of the normal working day made it impossible to devote her attention to one patient, no matter how much personal concern she felt. By midmorning the normal routines had cranked up to full speed and Jennifer found herself absorbed in the mind-wracking concentration demanded of each patient session. By lunch, she felt exhausted. The strain of the last few days was beginning to tell on her.

Especially trying was her session with Jeffrey. He now began to pour out the painful history of his past relationships. He was under the illusion common to many patients that changes in his life patterns could be accomplished merely by revealing what had been bottled up for so long. In spite of his exhilaration, Jennifer knew that a long road lay ahead before Jeffrey could assimilate his admissions and actually change the pattern of his own behavior. She also knew how delicate the next step would be, when Jeffrey's stay was terminated and the transfer to an outpatient program began. A whole new and perhaps more difficult transference would have to take place.

Jennifer tried not to think of the future. At the moment Jeffrey was like a novice skier ascending the lift to a new emotional level. The danger began when he started navigating the downslope. Without a drug buffer, any negative incident, no matter how minor, could send him back into the darkness. To prevent this from occurring, the staff had been instructed to monitor his movements more closely than usual.

In her session with Brae, Jennifer entered a different world. She did not really know what the effects of reducing his medication would be. No one could. That was something Jennifer had learned early in her training. She should have notified the orderlies to stand by with an unusually hostile patient. But because his drug reduction was unauthorized she said nothing, not even to Rita. If anything should occur, she had only the emergency button underneath her desk connected to the nurse's station. She wondered if it even worked. She had never bothered to test it.

Brae arrived a few minutes late. Jennifer detected little if any change at all in his outward demeanor. He was still guarded. His eyes were brooding and dark. Only his sarcasm was missing. He tolerated a few questions pertaining to his feeling profile before he abruptly sat forward and said, "I want to get out of here."

"The door is there," Jennifer said calmly.

"I mean out of this hospital."

"You're a voluntary patient, you can leave at any time."

"Anytime" he asked, as if he did not believe her.

"Unless there is a real danger to the patient or those around him. But that would have to be determined by the medical staff."

"Catch-22," Brae said tonelessly.

"Are you afraid we'll refuse your request?"

"No one will stop me?" he said sarcastically.

"Not unless you want them to."

"What is that supposed to mean?"

"You came here because you felt something was wrong. That feeling hasn't gone away, has it?"

There was a silence. Brae stared at her sullenly. "You think I'm sick, don't you?"

"It's more important to know if you think you're sick."

"Fuck this shit!" Brae jumped to his feet and headed for the door. "I'm getting out of here."

Jennifer saw the wildness in his eyes. Her heart began pounding but she decided to chance it. "Before you go, tell me about Mercedes."

Brae stopped with his hand on the knob. She watched his back hunch as if receiving a blow. Then he turned to face her. "You goddam bitch! Who told you about her?"

"I know. Isn't that enough?"

He crossed the room and placed his hands on her desk, leaning toward her, red-faced. "What do you know," he spat. His face was distorted, his eyes glazed, unnatural-looking. Jennifer knew he was out of control, but her hand froze on the buzzer. Without moving she locked her gaze with his.

"I want to help you. I want you to tell me about her."

Brae's eyes lost focus. He stared down at his hands. His

knuckles were white where they gripped the edge of the desk. His arms began trembling with the exertion. With an effort, he threw himself back into the seat. Jennifer could see the lines of exhaustion in his face. After a moment he brought his eyes to hers. When he spoke his voice was a rasp. "You want me to tell you how I killed her. Is that what you want to know?"

"I want to know whatever you want to tell me. Nothing more."

Something in Brae's eyes flickered, then he dropped his gaze and stared somewhere into space. The moment ebbed away. He said nothing, sitting with his arms spread on the arms of the chair. Ten minutes passed. No sound was uttered. Jennifer remained where she was, sitting rock still behind her desk. When the clock reached the forty-five-minute mark, she cleared her throat and reminded Brae that they could speak again tomorrow.

"I'll be waiting for you to come," she said softly as he let himself out.

It took Jennifer another five minutes to fully calm down. Keeping herself under control had taken a greater effort than she imagined, but it was imperative that she remain as steady as possible. He must understand that she was there whenever he needed her, without criticism or judgment.

A knock at the door brought her back to attention.

"Come in," she said, hearing the quiver in her voice.

The man who entered with a sardonic smile on his bearded face was Dr. Brady, the clinical psychologist. He carried a folder under his arm. "Got a minute?" he asked.

"Just about a minute," Jennifer said, trying to smile

"I just wanted you to see these," Brady said, coming into the office and placing the folder on her desk. "They're part of the work-up I'm doing on Laura, or trying to do since she's totally delusional. This is about all the response I've been able to get out of her." He tapped the folder. "The Rorschach test is fairly sketchy, with no consistent pattern at all. I followed up with a Thematic Apperception and got the same results."

Jennifer nodded her understanding. Both tests were based on a patient's interpretation of inkblots and dramatic picture situations. "What about the MMP?"

"Negative." The MMP tested personality and divided a patient's responses into clinical scales that separated behavior in categories such as paranoid, depressive, and hysterical. "It's weird. But the only thing she got agitated about were these," he said, opening the folder. He pushed several crayon drawings toward her, waved, and stepped out of the room.

Jennifer spread the half-dozen sheets of paper across the desk. All of them were a repetition of the same idea drawn over and over again. They pictured a woman's anguished face; from her skull radiated a corona of twisted lines.

Jennifer stared down at them for a moment, hearing Laura's words reecho in her mind. Then she tore open the bottom drawer and after searching under several folders, pulled out the crumpled drawing she had discovered in the filing cabinet that first night. She placed it alongside the others.

The similarity was startling. Why? What did it mean?

Without knowing where the first drawing came from, Jennifer could do little else but marvel at the resemblance. Was this something significant, or was it just coincidence? She had no time to consider them further as a glance at the clock revealed that her next patient was due in five minutes.

Jennifer shuffled the papers together, placed them inside the folder, and slid them back inside the bottom drawer. But she could not rid herself of a strange, nagging feeling. She began to experience the same haunting sensation of dread she had felt that first night after finding the drawing in Dr. Freedman's file.

With a sudden gesture, she rose and went down the corridor. Turning the corner she came face-to-face with Anne, who stared at her with surprise.

"You have Mr. Cochran scheduled, Dr. Westwood."

"I realize that," Jennifer said without breaking stride.

Jennifer unlocked the isolation chamber and slipped inside. Through the mesh window she could see Laura seated cross-legged on one of the mats. The restraints were tied loosely enough to permit her to move her arms in a strange manner around her head. Her movements were slow because of the sedative but Jennifer could see there was a definite pattern to her actions.

She unlocked the inner door and rang the emergency button. Within seconds two orderlies were sprinting down the hall. When they burst into the chamber, Jennifer said, "I want you to remove the restraints."

The orderlies looked surprised. "She's pretty unmanageable doctor," one of them said.

"Please, do it," she ordered.

The orderlies approached Laura cautiously. They unbuckled the fasteners and her arms swung up with a suddenness that took Jennifer by surprise. Instantly, Laura began tearing at her hair as if she wanted to pull the strands out by the roots. The orderlies tried to restrain her, but even sedated, Laura had amazing strength.

Jennifer went down on her knees in front of Laura. "What's wrong Laura? What are you doing?"

Laura's eyes stabbed toward her, filled with a desperate urgency. "Make them stop growing. Make them stop!"

"Yes, Laura. I'll help you. What do you want me to stop?"

"Pull them out!" Laura screamed.

Laura began to grasp her hair again but the orderlies wrestled her arms away.

"What should I pull out, Laura? What are they?"

Laura's face twisted grotesquely. Her eyes bulged as she stared at the imaginary serpents twisting around her skull. Jennifer stared at her and the image in the drawings became concrete in her mind. It was a Gorgon's head. *The living head of Medusa.*

"Doctor, please," one of the orderlies shouted, "we can't hold her."

"Put it back on," Jennifer said. She rose and watched the two men struggle to get the restraints back on. Laura fought them, screaming in terror.

Watching her Jennifer felt her own heart begin to pound. She stood on the edge of the dark chasm into which Laura had plunged. The image would shape her dreams for nights to come.

SEVEN

By the middle of the week, the test results were stacked in a neat pile on Jennifer's desk. The picture they painted was bleak. No medical evidence of organic damage could be found. Yet Laura continued to be delusional. Her case had been scheduled for grand rounds on Friday, which provided Jennifer with an even deeper cause of anxiety. Jennifer knew what the diagnosis was likely to be, but she could not rid herself of the conviction that the root of Laura's malady was not a psychosis—was not even psychological, as it were. It lay somewhere else, mysterious and as yet unknown. The week was not without its positive achievements. Jeffrey continued on his upward spiral. His mood changes were less rapid and extreme. He was interacting with the other patients and therapists and even made some sharply critical comments at the floor meeting that made Anne wince.

Jennifer's daily conference with Dr. Boise continued as usual. Boise acted as if nothing had occurred between them. Only when it came to examining the medication reports was there any friction. But Jennifer sensed he was biding his time, waiting for another incident like Jeffrey's desertion before calling her to account.

Jennifer had already committed a further sin by fudging Brae's records. After their critical confrontation on Monday he had cut his therapy sessions completely. Jennifer was surprised when each day passed and he still remained at the hospital. Brae might not be attending therapy or even eating regular meals but Rita Kahn reported that he was taking the medication she prescribed. Jennifer had reduced the dosages still further, until by the end of the week they were nothing more than placebos.

Jennifer expected Boise to find out what was going on but obviously Rita was covering for her. Exactly why, Jennifer could not fathom. But she was glad to have Rita as an ally. She surmised that she had become the beneficiary of some long-standing bitterness between Rita and Dr. Boise. But whatever it was, she felt herself lucky to receive the bounty.

In spite of Brae's absences, Jennifer could not help feeling some kind of breakthrough had been made. But she could do nothing but wait for Brae's next reaction. It arrived unexpectedly on Friday, just as she was preparing to leave for Laura's examination.

When he entered the office, Jennifer noticed the immediate change in his appearance. His unshaven face looked even craggier, more deeply lined. He looked as if he had lost several pounds and the dark patches beneath his eyes attested to his lack of sleep. The reduced medication had kept him on the edge of emotional turmoil without allowing him to go over. Jennifer knew she could not keep it up very much longer.

This time, instead of questioning him, she remained silent. Waiting. The impact of the last words he had said to her were still very much alive in her mind. They caused her to feel more than a little anxiety. The degree of tension Brae carried with him infected the room immediately, raising the level of Jennifer's own emotions and making it difficult for her to remain completely calm. She had the feeling that she was at risk, though she still had not taken any special precautions aside from testing the bell and finding that it was in working order.

Brae sat in a rigid posture with both arms extended on the arms of the chair, repeatedly clenching and unclenching his fists and staring intensely at her from beneath darkened brows. Jennifer could sense the struggle going on within him, but she remained silent, listening only to the tick of the clock.

When he finally spoke, the words seemed to fall like hammer blows. "You know why I'm here, don't you?" he said harshly.

"I think you want to tell me about Mercedes."

"I killed her," he said through tightened lips. "I sentenced her to death."

"She wanted to live with you, didn't she?"

Brae nodded.

"Do you think she would be alive if you had allowed her to stay?"

"I could have protected her," Brae said starkly.

"Could you really?"

Brae glanced at her sharply. "From those animals, yes."

"Then you know who killed her?"

"I know."

"But the police have no suspects." Jennifer stated, remembering Frank's words.

"That's because they're dead. All the suspects are dead." Brae's eyes fixed on hers harshly. "I killed them."

Jennifer was silent. She was sure Brae's statement that he had killed Mercedes was a guilt-related response to having turned her away. But she was not sure if what he had just confessed was part of the same response. The conviction in his eyes made her stomach tense. "How did you kill them?" she ventured softly.

"Very slowly and very painfully, doctor. Do you want all the details?"

"Only if you want to give them to me."

"I used a paring knife, doctor. Have you any idea of what it feels like to be flayed alive. I learned it from some friends of mine in the rackets. They once caught a guy who had raped a nun. What they left was not particularly appetizing."

Jennifer closed her eyes for an instant as a shiver of revulsion passed through her. Her hands were clasped on the edge of the drawer in front of her to prevent him seeing them shake.

"There isn't any greater pain, doctor," he said grimly.

"Perhaps there is," Jennifer said. "The pain of someone punishing himself for something he thinks he did."

"You think I'm doing that, don't you, doctor? Punishing myself for Mercedes' death."

"Yes," Jennifer said, looking straight into his eyes, "that's exactly what I think you're doing."

"Shouldn't the guilty be punished, doctor, or is that idea obsolete?"

"No. I don't think it is."

"Then don't you think I'm guilty?"

"No. I don't think you are. Did you really love her?" Jennifer asked with a probing glance.

A different expression crossed his face. Less arrogant, more unsure. "What difference does that make?"

"If you didn't love her, there was no point in your living together, was there?"

"I could have protected her."

"And what about the duty of self-protection you owe yourself? You can't protect everyone."

"I'm a cop. That's my job, isn't it?"

"Yes. But you're not Superman, are you?"

Brae stared at her intensely. He did not answer but this time when he left, he did not slam the door. Jennifer counted that as a plus.

The amphitheater was situated in the main wing of the hospital, convenient to all the other sections so that patients and staff could readily assemble for staff meetings and diagnoses. Most of Jennifer's section was there, along with faces she did not recognize. She would have preferred to sit beside Rita but no space was available. Instead she climbed to the third level and took a seat beside Dr. Brady.

Dr. Boise was already seated on an upper tier beside Dr. Murchison, who smiled at Jennifer when she entered. Anne occupied a place alongside. The hum of conversation came to a quick end when Brady looked up and said, "Ah, royalty." Jennifer followed his gaze and saw Dr. Kessler entering, flanked by two doctors in clinic coats whom she imagined were senior staff.

Jennifer realized that Dr. Kessler was moving directly toward her. She started to rise but he motioned for her to remain seated. His face wore a friendly smile but Jennifer felt her heart begin hammering.

"Dr. Westwood," Kessler began, "may I present Professor Palen and Professor Klein, both from our affiliated universities. They're here to evaluate your patient."

Jennifer shook both men's hands. Kessler touched her shoulder in a friendly fashion before he climbed toward the level where Dr. Boise was seated. Kessler's presence filled the room with a special kind of excitement. It was more than his reputation or even his position as head of the hospital. There was something about Kessler's presence that drew every eye and made him the focus of attention.

When everyone was settled, the presentation began. Dr. Boise spoke first in his dry monotone, running through Laura's history, the results of the various tests, and the sudden disturbance in her behavior. Brady spoke next, outlining the various psychological procedures that had been employed. After that, it was Jennifer's turn. She fought down the butterflies in her stomach and spoke about Laura's reaction to both medication and psychotherapy. When she was finished, Dr. Boise picked up a telephone from the console beside him and asked that the patient be brought in.

Laura was escorted by two orderlies. Her pretty face was distorted by the effects of the Thorazine, which had twisted her facial muscles grotesquely. Her terrified eyes darted from side to side, fixed on demons they could not see. Dr. Boise approached and asked several questions. Laura responded by turning her head from side to side and staring up with bulging eyes at the imaginary serpents growing out of her head.

When he finished, Boise glanced up at Kessler, who was huddled in conversation with the two professors. Kessler made a gesture and Laura was led away. Jennifer watched her go with a strange feeling of sadness. She felt part of herself go with Laura. Jennifer was called back to attention when several residents asked questions about Laura's background and family history. But everyone seemed to be waiting for Kessler to speak. Finally, the three sat back and faced the others.

Kessler first asked Dr. Boise his opinion.

In a sure voice, Boise said. "I believe the patient is suffering from a form of paranoid schizophrenia."

Dr. Brady echoed his diagnosis and Kessler turned to Jennifer. "And you, Dr. Westwood? What is your opinion?"

Jennifer paused before she answered. Her eyes swept the room for a moment. She saw the same conclusion in everyone's eyes yet something inside made her rebel. "I'm sorry. I can't agree."

There was a murmur, along with Kessler's raised eyebrows.

"And why not, doctor? All the signs point in that direction."

What Jennifer said next she knew might be damaging to her reputation. But she had to express the way she felt. "I know the evidence is against me, but I can't help feeling there is another reason for her behavior. Something organic that hasn't shown up on the tests. Not yet anyway."

"But all the indicators are present," Kessler stated. "Including the patient's age. Her family transactions indicate typically delayed maturation and conflicting expectations, leading to prolonged anxiety. The patient is in a state of pathological excitability. She's experiencing marked hallucinations and impulsive, destructive tendencies. There is a typical disregard of excretory functions, along with grotesque delusions centering on sexually obsessive serpent imagery tending toward a desire for self-mutilation. All of these factors would confirm your colleague's conclusions. What evidence do you have to support a different finding?"

In an earnest voice, Jennifer said, "I can only cite the complete absence of psychotic episodes in the past, the lack of a praecox reaction noted by her family as well as in my dealings with her. The patient's EEG also shows none of the stage-four sleep disruptions which are present in over fifty percent of schizophrenic patients."

"Inconclusive," Kessler said pointedly. "Stage four disruptions occur in cases of severe depression as well."

"The tests show no evidence of any chemical serum such as DMPE4 or Taraxein that are present in acute schizophrenics."

Dr. Kessler smiled tolerantly at Jennifer's insistence. "As you must be aware, Dr. Westwood, my own research has been directed toward the discovery of a biochemical defect in the subsystems of the brain which inhibits the interpretation of sensory data and stored memory traces. Specifically, the brain-cell antibodies in the septal region, which impair synaptic transmissions of vital information. However, much as I would like to diagnose the illness solely on biological grounds, there is still much too little concrete evidence. So I must concur with your colleagues. However, after fifteen years of marriage, I never underestimate the value of a woman's intuition."

Laughter filled the amphitheatre and Jennifer felt her face redden.

Then Kessler's face changed expression. "Some of us tend to forget that the bond that develops between a patient and his physician operates in both directions. Unfortunately, compassion is not a value that is compatible with scientific evaluation. I commend Dr. Westwood for feeling the way she does. Therefore, in the absence of any laboratory evidence to the contrary, I must concur in the diagnosis. The patient must be treated as a paranoid schizophrenic."

EIGHT

When she left the conference, feelings of depression settled over Jenifer like a dark cloud. While her mind agreed with the others, all of her instincts screamed out against the diagnosis. "A nice fool you made of yourself, Westwood," she whispered aloud, at one point. She could still feel her cheeks burning when she remembered how earnestly she had propounded her nontheory. They burned even redder at Dr. Kessler's little remark about women's intuition. His joke had knocked down her little house of cards and made her look even more ridiculous, showing her up for the inexperienced practitioner she was.

In spite of her embarrassment, something still nagged inside. Jennifer knew of certain disorders that cloaked themselves in the symptoms of other diseases. Knowledge of schizophrenia was still too murky to make any conclusion certain. Jennifer's depression deepened when she realized just how little time she had for any further research into Laura's condition. The burden of her schedule was already keeping her at the hospital well past normal hours—or did doctors ever have normal hours? Jennifer forced herself to analyze the situation unemotionally. The progress she was making with Laura promised a clear road to recovery and self-understanding. Never had she felt so certain about being able to help a patient. Never had the prognosis looked so promising. Now Jennifer felt cheated, as if some prize she had desperately wanted had been maliciously snatched away.

"Jennifer—hold up!"

She turned around and faced Mark Tobey, who strode toward her with a warm smile spread across his handsome face.

Jennifer stopped, realizing she had been so wrapped up in her thoughts she had walked halfway to the cafeteria without even realizing it. She smiled when Mark stood in front of her.

"Buy you a cup of coffee," he said.

"Sure," she answered, glad of the distraction his presence provided. They continued to the coffee shop where Jennifer allowed herself to respond to Mark's playful bantering.

"It's nice to see you smiling for a change," he said as they sipped the acrid taste of the coffee no amount of sweetener seemed to erase. "You look like the world is pounding you into the ground."

Jennifer shrugged. "I guess it is."

"I know what you're going through," he said, changing expressions. "And it can be dangerous."

"What do you mean?"

"Lady, what would you prescribe for a patient who spends twelve to fifteen hours a day at her job?"

"Valium. And lots of it."

"Wrong. Relaxation and lots of it."

"True. That is the best medicine."

"Okay. Since you won't write a prescription for yourself, I'll write one for you. You are hereby ordered to take tonight off and having a drink with yours truly."

Jennifer looked up into Mark's blue eyes and heard a voice inside shout, *Why not dummy? Go!* "Okay," she answered, "what time?"

"I'll come for you at nine sharp. I'll give you a guided tour of the poor man's Upper East Side." Mark glanced at his watch. "Got to push off. Remember, nine o'clcok."

Jennifer nodded, watching Mark navigate between the littered tables being cleaned by a slow-moving kitchen worker. Jennifer still had a half hour. She thought she might take a stroll outside, but she felt too weary to get up. Mark's offer had come at the right time. She was working too hard and putting in far too many hours. She needed some time off. Mark's company seemed just light and uncomplicated enough. Besides, she wanted to see more of the fabled East

Side nightlife. Since arriving in Manhattan, she had lived almost like a hermit.

"Do you mind if I join you, doctor?"

Jennifer looked up. Anne was standing beside her, clutching a tray on which was a container of yogurt and an orange.

"Please sit down," Jennifer said.

Anne took a seat, smiling with perfectly capped teeth that made Jennifer think of the bowl of waxed fruit her grandmother kept on her coffee table.

"Calories," Anne said, indicating her Spartan meal. It made Jennifer feel ashamed of her tasteless cruller and coffee.

"Terrible about Laura," Anne said opening the yogurt. "We all felt so bad about it. I don't blame you for the way you feel. She's such a lovely girl and so pretty."

The remark revived the sting of Jennifer's earlier unprofessional conduct at the conference.

"One good thing though," Anne continued. "I think I'll be able to convince Laura's parents to give permission to have Laura admitted to Dr. Kessler's research center."

Jennifer raised her eyebrows. She had been so concerned about the present she had given no thought to Laura's future. Treatment would no longer be provided for Laura at Montrose. She would have to be transferred to an institution for long-term care. Jennifer knew that thousands of mental patients had been dumped onto the streets when funds had been cut back. The state housed them in marginal neighborhoods where it was cheaper than keeping them institutionalized. Jennifer remembered the passionate way one of her fellow interns had described seeing these patients wandering aimlessly through the streets, talking to themselves and picking through garbage cans or aimlessly riding the subways, prey to every kind of street predator. The thought made Jennifer shudder. Laura needed special care and years of intensive therapy once high doses of Pentothiazine brought her out of her delusive state. It was the kind of care she would get if Kessler accepted her.

"Is Dr. Kessler willing to accept her?" Jennifer questioned.

"Oh yes. We were very lucky there. Imagine if she had been admitted to a state facility."

Jennifer nodded. In her present condition Laura would be unable to fend off assaults, sexual or otherwise. Jennifer's experience with state facilities made her understand the danger. Laura's admission to Kessler's center would be a blessing, providing the best chance of recovery and the finest care. For that, at least, Jennifer was grateful.

At four o'clock, Jennifer accompanied Laura and two orderlies through the hospital to the second floor cat walk connecting Montrose with Dr. Kessler's research facility. The sight of two Oriental nurses in immaculate blue uniforms waiting to receive her revived Mark's comments that first day, when he described Kessler's center as the inner sanctum. The nurses provided a sharp contrast to the casual dress of the orderlies. They took control of Laura's wheelchair and her records without a word or smile. Jennifer felt as if she were part of the furniture for all the recognition she received.

A thick glass door opened and the chair was wheeled inside.

"Wait!" Jennifer said.

The chair was halted, allowing Jennifer to kneel in front of Laura and scan her distracted face. But the spark of recognition she hoped for did not appear. Laura's eyes were focused elsewhere, torn by an anguish Jennifer could only imagine.

She rose and stepped away. The nurses continued into the passage and the glass door slid shut noiselessly behind them. Jennifer waited until Laura was wheeled all the way across before she walked away, rent by an aching feeling of loss.

The downstairs buzzer sounded at nine sharp. Jennifer had to scramble to answer it, clad only in her bra and panties. By the time Mark reached her floor, she had slipped into jeans and a sweater. Mark appeared in the doorway looking like a preppy's dream in a tweed jacket with leather elbow patches, white turtleneck, and gray slacks. He stared down at Jennifer's bare feet and told her she might find going barefoot a little tricky.

Jennifer laughed and went into her bedroom to pull on her boots and a corduroy jacket. Emerging, she found Mark staring at her still unhung lithos. Embarrassed, she said, "I still haven't found the time to do anything with this place. Including clean it."

"Are you kidding? This is a palace. You should see my dump. It's awful."

Jennifer reached into the hall closet for her handbag and Mark saw the bicycle wheel. "Do you ride?" he asked.

"Oh that," she said, glancing down. She had completely forgotten its presence. "It belonged to Dr. Freedman. One of my neighbors was holding it for him. I meant to send it on."

"Too bad about Freedman."

"Did you know him?"

"Not really. He was kind of a loner. But one of the residents on my service was a buddy of his."

Jennifer closed the closet and locked her door and they set off on their expedition. Mark took her along First Avenue with its elegantly decorated saloons packed elbow to elbow with professional business people of both sexes. Jennifer was immediately conscious of eyes sweeping through the room like industrious bees seeking a hospitable flower. She felt glad of Mark's protection, but when he stepped away to the john she was immediately hit upon by two men almost at the same time, each insistently offering to buy her a drink. When Mark returned they set off to yet another place, but Jennifer had had enough.

Mark looked a little disappointed. He thrived on the hectic atmosphere, having the ability to focus on what she was saying, while his eyes conducted little flirtations up and down the bar.

They wound up at a comfortable neighborhood bistro across the street from Jennifer's apartment house and almost immediately became involved in an irritating argument. It began when Mark began enthusiastically extolling the virtues of the new generation of antidepressants and the almost miraculous cures they were effecting.

"Cures?" Jennifer reacted skeptically. "That usually means a patient no longer needs medication. How can you have a cure when the patient is kept on drugs more or less permanently?"

"I'm talking about the possible," Mark said, "not the impossible dream. There are no cures."

"Is that all you think psychotherapy is, an impossible dream?"

"You tell me," he shot back. "Isn't it better to control the symptoms rather than spending half your life on the couch and still feeling miserable?"

"I think it just takes work and a whole lot of caring," Jennifer said forcefully.

"And time. How many patients are willing to invest twenty years with no guarantee. Would you?"

"I don't know," Jennifer answered. "But I think you're putting the cart before the horse. I'm not putting the new drugs down. I just think they should be used as a supplement to therapy, not in place of it. You can't treat the symptoms and ignore the basic cause of a problem."

"Listen, doctor," Mark said passionately. "I've been working with a six-time loser. She's a successful artist. Married, has two kids and everything to look forward to, only she's been in and out of mental hospitals half a dozen times. She's had therapy up the wazoo, and I'm talking the best. She's tried individual, group, even orgone boxes. Every fad from est to Primal Scream. But nothing worked. Not even lithium, which made her dizzy and blurred her vision—which is great for a painter. Then I put her on tetracyclics, and bingo, she's flying. She was admitted three weeks ago and I'm ready to discharge her. And without any noticeable side effects. No drug hangover. No arrhythmias. No palpitations. If that isn't a miracle, you tell me what is. This lady doesn't want any more analysis. She doesn't even care what the cause of her depression is. She's free. That's all that counts."

"As long as the drugs keep working. What if they don't? No one knows the long-term effects."

"Does a diabetic kick because he's got to inject insulin every twenty-four hours? He's alive and functioning. That's the important thing."

"You're experimenting with human guinea pigs," Jennifer stated firmly.

"Don't give me that old saw. Every medication developed depends on some kind of human experimentation somewhere down the line. Usually starting in small control groups of incurables. There wouldn't be a single advance without it."

"So we just prescribe pills. No more therapy, support, or caring."

"We're not in the furniture business, Jennifer. I'm not interested in saving the couch. Only in what works."

"Even if you never have to see your patient?"

"I wouldn't care if I sent him the pills by mail, as long as I know they'll make him happy."

"Jesus, Mark! Why did you bother going to medical school. You should have set up a business in Bogotá and been our Colombian connection. Just ship your drugs through the mail and everyone's happy."

Mark snickered at her remark but Jennifer was feeling a dull ache in her stomach. The drinks were having the opposite effect she intended. The whole subject was beginning to irritate her anyway. Mark's enthusiasm for the new psychopharmacology ran completely counter to every reason Jennifer had ever given herself for becoming a doctor. She could never become a faceless dispenser of prescriptions. Laura was a case in point. Her therapist would be her lifeline back to reality. No drug could replace that or integrate a personality that had been disintegrating for God knows how long.

Sensing her mood change, Mark signaled for the check and eased her outside. Jennifer found herself offering him a cup of coffee almost by reflex. Mark accepted and they went back up to her place.

Jennifer turned on the radio and went into the tiny kitchen, praying the milk she had bought over the weekend had not spoiled. It turned out to be okay and she put on a pot of ground coffee which had earned her a reputation as a gourmet in her med-school dorm.

"Smells wonderful," Mark said, coming into the kitchen behind her. Jennifer turned and found herself snared in his arms. His mouth brushed her cheek, then swept across her lips. She accepted the kiss but resisted his probing tongue. She pulled away a moment later.

"What's the matter?" he asked with surprise.

"Let's not, okay?"

"Why not. We're big boys and girls."

"Exactly, so you won't commit hari-kari if I decline."

"You decline and I fall," he said, clutching his heart.

"Don't take it personally," she said stepping away. "This is resident rejection month."

"Was it our little argument?"

Jennifer shook her head. "I don't know what it is."

"Overwork is what it is. That's why I'm presenting myself as the only sane alternative," he said trying to take her in his arms again.

"No Mark, please."

"Okay. But brother Mark has a big shoulder if you want to talk about it."

For a moment Jennifer was tempted to discuss Laura with him but she resisted the impulse, afraid of the same reaction she received at the conference. Her intuition would be crushed beneath a steamroller of medical evidence.

"It'll pass," Jennifer said.

"Let's hope so, Dr. Westwood. Because I intend making another pass. Not tonight. Only one seduction to a customer. But be warned."

They both smiled, then she poured the coffee. They spent a half hour discussing hospital gossip before Mark left. Jennifer detected an eagerness to return to the hunting grounds.

"Good night," he said at the door.

"And good luck," she countered.

"How well you know me," he said with a good-natured grin. "Friends?"

"Friends," she responded letting him kiss her again. Then he waved good-bye and clattered down the stairs. Jennifer locked the door, relieved that Mark was gone. She had experienced her share of short-term romances in her college and med-school days. There had even been one serious affair during the summer of her first year as an intern. Paul had stirred her in a way she had never been stirred before, though both of them placed less of a premium on their feelings for each other than on their separate careers.

In spite of their relationship, Jennifer had felt relief when Paul left for a residency on the West Coast. His presence had been too much of a distraction. Jennifer sighed and threw herself down on the couch and stretched her long legs, allowing Paul's memory to wash over her. Closing her eyes, she could still feel the power of his hands when they caressed her body. She shivered, remembering the way he took possession of her, making her reach a climax merely by the touch of his fingers.

She opened her eyes and drove the thoughts away, wondering how long it had been since she last had sex. She recalled a short visit home and a brief encounter with an old friend's ex-boyfriend some six months before. Still, that had been more out of friendship than passion. She wondered why she had resisted Mark. He was more than attractive enough. Perhaps that kind of encounter no longer satisfied her. Not that she felt ready for any kind of relationship at the moment.

Her relationship to Montrose was much too demanding to allow a rival.

The thought of the clinic set off a chain reaction and she found herself thinking about Brae. Laura's conference had shoved everything else out of her mind. Now that Laura was no longer under her care, Brae became her most important focus. What he had imparted in their last session now began to trouble her. The implications were extremely serious, she realized. It was one thing to release him to an outpatient situation once his condition warranted it, but the string of revenge killings was another. Provided what he told her was actually true.

Jennifer undressed and showered, but when she crawled under the covers she could not sleep. Her thoughts were haunted by Brae no matter how she tried to focus on other things. Finally, she threw off the blankets and slipped into a robe. She went into the living room, picked up the phone, and dialed the number Frank Richie had given her.

The precinct would not tell her where Frank was. Only that they would relay her message. Jennifer pulled out her notebook and began planning therapeutic strategies when the phone startled her. Frank was on the other end of the line.

"What's the problem?" he asked in a clipped manner.

"I'd like to talk to you about Brae. It's important."

"Sure, when?"

"Tonight, if it's all right with you. There's a bar across the street from my house."

"What's the address?"

A half hour later, Frank was shouldering his way between the patrons toward the rear booth where Jennifer and Mark had sat only two hours before. If the bartender was surprised at her change in partners, he did not show it.

Frank eased into a seat opposite Jennifer and ordered a coffee, while Jennifer ordered another beer. The clientele had thinned out, making it easy to converse.

"I'm glad you've come. Are you on duty?"

"My partner's outside covering the radio. If there's a problem, I'll have to split. What's the matter?"

Jennifer waited until Frank was served his coffee before she spoke. "I'm worried about something Brae told me. He said after Mercedes' death he committed several revenge killings."

Instead of surprise, Frank merely nodded as though he had been prepared for her revelation. "Here's the way it is, doctor. I understand your concern but there were no revenge killings. It's all in Brae's head."

"You're not trying to protect him, are you?"

"Of course, I'm trying to protect him. Aren't you? Isn't that why you got me here?"

"Yes. But you've got to understand. I can't recommend his release, knowing he might kill again."

"Lady, I've been a cop for nineteen years. I'm not about to ride around this town with a homicidal maniac as my partner. I'm telling you, Brae didn't kill anyone. I checked it out."

"Can I believe that?"

"That's up to you. But see, he told me the same thing, making me swear I wouldn't tell anyone. That's one of the reasons I got him to check himself into the hospital."

Frank glanced up. A stocky black man in a raincoat had entered the bar and signaled with an upraised hand.

"I gotta go."

Frank rose and stared down at Jennifer. "On this job you get to know your partner better than you know yourself. Brae didn't kill anyone."

Jennifer did not respond. She would have to discover the truth for herself. To do that she would have to risk taking Brae off medication completely. She knew she would have to deal with the crises it might provoke, even if the greatest danger was to herself.

NINE

———— •◦ ──◦◦◦◦── ————

The crash Jennifer had been expecting arrived sooner than she thought. Brae left the clinic at eleven the following morning, plunging the floor into a dangerous state of excitement. Montrose's open-door policy was never without risk. But once a patient left, the doors were locked to prevent the action from being repeated. It was amazing to Jennifer how quickly the other patients knew one of their number was missing and how many of them wanted to follow suit, creating enormous difficulties for the already overburdened staff.

When she got the message that Brae had slipped out, Jennifer went to the nurses' station where she found Dr. Boise and Anne. Boise was going through Brae's medication charges when Jennifer entered. The look in Anne's eyes promised trouble but, strangely, it failed to happen.

Boise made a few perfunctory remarks about maintaining normal routines, but the look in his eyes was one of satisfaction. Jennifer knew he had one more piece of ammunition against her. When Boise left, trailed by Anne, Jennifer stepped over to Rita's desk and glanced at the medication slips. Boise had taken copies of each record.

Jennifer went through the next few hours acting out her role. But while she remained outwardly calm, inside she felt like a prisoner waiting for the guillotine to fall. Her remarks at the conference had opened a crack in her credibility. Should something happen to one of her patients because of her insubordination, then Dr. Boise's case against her would be clinched. She had not only jeopardized her own career but Dr. Kessler's status. Jennifer realized she had no real defense. She had reduced Brae's medication and exposed him to the very danger that brought him to Montrose in the first place, all in a vainglorious attempt to prove he would respond to the talking cure. What if he killed again?

Jennifer skipped lunch, waiting vainly for word. By three she knew she had to get off the floor, even if it was only for a few minutes. She let herself out with her key and went down to the cafeteria where she tried to eat a sandwich and drink a container of milk. The effort was wasted. She left after ten minutes and rushed back to her wing.

She waited for an elevator on the first floor but one failed to arrive. Impatient, she decided to walk, when the doors finally slid open and several people rushed out. One of them was Mark. Jennifer started to call to him but the expression on his face stopped her. The easygoing mask of self-confidence he usually wore was gone. In its place was a look of troubled concentration. He rushed away in the opposite direction without seeing her. Jennifer wondered what his problem was, but she took no comfort in knowing there were other crises besides her own.

"Dr. Westwood."

Jennifer looked around and was surprised to see Frank Richie bearing down on her. The detective's face wore a concerned expression that almost matched Mark's in intensity.

"Can I talk to you for a minute?" he asked when they were facing each other.

"Sure," Jennifer said, looking around for some place private. The chapel was only a few feet away. Fortunately it was empty. Jennifer led the way inside and stopped to face Frank when she was beside the first pew.

"It's what you said last night," Frank said softly. "About Brae taking revenge."

"Yes." Jennifer said, feeling a tightness in her throat.

"I'm still sticking by what I said. But I thought you should know the guy Mercedes was running with, the technician who sold dope; he was killed about two weeks before Brae signed himself in here. I just found out this morning."

"Why are you telling me this if you didn't think Brae killed him?"

Frank's eyes filled with a look of distress. "I don't know.

There are no real leads. The guys investigating think it was drug-related."

"But you're not sure?"

Frank shrugged. "I just thought you should know."

Jennifer stared at the detective, trying to fathom what he really thought, but his face was impassive. "I understand and I appreciate your coming to tell me."

"I gotta run," Frank said, and together they walked out of the chapel. "If anything breaks, I'll let you know." When they were outside, Frank waved and ambled toward the exit.

Instead, of returning to her floor, Jennifer continued back through the lobby to the rear of the building. She needed time to absorb the information Frank had just given her, but her mind would not function. She was too emotionally wound up.

Without realizing it, Jennifer had walked through the ground floor to the rear of the complex. She continued through the double glass doors into the garden and took a series of deep breaths. The air was crisp and sweet. It felt good to be outside. Dry leaves blew up in little swirls as she continued on the path and turned the corner of the clinic. Ahead, she faced the research center and the tube of glass and steel through which Laura had been wheeled. Jennifer glanced at her watch. She still had forty minutes before her next patient. On impulse, she turned and reentered the complex, following a blue line on the floor that led her around a series of turnings to a bank of elevators.

Reaching the second floor, she stepped out into a glass-walled vestibule that faced the catwalk. Through a glass window the center appeared, surmounted by its dome. A TV monitor manned by a security guard faced her across the linoleum floor near the entrance to the walkway.

Jennifer stepped over to the gray-uniformed guard and announced her intention of visiting the complex. She gave her name and Laura's, the patient she wanted to visit. The guard relayed the information into a telephone, then told her to please have a seat.

Jennifer was much too agitated to sit. Instead she paced back and forth in front of the glass, peering out at the center, allowing her eyes to curve around the windowless walls and the line of electrified fencing.

"Dr. Westwood?"

Jennifer turned to face the guard expectantly.

"Dr. Boise would like to see you in his office, immediately."

Surprised, Jennifer's brows knit with puzzlement. How did Boise know she was here? And more important, what did he want?

Waiting for the elevator, Jennifer's mind filled with the worst. The knot in her stomach told her they had found Brae.

Retracing her steps, she reentered her own wing and took the elevator to the fifth floor, where Boise's office was located. He occupied an office at the end of a long corridor lined with other functionaries. The outer office Jennifer entered was filled with filing cabinets and occupied by three secretaries, one of whom told her to go right in.

With a bold step, Jennifer opened the door to Dr. Boise's private office and stepped inside.

The chief of service was sitting behind his desk, leaning back in his chair. Light speared through the blinds behind him, creating an unflattering gleam on his bald dome, which the few strands of hair failed to conceal.

"Sit down, doctor," Boise commanded, harshly.

Jennifer felt herself rebel at his tone, but she took one of the wooden chairs set before his desk without saying a word. Darts of anxiety shot across her chest as she felt his hardened stare. His clinic coat was pulled back to reveal his vest, ribbed with rolls of fat. What he said next took her completely by surprise.

"Just exactly what were you doing at Dr. Kessler's clinic?"

"I wasn't at his clinic. I never got near it. I merely put in a request to see Laura."

"For what purpose?" Boise asked in the same reprimanding tone.

"She was my patient."

"Not any longer," Boise snapped. "Requesting visitation is an unprofessional trespass on the jurisdiction of her treating psychiatrist. Aren't you aware of that, doctor?"

"I don't understand," Jennifer stated.

"You don't understand?" Boise echoed sarcastically. "Professional courtesy requires you to wait for a call from her treating physician. You've worked in hospitals before. Don't tell me you're not acquainted with such a procedure?"

"I didn't think it applied to a treating psychiatrist."

"Dr. Westwood, you have a peculiar disregard for the traditional courtesies of your profession."

Jennifer's eyes blazed. "I'm not concerned with tradition where the welfare of one of my patients is concerned."

"Laura is now Dr. Kessler's patient and under his jurisdiction. Should he want your professional opinion, I'm sure he'll request it."

"I'm sorry. I don't accept that."

Dr. Boise raised his brows. "*You* don't accept? Doctor, may I remind you that you are merely a resident in this hospital and subject to its rules and regulations. One of which is the proper professional relationship between a patient and his treating physician. A relationship I suggest you reduce to its proper focus. Doctor, for your own good I suggest you begin developing the dispassionate attitude required of a professional."

Clenching her fists to keep from exploding, Jennifer said, "Is that all, doctor?"

"For the moment."

Trembling with anger, Jennifer rose. With stiff steps she left the room and crossed the outer office. Her face was blazing. Her eyes were filled with tears. She felt humiliated. There was a women's room opposite the elevator. Standing with her hands on the edge of the porcelain sink, she stared at her face in the mirror. She felt like a high-school student who has just been reprimanded by the dean.

"That bastard!" she cried aloud.

After washing her face with cold water, she left the white-tiled room and waited for the elevator to return her to her floor. When the doors opened she stepped inside and came face-to-face with Mark.

She was about to speak but something halted her.

"What's wrong?" she said, staring into his distraught face.

Instantly she knew. Two orderlies stood behind him, struggling with a female patient. Jennifer stepped back as the woman began fighting against their grip. Her eyes were wide with terror. From her lips came an incoherent babble of sound.

"Get back," Mark ordered as the woman broke free for a moment. The woman was obviously Mark's patient. When the doors opened on four, Mark stepped out, drawing Jennifer out with him to keep her from being hurt. The orderlies managed to get the woman off and began dragging her down the hall.

Jennifer had never been on Mark's floor before. She knew it was for seriously disturbed patients. It resembled her own floor except for the lack of windows in the doors.

As if expecting their arrival, a nurse rushed out of the station and quickly opened the isolation chamber. Struggling and resisting, the patient was dragged inside. Before the doors closed Jennifer heard her scream.

"Stop them . . . cut them off. They're biting! Help me!"

For an instant, Jennifer envisioned Laura's face. There was something identical about this patient's actions.

Jennifer moved closer as Mark followed the nurse inside. The orderlies were trying to slip the young woman's arms into the restraining jacket. One of the woman's hands tore free, grazing Mark's cheek. He jumped back but Jennifer could see she had not meant to attack him. Instead her hand began tearing at her hair. Trying to pull it out of her skull by the roots.

The nurse grabbed the woman's hand and twisted it behind her as a second nurse rushed inside with a hypo and handed it to Mark. He located a vein and jabbed it in, while the orderlies tried to hold her thrashing body still. Again and again the woman screamed, *"Cut them away . . . tear them off me . . . stop them!"*

Mark's hands were shaking when he handed back the needle. She saw how hard it was for him to master his feelings.

"Are you all right?" she asked when he stepped outside.

"It happened in RT," he said, speaking like someone in shock. "She just went haywire. She attacked one of the other patients. I was going to discharge her at the end of the week."

"I'm sorry," Jennifer said.

"You're sorry. Christ. This is Carla DiMatteo, the artist I told you about. The six-time loser I thought I had under control. Jesus, this is completely crazy. Something must have gone wrong with the dosage."

Mark stormed into the nurses' station, demanding the medication book. Jennifer went back to the elevators but her mind would not rid itself of the image of the terrified young woman and the horrible fear in her eyes—the same fear she had seen in Laura's.

When the elevator doors opened on her own floor, she was surprised to find the entrance unlocked. Almost as soon as she reached the nurses' station Rita came out to greet her. "You can relax. Brae's back. He walked in here twenty minutes ago."

"All in one piece?"

"Luckily. He's waiting for you in your office."

As calmly as she could, Jennifer walked toward her office. Her heart beat with relief. She had triggered a crisis without being able to predict the outcome. Knowing every therapist faced the same situation at one time or another did not help. It was a toss of the coin whether she had helped Brae or caused him irreparable harm. She opened the door to her office with a trembling hand.

Brae turned to face her as she entered. His eyes were dark pools of anguish. He sat before her desk, head bowed over his clasped hands, his posture one of defeat. The orderly who sat inside got up and left when Jennifer came in, whispering he would be waiting outside.

Jennifer took a seat behind her desk and waited. A moment later Brae raised his eyes to hers. "I tried to do it," he said in a trembling tone. "I made it all the way to the bridge."

Jennifer tensed, visualizing the height of the massive structure spanning the river between Manhattan and Queens.

"I stood looking down at the water. It looked so far away, so deep and calm and right. I didn't think about the fall or the cold or what would happen to my body when I struck the water. None of that seemed important. I just knew it was right for me to do it." He looked up and his eyes were glistening. "But I couldn't. I just couldn't do it."

Jennifer said nothing, merely nodding her understanding.

"I thought about her and how because of me she was dead. And not wanting to live because of it. But I still couldn't jump. What held me back?"

"I don't know," Jennifer said softly. "But we could begin trying to find out, couldn't we?"

Brae looked confused for a moment. Then he said, "I don't know . . . I don't know. . . ."

Jennifer used her own keys to gain admission to the fourth floor. She did not bother checking in at the nurses' station. She had tried phoning Mark first but no one picked up. Mark would not have left the hospital this early, she knew. But she was glad he was not in his office when she peeked inside. She had decided not to do anything until she spoke to Mark first. But when ten minutes passed and no one appeared, Jennifer stood up and glanced at herself in the mirror in Mark's bathroom, then with a determined step went out of the office.

The corridor was silent. No patients were visible. Checking her watch, Jennifer realized they would all be at dinner. The nurses' station was locked. They were most likely in conference, where she should have been. But the thought of facing Dr. Boise twice in one day was too abhorrent. She would take a chance and accept the consequences.

Jennifer opened the outer door with the passkey on her key ring and stepped inside the isolation chamber. Through the inner door she could see Mark's patient making a slow circuit of the room. Although still in restraints, she was turning her body in a strange corkscrew motion, keeping her head tilted toward the wall as she turned. Her eyes strained upward, staring at some imaginary object that seemed to float around her face.

Jennifer stepped inside the room, assailed by the pungent odor of disinfectant. She stood in silence, watching Carla continue her oddly stylized motions.

Jennifer took a step closer when Carla reached the corner.

"Carla," she whispered, "what are you looking at?"

An anguished cry escaped Carla's lips. She stopped moving and tried to wedge herself into the corner. Her eyes grew even wider. The pupils flicked back and forth as if she were being attacked from several directions.

Jennifer stepped closer. "What's wrong, Carla? What do you see?"

The moan grew louder. Carla's body began to shake and twist as she tried to raise her arms. But the restraints were buckled too tightly.

"Let me help you, Carla. Tell me what to do."

"Get them away!" Carla screamed.

"What are they? Tell me. Carla, what do you see?"

Carla shrieked and cringed against the wall, crouching down as if the creatures were swarming all over her.

With a quick movement, Jennifer unbuckled the restraints, allowing Carla to move her arms though they were still covered by the long flapping canvas sleeves.

Carla sprang away, flailing her arms around her head. Wailing and crying, she fought to drive away the demons.

Jennifer reached around as best she could and unfastened the other buckles. In a few minutes, Carla had fought free of the jacket and lay writhing and moaning on the floor as her hands began tearing at the strands of hair.

Jennifer fell to her knees beside her and tried to hold her wrists away from her head.

"Make them stop," Carla cried. "Make them stop."

"What is it, Carla? What are they?"

Carla broke free. Her hands tore at Jennifer, grasping handfuls of her hair. Jennifer's head was twisted sideways, throwing her off balance.

Carla sprang over her, sharply turning her neck until her face was pressed into the foul-smelling mat. Jennifer could not defend herself against the power of the deranged woman's attack. She felt the air being choked from her lungs. One of her arms had been pinned beneath her, making it useless for defending herself. With the other she tried to grasp Carla's body but she was unable to pull her off. Her chest felt as if it were on fire, her vision blurred. She could hear her pulse jackhammering in her ears. She struggled to breathe but Carla's knees were jammed into her back. Her head began to swim. Light whirled beneath her closed eyelids as she struggled to suck air into her burning lungs. Then darkness began to roll over her in an endless suffocating wave.

Suddenly, the weight was torn away. Hands were pulling her to her knees. She struggled to breathe as a voice came from far away. "That's it, take deep breaths. That's it."

Jennifer opened her eyes. The hands helping her to her feet belonged to Mark. A confused mass of arms and legs sorted itself out into nurses and orderlies, all struggling to restrain Mark's patient.

Mark guided her out of isolation. "What the hell were you doing in there?" he shouted. But Jennifer could not speak. It took several moments for her to come to herself after he brought her into his office and seated her in a chair beside his desk. Then all she could manage were the words, "I'm sorry . . . I shouldn't have."

Mark held up his hand. "Take it easy." He handed her a cup of water and she drank. Mark took a seat at the edge of his desk and placed a soothing hand on her shoulder. "You're a pretty crazy person, you know that?" he said with a perplexed expression. "What were you trying to prove?"

It took an effort but Jennifer managed to get out the words. "I wanted to see . . . if . . . if she exhibited the same symptoms as one of my patients."

"That's one hell of a way to find out. You're damn lucky she was scheduled for an EEG right after our conference. If we hadn't come by, I don't know what would have happened."

"I know . . . thank you."

"Well, did she exhibit the same symptoms?"

Jennifer nodded. "That's the strange part. She did."

"You think that's strange? I still can't figure how this happened. I was getting ready to discharge her—then this."

"Did you check her medication?"

"Damn it, yes! Nothing. Not so far, anyway. I sent samples of the batch down to the lab for analysis."

"And this episode happened right out of the blue?"

"That's right. She was up in RT and the therapist noticed her sitting in a corner, doodling. He thought it was weird since Carla is a very talented artist. But there she was drawing the same picture over and over again. When the therapist asked her what she was doing, she went berserk."

"Can I see the drawing?"

"Sure. I have it right here."

Mark opened a drawer and handed Jennifer a piece of paper, pieced together with scotch tape. Even before she looked at it Jennifer knew what she would see.

A woman's face stared out at her with saucerlike eyes and hands clenched tight on either side of her open mouth, from which came a soundless scream. Jennifer stared at the drawing in wide-eyed disbelief. From the woman's skull grew a writhing mass of oily black snakes.

TEN

————————••————••————••————————

Jennifer had seldom experienced a state of excitement as she felt surging through her when she left the hospital that evening. Mark had allowed her to keep Carla's drawing after he made a copy. She placed it side by side with the one Laura made and the one she found in Dr. Freedman's file drawer. Together the three produced a startling effect. Bizarre and terrifying.

The similarity of the images they portrayed could not be denied. Whether drawn in the primitive manner of the first two or in Carla's more sophisticated rendering, they still represented the same grotesque object. A Medusa head of living horror.

What did it mean?

As she rode the tram back into Manhattan Jennifer was assailed on one side by the possibility of making some radical new discovery and on the other by the gnawing doubt that the drawings were merely coincidental. Serpents were a recurrent image in mental patients' drawings and could symbolize anything from actual snakes to genitalia. They were as common as the images of empty rooms and twisting streets which patients used to represent the terrain of their unconscious minds. Yet something inside her resisted the idea that the similarity of the drawings was only coincidence. The women were too close in age and situation.

But that was all they had in common—so far.

Jennifer grabbed a bite at a pub on First Avenue and did

some food shopping before she returned home. She was half-way through the door when the thought struck her that all three women might have been treated with the same drug. She knew she was committing a heresy to think this, but so many of the drugs being used at Montrose were new. It was just possible they might react in some damaging way in a particular kind of patient under a similar set of circumstances. Of course, she would need to investigate the similarities among the women's cases before she could go further. But unless Carla showed some kind of startling reversal, she too would be diagnosed like Laura. Jennifer realized, if she could bring enough factual material forward to show a similarity between Carla's case and Laura's, then she might just have the evidence she needed to convince Dr. Kessler that the condition was something other than schizophrenia.

The idea of both young women doomed to a life of incurable insanity made her stomach knot up. But she would need real evidence this time, not intuition. Gripped by these thoughts, Jennifer found sleep next to impossible. Her mind churned with possibilities. It was only after two that she was able to drift into a troubled sleep in which she wandered through an endless portrait gallery of women whose hair turned into masses of living black snakes.

New day, new problems.

Getting a copy of Carla's records was not as easy a task as she first imagined. Mark turned out to be her first obstacle. He was anything but receptive when she met him in his office before patient sessions and explained her theory. His usual smile quickly faded when she outlined what she wanted.

"Hell, Jennifer," he said with annoyance. "You know giving you these records is completely against hospital rules as well as a complete waste of time."

"Why?" she asked, wondering at his sudden change of attitude.

"I'll tell you why. The linkage you're proposing doesn't exist. The only thing similar about them is their ages. They weren't even on the same drug for God's sake. What you're proposing makes no sense."

"Why don't you just let me have the records. I'll be the judge of whether they're similar or not."

"You're a ball-buster, Jennifer. You know that?"

"It's a compliment I can live with."

Reluctantly, Mark slipped out to the Xerox machine, concealing the records in his medication file, and Jennifer realized just how much of a team player Mark really was. She had already learned the kind of premiums young doctors placed on being good little soldiers and not rocking the boat. They rarely questioned a procedure or a superior. Making one's way up the anthill was as important—no, more important—than the patients they attempted to help.

Mark returned with the material, handing the pages across to Jennifer with annoyance. "If anyone sees this, it's my ass, you realize that."

"You've got a spare. What are you worrying about?" Jennifer remarked dryly. "And thank you darling," she whispered, leaning across the desk and pressing her mouth to his startled lips.

"Hey, what about tonight?" she heard him shout as she slipped out the door.

"Opportunist," she called back over her shoulder.

Unfortunately, when she got the record back to her office and laid it alongside Laura's, she discovered Mark had been right. There was little in them that matched. The only things that were identical were the hospital procedures. Both had been given a CAT scan because of slight irregularities in their EEGs. But nothing concrete had been discovered in either case. Of course that opened the possibility that the medications both women were taking caused a negative reaction for exactly that reason—some brain irregularity, which, when exaggerated by the chemical compounds in the drugs, produced schizoid symptoms. It was plausible, though farfetched, she realized, and in any case it would take a full-scale research project to be certain. And that was well beyond Jennifer's capabilities. Which left the possibility of a missing link: Dr. Freedman's mystery patient, the one who had done the third drawing.

Now all she had to do was examine Dr. Freedman's patient records. And that was where the fun began.

The first call Jennifer made to Patient Records led to a cul-de-sac of bureaucratic red tape. All requests for records had to be countersigned by the head of service or the head of administration, since each record not actually assigned to a treating physician was protected by a maze of legal restrictions designed to protect a patient's privacy.

Asking Dr. Boise was out of the question. The mere idea that he might help her work on an unauthorized hunch defied the laws of probability. If she was to find out anything, she would have to act on her own. And considering her present status, she'd better proceed as carefully as she could. Unauthorized investigations would only add more weight to the case Dr. Boise was building against her.

But where could she start? Picking up the phone, she dialed Mark again. This time his irritation level was at a maximum. "What the hell do you want now?"

"You once said that Dr. Freedman had a friend, a buddy on your service."

"You've got a great memory for everything except your social life."

"What's the resident's name, then we'll discuss it."

"Malkoff. Dr. Karl Malkoff."

"Thanks," she said, starting to hang up. She was unsure just how much farther she could trust Mark, but she needed help. "I'm having some trouble getting hold of Dr. Freedman's patient records without going through the whole rigamarole."

"Hell, why not just ask your social worker. They usually keep capsule records on all of their patients. Not day-to-day medical notations but diagnoses and what kinds of therapies were used. Stuff like that."

"Mark, you're a genius. Thanks."

"Hey. What about tonight?"

"I'll call you later," she said and hung up. Asking Anne for the records was the same as asking Dr. Boise. *Shit!* She was right back where she started, unless . . . The records were in Anne's office. All she had to do was wait until Anne left for the day. Then she could slip inside and take a look at them without anyone knowing. Not a bad idea, she thought excitedly. There was only one obstacle. Anne's office was usually locked. She would have to find a way to get hold of a key.

If Jennifer surprised herself with the realization of what she intended to do, she was even more surprised when Brae actually showed up on time for his session.

Something had changed in the last few days since his return. Jennifer could see it as soon as he entered and took the seat across from her. Brae seemed less intense, less rigid. But without the safety of the drug buffer, Jennifer did not really know what to expect. She knew that patients like Brae, who went into a sudden and deep withdrawal, could climb out of it again just as quickly. Sometimes a shock of some kind had an even more positive effect, relieving symptoms altogether. She had seen patients come out of depressions within days, even hours, appearing to act completely normal and having only the foggiest recollection of their own illnesses, as if the whole experience had only been some kind of bad dream.

"I'm glad you came," she said meeting his gaze. "Would you like to tell me how you've been feeling?"

"Let's skip it, okay."

"Okay. Then what would you like to talk about?"

"The men I killed."

"All right. What would you like to tell me?"

"How they died."

Jennifer braced herself, trying to appear as calm as possible.

"I told you I used a knife, didn't I? A hunting knife."

"No. You said a paring knife."

"Yeah," Brae said as if it was a struggle to remember. "It doesn't matter."

"Wouldn't it matter, as evidence I mean?"

"What is that supposed to mean?" he questioned with narrowed eyes.

"Aren't you afraid the knife would be found and traced back to you?"

"No one will trace it to me."

"Then where did you hide it?"

Brae's face went blank for a moment. "I hid it."

"Where exactly? Don't you remember?"

"What's the difference?" he shouted.

"I'm sorry. I just wanted to know."

"That's my business, not yours!" he said in the same explosive tone. "Why do you keep getting me to talk about what kind of knife I used. I used a knife, that's all."

"All right," she said calmly. "Please go on. You were going to tell me how you killed them."

"How I killed them," he repeated, groping for the words.

"I made them feel the pain, the same pain she . . . she felt. Every second of pain and more . . . much more." Brae stopped and stared fixedly into space.

"Where did you hide their bodies?" Jennifer asked quietly.

"Their bodies," Brae repeated. His face was flushed. Sweat was popping in little beads on his forehead. The veins along his temples were visible from the strain.

"You had to hide them afterwards, didn't you?"

"I hid them," he said, as if he was having trouble remembering.

"Where?"

"I can't tell you."

"You don't have to, just as long as you know," she whispered.

"I know where they are," he said forcefully, but Jennifer could see the confusion in his eyes, as if one part of his being disbelieved what the other part was saying.

"You don't have to worry about my telling anyone," Jennifer said. "What you tell me is privileged information. I couldn't testify against you."

"No . . . you couldn't," he faltered. "You couldn't testify."

"But you would have to stand trial, if the bodies were found, wouldn't you?"

Brae stared straight ahead with glassy eyes. "Trial?" he echoed, struggling to comprehend. Jennifer could almost feel the turmoil raging within him.

"You did kill them didn't you?" she questioned softly.

Brae's pupils focused on her. "I had to kill them; they raped her."

"Who raped her?"

"They did . . . the men."

"How many men?"

"How many?" he repeated. "Two. No three. There were three."

"Aren't you sure?"

"There were three."

"Can you describe them? Were they tall men? Dark or light? Black or white. Frank would want to know, wouldn't he?"

"Yeah," Brae nodded. "I'll have to tell Frank. They were white. No . . . some of them were black. Latins."

"How many Latins?"

"All of them were Latins. Mercedes was Latin. They wanted revenge because I took her away from them."

"Is that why all three of them killed her?"

"All three?" Brae said. Sweat was pouring down his face.

"You said there were three."

"I can't remember now." His eyes were darting back and forth.

"Why can't you remember? You killed three men. You have to remember them."

"I don't know," he said blankly.

"Is it possible you didn't kill them? Maybe you made a mistake."

"I had to. They raped her," he said tensely.

"Maybe they weren't the ones. Isn't that possible?"

"Yes." He nodded. "No . . . I don't know."

Jennifer watched his hands tighten on the arms of the chair. He seemed about to spring. The conflict was reaching a climax.

"We could go and dig up the bodies, then we would know for sure, wouldn't we?"

"Yes. We'd know," he said in a mechanical tone.

Jennifer knew she was nearing the edge. But she could not stop. Her eyes glanced up at the clock. They had reached the end of the session. She knew she must conclude, but she sensed how close they were to a breakthrough. Brae's knuckles showed white where they gripped the chair. His lips were twitching soundlessly. His eyes were fixed points of focus. He seemed to be in a kind of trance.

"You didn't kill those men, did you?"

He did not respond but she could see the effect of her question. His body tensed even further. His face flushed.

"Could it be, you thought you killed them, because you felt you had to punish someone for what happened to Mercedes?"

Brae's eyes fixed on her, like tiny lasers.

"Who is it you wanted to punish, Brae? It's you, isn't it?"

The moment lengthened but he did not speak. His eyes remained locked with hers.

"But you're really not to blame, are you? You weren't sure you loved her enough to let her live with you. You needed more time to be sure. Her death isn't your fault, Brae. Is it? You don't have to blame yourself." Jennifer watched his eyes. She could see him struggling to piece together what she had just said. In a gentle tone, she said, "If you want to, we can talk again tomorrow. I have someone else waiting."

Brae raised his eyes to hers for a moment before he rose. He went to the door, pausing before opening it. He turned to face her with an expression she could not quite understand. But the former hostility was no longer there.

When he closed the door behind him, Jennifer exhaled and slumped back in her seat. The session had exhausted her. Her hands were trembling from the strain. But she knew they had made a breakthrough. That was all that mattered. Brae had gone through an ordeal. Now he would have to find the footing to make his understanding permanent.

Checking her calendar, Jennifer realized Brae was ending his thirty-day stay in less than a week. It gave her very little time to prepare him for an outpatient situation. But she knew the next few days would be critical in consolidating the effects of the breakthrough. She prayed he would return tomorrow.

When she heard the knob turn, she quickly closed Brae's folder and opened the one beneath it. But the individual who entered was not her next patient, but Dr. Boise. The look of annoyance on his face was unmistakable.

"Mr. Bradley just wandered down to the nurses' station complaining that when he arrived for his session your door was locked. Would you kindly explain?"

"My last patient was experiencing an important crisis. I could not jeopardize it."

"Oh, I see," Boise said sarcastically. "But it's all right to jeopardize Mr. Bradley."

"I didn't think Mr. Bradley would be hurt by the delay."

"You didn't? Don't you understand by keeping your last patient over the time limit, you've taken away Mr. Bradley's time and all your other patients' down the line."

"I intend to make it up by keeping each the required time."

"And what happens to their schedules? We don't have enough personnel to take them to their various therapies individually. That's why maintaining the schedule is so important. Not to mention the nurses' overtime, because your own schedule will be so seriously overextended."

"I understand, Dr. Boise," Jennifer said tamely. "I'll try not to let it happen again."

Boise glared at her for a moment. "I wish I could believe

that, doctor. Unfortunately the pattern of your behavior seems to contradict it. The rules of this hospital mean very little to you. It should not surprise you that the incident on the fourth-floor isolation chamber with Dr. Tobey's patient was reported to me this morning. You put both yourself and the patient in a position of extreme danger."

"I would like to explain," Jennifer said, as the blood rushed to her cheeks. For an instant she almost blurted out all of her suspicions to Dr. Boise. But his manner cut her off abruptly.

"I'll give you a word of advice, Dr. Westwood. Without mincing words. You know you're undergoing a period of probation. You're on trial in more ways than one. Dr. Kessler advanced your name over several equally qualified applicants. Frankly, your actions very much reflect on him. I did not approve his choice, but I went along with it because of his wishes. I have no desire to see him embarrassed because of your behavior and I won't allow you to compromise me. So far I have refrained from making any negative reports, though several members of the board would not mind seeing Dr. Kessler taken down a peg. Everyone wants to be a star, but no one likes working alongside one. Am I making myself clear enough for you, doctor?"

"Abundantly," Jennifer responded.

"Needless to say, if your conduct continues along this path, it will be my responsibility to bring you up on charges before the administration and have your residency terminated."

Dr. Boise turned and hurriedly left the room. Jennifer wondered what his reaction would be if he even suspected what she had planned for later that evening.

ELEVEN

Visiting hours ended at nine. Jennifer waited another two hours for the floor to settle down, using the time to catch up on her backlog of paperwork. At eleven, she locked her office door and headed toward the nurses' station. The shift changed at midnight, but Jennifer knew that the personnel took turns slipping down to the lockers a half hour before to begin changing. That meant only a skeleton crew manned the floor.

Jennifer smiled at the two nurses on duty when she entered.

"Working late tonight, doctor," one of them said, smiling.

Jennifer made a harried gesture and busied herself with the medication log until one of the nurses left to make her rounds. Jennifer struggled to find a way to distract the other nurse, but before she could concoct a scheme, one of the public phones began ringing. With an exasperated sigh, the nurse stepped outside to answer it.

Jennifer rose and stepped over to the board where the keys were kept. She slipped one of the masters into her clinic coat and hung another set of keys in its place.

A moment later the nurse returned, shaking her head at the nerve some people had calling at that hour. Jennifer grimaced her understanding, then rose and left the room, uttering a brisk good-night.

Her pulse accelerated as soon as she passed the large glass window fronting the station. A few steps past it and she was at Anne's door. The master slid into the lock, and after a stubborn jiggle it opened.

There was no light inside the tiny vestibule. Closing the hall door behind her, Jennifer felt her way toward Anne's office. She slid her hand along the smoothly polished wood and found the knob. The key slid in without difficulty and the door opened. Jennifer stepped inside and moved cautiously to the desk. She turned on the lamp, filling the small room with an amber glow.

Anne's files were inside a wooden filing cabinet beside the window. Jennifer opened the first drawer, which contained hospital records. The second contained the case files. A drawer divider still had Dr. Freedman's name typed across it. Jennifer found her own new admits behind the divider, then Dr. Freedman's cases behind it. Jennifer read Jeffrey's name, then Brae's. Laura's came a few cards down. After that Jennifer only concentrated on the diagnosis typed on each card, looking for any depression admits who developed schizoid symptoms. It suddenly struck her that she was doing something outlandish. Mark was right, this made no sense.

That was when she found them.

Not one but two cards, one behind the other. Excitedly, Jennifer pulled out both cards, flipping the card behind to mark her place. She brought them over to the desk. Incredibly enough, both patients had been admitted with affective disorders. Both had developed schizoid symptoms within two weeks and both patients were women.

Using a pen and pad she found on the desk, Jennifer noted their names and the details of their cases. The first card listed a twenty-seven-year-old housewife named Leah Redmond, a mother with two children. The second was a fashion model named Mary Ann Spreull, age twenty-three.

Jennifer returned to the cabinet and slipped both cards back into the file. She had just started to close the long drawer, when she heard a click. The knob was beginning to turn. Someone was trying to unlock the door.

With a quick step, Jennifer reached the desk and turned off the light. She squeezed back against the wall. The door opened slowly. There was just enough light to make out the shape of an entering figure. Jennifer pressed her palms against the wall, not daring to breathe.

A body brushed against the desk and moved past her. Jennifer froze. What reason could she give for being here? Why had she so stupidly turned out the light? She heard the bathroom door open and an instant later light flooded the room. The figure stepped back inside and turned around. With a shock, Jennifer found herself facing Brae Haskill.

He had just put a cigarette to his lips and was about to stroke a match when he saw her. "Jesus!" he exclaimed, jumping back.

"What are you doing here?" Jennifer asked.

Brae's eyes moved to the pad on the desk, then to the open drawer of the filing cabinet. "I could ask you the same question, doctor?"

"I'm here ... because—"

"Skip it," he said, lighting up.

"You came in here to smoke?"

"That's right. They don't allow it after ten."

"Then what you're doing is against regulations."

"Tell you what, doctor," he said with a mischievous smile. "I won't tell on you if you don't tell on me."

Jennifer felt her pulse rate returning to normal. But the look in Brae's eye was decidedly unnerving. "Just how did you get in here?"

"I used this," he said holding up a bobby pin. Jennifer tried to look reproving, but she could not help noticing how clear his eyes were. The distracted tension was no longer there. In fact, his eyes wore a look of frank appraisal that one gave to a desirable woman, not to one's doctor. Jennifer began to feel uneasy.

"I think you should go back to your room now," she said firmly. She closed the drawer of the cabinet.

"You're the doctor," he said, taking a final drag. Then he stubbed out the cigarette on the sole of his shoe and flipped it into the toilet. He flushed it and made a gesture for Jennifer to go first.

She opened the door and slipped into the corridor.

The door closed behind her. They were alone in the dark.

"I'll see if it's all clear," he said, moving past her. She jumped back as his body brushed against hers.

He opened the door a crack and peered out. "All clear," he said in a whisper. Jennifer ducked outside and started back toward her office.

"Good night doctor," she heard him whisper slyly.

She did not answer, nor did she turn around to reveal the deep flush of embarrassment that seared her features.

The night shift had already changed when Jennifer returned to the nurses' station. With only one nurse inside and the orderlies making rounds, it was a simple matter to return the key to the rack without being observed.

Downstairs, she asked security to call her a cab. It took longer than she thought and she impatiently paced back and forth across the empty lobby, keyed up in spite of her fatigue.

When the lights of a cab approached, Jennifer went through the glass doors impatiently, but the vehicle sped past her, heading toward the research center. Jennifer glimpsed several Oriental faces in the rear and followed the cab with her eyes as it turned around the bend. The dome was backlit by the glare of lights, causing a strange chill to pass through her. How many nightmares were contained within its walls? she wondered. The line between reality and terror was so thin it made her feel the fragility of human sanity. The building she stared at represented the best hope humankind had against the darkness, but in her present mood the sight of it failed to fill her with any warmth. She was obsessed with the need to get her hands on Dr. Freedman's medical records. Only then would a pattern reveal itself.

Or would it? Again Jennifer was assailed by doubt. Finding the two cases tonight was so startling she had forgotten that schizophrenia was the most common of all the major psychoses. She remembered the statistics. Sixty percent of the population of all state hospitals suffered from the disease. The risk factor for the entire population was one percent or one out of every fifty people in the entire country. Looked at that way, the cases were not even surprising. Nor was the prior diagnoses. Mistaken diagnoses were common enough in medicine. Certain types of schizophrenia often masked themselves in psychoneurotic symptoms. It was more than possible that she was wasting her time, led on by her own identification with Laura. But having gone this far, she felt a need to see it through to the end—whatever it might be.

If she could just find a link between the cases. Even the same delusional symptoms might be enough to aid her cause. But she needed those records to determine just what kinds of medication had been given. Even if she was able to obtain them she would still have to discover if the women's reactions were similar. But to discover that she would have to examine each of them face-to-face.

Both patients had been admitted to Dr. Kessler's center. She could not risk another assault on his fortress, not without an invitation, as Dr. Boise so forcefully pointed out. For a fledgling resident like herself there was no reason why one would be extended. She could approach Dr. Kessler, but she hardly thought that feasible. Not after the way he had handled her suspicions at the conference. She needed evidence. She would have to find a way through the bureaucratic tangle, *unless* . . .

The idea was so startling Jennifer did not see the taxi until it stopped a few feet from her.

"Are you the Manhattan fare?"

"Yes. Thank you," Jennifer replied, rushing to pull open the door. She saw nothing on the way home. Her mind was completely absorbed in working out the audacious idea she had concocted.

TWELVE

———◆◆◆———

The plan was so incredibly simple Jennifer was almost afraid it would not work. She was so used to complexity she mistrusted anything so straightforward. But it *would* work. It had to. She would visit Dr. Kessler's center not as a psychiatrist, but by pretending to be a relative.

The idea had some risk, she realized. It was just possible she would be discovered, but the chances of this were slight. No one would be expecting it. Of course if she was found out, it would be the end of her career at Montrose or anywhere else for that matter—once the facts were typed into her record. Yet she was determined to chance it.

Jennifer lay awake for an hour before sliding into sleep, figuring every possible angle. She woke an hour early and continued to fine-tune her plan. By the time she had breakfast, dressed and made her way to the tram, the scenario had taken a positive form. Ironically, it was her acting training that gave her the confidence to go through with it. Stopping at several pharmacies, she was able to purchase the supplies she needed. Now all she had to do was make the arrangements.

The procedure turned out to be far less difficult than she imagined. Jennifer waited until her first therapy session was over before she dialed Patient Information at the center. A crisp voice with a slight Oriental accent informed her that all visits had to be scheduled at least eight hours in advance and were granted entirely at the discretion of the hospital.

Jennifer told the clerk she was a first cousin of Leah Redmond and was put on hold. After a few minutes of butterflies, the voice came back on. Since Leah's quotient of visits was still unfilled, she could receive a visit that evening. The clerk asked for Jennifer's name.

Jennifer started; she had not expected results so quickly. The name of her college roommate flew into her head. "Sarah . . . Sarah Redmond."

"Very good, Miss Redmond. Your visit is scheduled for seven."

The phone was hung up, leaving Jennifer quivering. Seven did not give her much time to prepare. She would have to return to her apartment by six at the latest. It would be tight but she would have to manage it.

Lunch was spent tracking down the elusive Dr. Malkoff. Jennifer finally found him seated alone in a corner of the cafeteria cramming a chef salad into his mouth while trying to keep bits of food off the book of poetry he was reading.

"You'll ruin your eyes that way," Jennifer said, taking a seat opposite him.

"It's okay, I eat a lot of fish. Who are you?"

"My name is Jennifer Westwood."

"If you're trying to pick me up, I want to warn you I don't like long-term relationships."

Jennifer laughed. "Not really. I'm replacing Dr. Freedman and I understand you were a buddy of his."

Malkoff shook his bearded head. "Buddies? That's one way of putting it. Buddies we were not. Freedman was devoted to long-distance cycling and his caseload."

"I guess I was misinformed."

"I guess you were. I suppose we did spend some lunch hours together but Freedman was the quintessential loner. I think he became a strict Freudian so he didn't have to talk to his patients."

Jennifer smiled, watching Malkoff's eyes twinkle at her response to his joke. "I was just wondering if he ever mentioned any special patient problems."

"To Hank all his patients were special problems."

"This would concern a sudden onset of schizophrenia where there had been no evidence of it before and the admitting diagnosis was for an affective disorder."

"I thought that's what schizophrenia was all about," Malkoff said with a smile. "But no, Hank never mentioned any such concern. But I don't think he would have taken me into his confidence."

Jennifer thanked him. He made a not-to-worry gesture and delved back into his book. Jennifer went over to the food counter and selected a ham sandwich and a container of coffee. She started back inside looking for a place to sit when she saw Rita at a table by herself.

Jennifer made her way over and asked if she could join her.

"Sure, have a seat, doctor. You look a little tired."

"I am," Jennifer said, sitting alongside her. "Dr. Freedman left me with a full load."

Rita smiled and hooked a wriggly square of jello onto her fork.

"I should have chosen that," Jennifer said regretfully. "How did you and Dr. Freedman get along? I understand he was kind of a loner."

"Oh, he was."

"Did he ever discuss any of his patient problems?"

"At the staff conferences, of course."

"No. I meant with you personally."

"Not that I remember. Why?"

"Oh, it's really nothing. It just would have been helpful if I had some of his cases to work with, just as background in dealing with the ones I inherited."

"You should discuss that with Dr. Boise. He's the only one who could get the records for you. Would you excuse me," Rita said abruptly. "I was supposed to meet someone."

"Sure," Jennifer answered, watching Rita pick up her tray and head toward a table where a resident Jennifer had never seen before rose to greet her. Watching them interact made it obvious that Rita was interested in more than a medical discussion. Strike two, Jennifer thought, getting up to dump her tray.

She was not looking forward to her conference with Anne. Guilt over violating her office had set in. But Anne would not be denied. She arrived in Jennifer's office with a brisk step and began her usual high-speed rundown. The session ended without incident. But when Anne got up to leave, Jennifer stopped her with a question. "Anne, I was curious just how Dr. Freedman handled the Spreull case."

Anne turned to face her. "The Spreull case?" she questioned. "What do you mean?"

"Well, I heard the symptoms were very similar to Laura's. And I thought, what with both cases happening in such a short time . . ."

"I really don't know what you mean."

"Weren't both cases similar?"

A strange look appeared on Anne's face, blending caution and curiosity. "Who told you that?"

"Oh, I just heard some comments in the nurses' station."

"Well, I don't know what you heard, but the facts were not at all similar. Both were eventually diagnosed that same way, it's true. But that's not at all uncommon."

"She was also transferred to Dr. Kessler's clinic, wasn't she?"

"Yes. I believe she was."

"Wouldn't you have arranged that?"

"I suppose I would have."

"Aren't you certain?"

"Have you any idea of the amount of placements I make in a single month?"

"Don't you keep records?"

"Not after the patient has been transferred. The records are sent ahead and kept in our computer. If I didn't keep current, my little office would be buried," she ended with a laugh.

"I understand. I just wondered, that's all."

"Well, if that's it," Anne said and quit the office with a wave.

When the door closed behind her, Jennifer was left with an uneasy feeling that Anne had something to hide.

It took less than an hour for Jennifer to tint her hair the light brown color she had purchased that morning. Using makeup she darkened her lips and changed the shade of her eyebrows. She used blush to tint her cheeks and pasted on false eyelashes, then brushed her hair long over her shoulders. A loose-fitting green cape and high tan boots completed her outfit. It was so different from her usual image she doubted if anyone at the hospital would recognize her. Besides, she had been there too short a time to get to know anyone other than the few people on her floor, and most of those would be off duty by the time she arrived.

But to avoid the chance of a meeting, Jennifer took a cab over the bridge. Fortunately, the driver agreed to wait and ferry her back to Manhattan.

The first part of the plan worked perfectly but did not prevent her from feeling an almost paralyzing case of stage fright. Her palms were sweating and she did not need a stethoscope to record the accelerated rate of her heart beat.

She arrived at the entrance to the center almost before she realized it. Fortunately, darkness added to her cover. She instructed the driver where to wait, then left the cab and headed inside the ultra-modern complex.

A set of double glass doors opened to admit her. The reception area was actually smaller than Jennifer had imagined. It was also almost devoid of furnishings, except for a long leather couch. Unlike most hospital lobbies, with corridors going off in all directions, this area was almost hermetically sealed, except for two sets of metal doors at either end.

No other visitors were waiting when Jennifer approached the reception desk and gave her name to an attractive Chinese woman of twenty or so in a high-necked blue uniform. The woman typed her name into a computer terminal. When Sarah Redmond's name appeared, she nodded approvingly and slid a plastic pass toward her.

"Which way?" Jennifer asked stepping away.

"One moment, please."

Jennifer watched the woman beckon for her to return to the counter. In front of her was a small ink pad and a form. Jennifer realized the woman wanted to take her fingerprints.

For an instant she froze. Her own prints were on file in the administrative office.

"Is this essential?" she asked, as her mind whirled. If both terminals were connected, she would be immediately discovered.

"I'm sorry. Security requirement. Please."

The woman held her hand out. Jennifer made her decision and allowed the woman to take her hand and make an imprint. She was gambling that the records of the center and the hospital were kept separately. As the woman rolled her thumb on the pad Jennifer realized that her thumbprint was not all that was being taken. A small aperture she had not noticed before opened behind the counter and Jennifer made out the lens of a camera behind a sheet of glass. She was also being photographed.

Before she could react, a buzzer sounded and the set of doors at one end of the room opened. An Oriental nurse in the same pastel blue outfit stood in the doorway waiting.

"That way, please." The receptionist gestured. Jennifer's stomach twisted into knots but she started toward the doors briskly.

"Miss."

Jennifer froze. She turned around, expecting the alarms to begin going off. Instead, the receptionist offered a small packet for wiping off her fingers. "Thank you," Jennifer said. Blood began flowing through her arteries again.

The nurse signaled for Jennifer to follow and led her along a sleek-looking corridor lit by overhead tubes of fluorescent light. Doors faced each other on either side while another set of double doors sealed the area at the far end. The nurse stopped at one door and pressed a button. The door opened and Jennifer was ushered inside.

The room was comfortably furnished with two facing couches and was as softly lit as the corridor outside. A young woman sat on one of the couches beside another Chinese nurse. The nurse who had escorted Jennifer stepped outside and closed the door, leaving Jennifer alone with the two women.

Leah Redmond was a petite blond with regular features, whose hair had been set in an out-of-date bouffant style. Jennifer could see she had been made up for the occasion. She wore blue mascara, blush and lipstick, and had been dressed in a frilly blue frock, like a child's doll. She looked less like a woman than a waxwork. Jennifer counted on Leah's delusional state to cover what would be an obvious lack of recognition. But that ceased to be a worry from the moment she entered. Leah sat in the druglike trance, as silent and distant as a portrait.

The next ten minutes became pure torture when Jennifer realized the nurse intended to remain throughout the visit. Jennifer was forced to improvise a one-way conversation in which she related the details of her life as an aspiring actress in daytime soaps. Through it all, Leah never moved. She only blinked her eyes.

Jennifer realized her time was quickly running out. If she was going to elicit a reaction, it had to be now. With a casual gesture, she leaned forward to kiss Leah good-bye, at the same time spilling the contents of her bag all over the floor.

The nurse, who up to now had been as silent as Leah, reacted immediately, bending to aid Jennifer in gathering up her things. At that moment Jennifer slipped her hand inside the cape and drew out the picture Carla had drawn. She placed it directly in front of Leah's glazed eyes.

The transformation was instantaneous. As Leah's lifeless eyes scanned the picture a sound began building in her throat. Her eyes began to bulge. Her mouth opened in a strangled cry and her hands rose toward her hair.

The nurse sprang instantly, grasping Leah's wrists and trying to pull them away from her head. The scream that broke from Leah's lips was a subhuman howl. "Stop them . . . get them away. . . ."

Leah's eyes darted back and forth with the same expression of horror Jennifer had seen on the faces of Laura and Carla. Her fingers tried to clutch at the imaginary shapes that were writhing around her head.

The door sprang open and two male orderlies rushed inside. Jennifer was shoved out of the way as they twisted her arms behind her.

"You go. Now!" the nurse shouted.

"My things . . ." Jennifer cried pointing to her fallen bag.

"We bring. You go now!"

The blue-clad nurse who had escorted her inside now appeared and gripped Jennifer's arm, drawing her out of the room. No one seemed to notice the picture that Jennifer tucked back inside the pocket of her cape. When she turned around the door had already closed.

At the front desk the nurse and receptionist looked extremely annoyed. A young Oriental male with a sleek haircut and a dark blue business suit brought her the handbag. Jennifer pretended to examine her things as she was gently but firmly led outside. She had brought nothing that could reveal her true identity, but everything was there anyway. The glass doors closed behind her as she swept toward the waiting car.

Her pulse was beating like the oscilloscope of a patient about to undergo a coronary bypass.

Jennifer's mind raced as quickly as the car returning her to Manhattan. She was filled with a sense of excitement she could not suppress. All her instincts told her she was on to something much larger than she first imagined. She had the feeling it was something she could not really handle alone, but there was no one she could trust to help her.

If the new drugs were responsible for the conditions of these women, then a great deal more than a single reputation was at stake. Jennifer's mind refused to consider the implications beyond realizing she might be about to upset a mighty big apple cart. What the consequences might be for her personally she could only guess. But whatever the risk, she was prepared to accept it. Too many of her colleagues had conditioned themselves to achieve "success *über alles,*" as she liked to put it, and in so doing forgot the very basis upon which medicine rested. It was not a science that existed only within the covers of some text books or the sterile confines of a laboratory, but a living body of knowledge that was based on the very suffering of its patients.

Jennifer had never been able to condition herself to the lack of feeling she saw in so many of the doctors around her. She felt a sensation of dread every time she remembered the living nightmare she saw revealed in the eyes of the three women. How many more like them there were she could only guess. She still had one more of Dr. Freedman's patients to examine. How she could accomplish it without having her prints matched was still something she had to work out. In the meantime, she had to devise a way to get her hands on the records. The entire problem formed an unbreakable circle. She needed permission but permission would not be granted.

Jennifer stared ahead with an unblinking gaze, ignoring the spectacle of Manhattan's skyline rushing toward her as the car crossed the Fifty-ninth Street Bridge. She had failed to find a way to scale the walls. Now she would try knocking at the front door.

THIRTEEN

The computer library was located in the Tobler Wing along with the major administrative offices. It was reached by elevator from the main lobby and, like most computer sections Jennifer had ever been in, was protected by special doors against changes in the atmosphere and dust.

The people inside seemed similarly insulated. Jennifer always associated computer technicians with the priesthood. The similarities went beyond the special uniform both were required to wear. They often acted as if the information contained in their rolls of tape was nothing short of Holy Scripture. Even worse was the doctrinaire quality of their procedures, something she found particularly annoying.

The morning she entered was no exception. The clerk who faced her had all the smugness of the breed. On her coldly impassive face was an expression that said, "You may have finished eight years of school, young lady, but I am the guardian of the knowledge you need and you had better be damned polite about asking for it."

Jennifer had taken courses in computer technology and was capable of operating a keypunch but Montrose denied its physicians direct access to the record tapes on legal grounds. So Jennifer stilled her irritation, smiled and courted the clerk who handed her a long yellow requisition form. As she expected, the clerk returned in less than five minutes with the information that none of the records could be released without the proper authorizations.

"I didn't know," Jennifer said, acting as if she had learned this for the first time. "It's just that I've taken over Dr. Freedman's practice and I thought . . ."

"Oh I see," the clerk said with a sympathetic look. "Wasn't that a shame. He was so young."

Jennifer produced a matching expression. "Yes, it was terrible. That's why I thought the records had been sent down for me to look over."

"But these patients were no longer on Dr. Freedman's service when he was killed," the clerk said, looking down at the form.

"I know. But it's a way of familiarizing myself with his methods, so I can continue treatment for the patients I've inherited."

"That makes sense. One moment, I'll check again."

Jennifer pretended to study the regulations chart until the clerk returned. "Well, doctor, most of the ones you want will still need legal authorizations. I'm sorry. Besides the records were sent over to Dr. Kessler's center."

Jennifer glanced down at the form. The names of Leah Redmond and Mary Ann Spreull were checked. There were no others. "Well, thanks a lot," she said, starting to move away when the thought suddenly struck her. "I wonder. Were there any requests from Dr. Freedman that he didn't have a chance to pick up?"

"I'll check."

Jennifer waited with a feeling of tension. Her inspiration was really off-the-wall. It meant that Dr. Freedman had suspected something. That possibility had never crossed Jennifer's mind until that moment. She had no idea why it should have. She was probably just wasting her time.

The clerk returned in less time than she expected, laying a series of forms on the counter in front of her. "As a matter of fact, Dr. Freedman did make several requests. Here they are."

When the clerk turned the forms toward her, Jennifer felt needles begin shooting along her spine. What she read amazed her. Freedman had requested the names of all patients diagnosed as schizoid over a period of two years. He also requested the names of all patients admitted to Dr. Kessler's center, along with their CAT scans and medication records.

Trying to appear calm, Jennifer looked up and said, "Were these requests ever authorized?"

"Oh yes, they were signed by Dr. Boise."

"I thought they had to be authorized by the administrator?"

"Well they do, actually. But Dr. Boise's signature is usually all right. Especially if we get a verbal okay from Administration."

"Did you get the okay?"

The clerk examined the requests and looked embarrassed. "I don't see it noted here. But I'm sure the call was made."

"Oh sure," Jennifer said with a smile. She did not want to make the woman any more ill at ease than she already was.

"I suppose Dr. Freedman never got a chance to pick them up?" Jennifer said with a quickening pulse, praying the answer was no.

"I see he did," the clerk said and Jennifer's heart sank.

"But they haven't been returned. As a matter of fact they should be, since they're legally protected information."

"Can I see when he signed them out?"

"Surely," the clerk said and turned the requests toward her. Jennifer read the date. It was made one week before she started at Montrose. One week before Dr. Freedman died.

"The records aren't in his office are they?" the clerk said with a look of concern.

"No. Everything was cleaned out."

"Then I'll have to check with Dr. Boise."

"I could do that for you, if you'd like," Jennifer said quickly.

"Would you? That would be a convenience. We're so jammed up right now. Two of our staff are on vacation."

"Oh sure. No problem."

"Thank you, doctor," the clerk said gratefully. Jennifer left the section and took the elevator back down, trying to filter the sensations flowing through her. Incredibly enough, Freedman had begun an investigation parallel to her own. *Why?* Had he also suspected something was wrong? His request for the medication records seemed to prove it.

Jennifer's brain was on fire. What was actually going on? The sensation of excitement from the previous day was replaced by something else, a feeling she could not explain. What she had embarked upon was more than just stepping on some administrators' toes. Something very serious and very wrong was going on at Montrose. But she needed those records to find out just what it actually was.

Patient routines forced Jennifer's mind to release its hold on her suspicions. But she could not help finding out one fact more. Her casual questions in the nurses' stations elicited the information that Dr. Freedman's apartment had been packed by someone from the hospital, though no one could say who. Jennifer covered her questions by saying several things of the doctor's had been returned by neighbors and she had promised to send them on.

"Wait a sec," Rita said. "I'll find out where you can send them. Jennifer wanted to stop her but was afraid that might look unnatural.

A few minutes later, Anne came in holding an index card. "Rita just told me you had some of Dr. Freedman's things. This is his parents' home phone and address," she said in her efficient tone. "Get a receipt for the postage and the hospital will reimburse you."

Jennifer thanked her for going to so much trouble.

"It's no trouble, doctor," Anne said with a smile. "That's what I'm here for."

Anne was almost through the door when Jennifer called to her. "I wonder if I could bother you about something else? You wouldn't know who packed up the office, would you?"

"I could find out, why?"

"I think they broke the lock on the filing cabinet," Jennifer lied.

"Well, it's probably best if we just get it replaced. You know how touchy the custodial staff can get." Anne made a disparaging gesture before she stepped outside.

Jennifer smiled a thank-you and continued back to her own office with an expression of professional calm. Inside, she was just the opposite. She locked the door and placed the card in front of her while she picked up the phone and dialed.

A woman's voice answered.

"Mrs. Freedman?"

"Yes."

"I'm sorry to disturb you. My name is Dr. Westwood. I'm calling from Montrose. I wonder if I could bother you for a moment?"

"What would you like?" the woman said, her tone changing to hollow weariness.

"First, I'd like to say how sorry I was about your son."

"Were you a friend of his?"

"No. Actually I've just taken over his service."

There was a pause. "What can I do for you?"

"I think some hospital records might have gotten packed away along with your son's things."

"I don't think so. I unpacked them myself and I don't remember any."

"I hate to ask you this but it's very important. Could you double-check? It's especially important that they be returned."

"Would you like me to call you back?"

Jennifer checked the clock. "No. I can hold for a while, if it's not inconvenient."

"One moment please."

Jennifer waited with the phone pressed against her ear. She tried not to think. Instead she listened to the sound of children's laughter drifting up from one of the nearby playgrounds. She did not want to picture the woman who was going through her dead son's belongings to please the stranger who had taken the place that should have been his. How much sacrifice had his family made, seeing him through a medical education? How much pride had been taken in the accomplishment only to have it snatched from them? How much emptiness was there left to face?

For the first time, the doctor whose life she inhabited took on the coloration of a real person. Before that he had been only a one-dimensional cutout. Jennifer had not wanted to know more about him. Living in his apartment and occupying his office was enough. Now all that had changed. What she had learned that morning made her feel something like a sense of identification.

The woman's voice startled her when it came back on the line. "I'm sorry," she said in a hoarse tone. "Nothing like that was in with my son's things. Is there anything else?"

"Nothing else, thank you. And I am sorry."

"Well, good-bye then."

There was a click and Jennifer put down the receiver, feeling a sense of remorse for having caused the woman more pain. She rose and went to the window, realizing she had come to a dead end. Carla's conference was scheduled for the middle of next week. It would be the perfect moment to introduce new evidence. Jennifer was sure that if she could establish a connection between the symptoms and the medication, it would prompt Dr. Kessler to okay her line of research. Someone like Kessler was beyond the petty power plays of a Dr. Boise and the other *wunderkinds* of his staff, who may have been recklessly misusing the new drugs to enhance their own reputations.

Jennifer felt like a butterfly transfixed on a pin. No matter where she turned she always came back to the same thing. She had to get her hands on those records. Now that she knew they were not in with Dr. Freedman's things, other possibilities presented themselves. Dr. Boise was the obvious choice. As Freedman's superior he would have supervised the packing of the office, gone through the files, and removed the records. That was her next step. It meant a search of Boise's office. The question was, how?

At the thought of the risk she was running, Jennifer's mind blanked. She could not think of pentrating Dr. Boise's defenses without thinking of the chance she was taking with her future. Instead, her mind switched to a different track, one she had ignored as long as Freedman had remained the cutout she had preferred to make of him. Now that he had assumed the dimensions of flesh and blood, certain questions began nagging at her. First and foremost was how Freedman, who was by all accounts an expert cyclist, met his death on a bicycle in Central Park one week after beginning his own investigation? Had he stumbled upon something so important that he was killed to protect it?

The thought was so bizarre it made Jennifer wince. It was preposterous for her to be thinking this way. It was as exaggerated as one of her patients' delusions. But the idea would not vacate her mind. Along with it came the image of the research center with its aura of mystery and the hint of corporate sabotage.

Were certain patients being given drugs that were still so experimental they were not yet even approved for testing by the FDA? If so, and IPC was behind it, then exposing the practice would jeopardize the company in several ways. What she knew of corporate practices left Jennifer with few illusions as to how far the conglomerate would go to protect its interests. Murder would be an expedient solution to prevent exposure. This possibility haunted her through her next few patient sessions. But it was only when she was closeted with Brae that the idea took concrete form.

Brae's advance was clearly ascertainable. His progress was a clear and direct line, rising as steeply as it had fallen. His success in dealing with the breakthrough and his continuously stable behavior prompted Jennifer to moderately increase his dosage of tetracyclics. The medication was markedly beneficial in maintaining his emotional equilibrium. Jennifer had already settled on a release date. Her only problem now was locating a suitable outpatient therapist so he could begin the long haul toward self-discovery.

Their sessions produced several satisfactory results, including Brae's willingness to at least meet another psychotherapist. It was because of his progress that Jennifer was prompted to commit another unpardonable heresy.

Two days after her call to Dr. Freedman's home, toward the end of Brae's session she suddenly blurted out the words: "Before you go, I'd like to ask you something."

"Don't you always?" he said with a wry smile.

"This is not patient-related."

"Oh. Then it must be serious."

Jennifer ignored his attempt at humor. "What I'd like to know is how I could go about discovering the facts of an accident?"

"What kind of accident?"

"An accidental death."

Brae gave her his most professional glance. "You want some advice from a cop?"

"Yes," she answered.

"Well, first you've got to get hold of the investigating officer's report."

"How could I go about getting that?"

"Unless you were an attorney connected with the case, you would have to go through department channels. There are forms and more forms. It could take months."

"Isn't there any way to speed up the process?"

"Sure, if you had a friend inside the department who knew how to pull a few strings."

Jennifer glanced at Brae and her brow furrowed. "Suppose

I had a patient inside the department who was willing to pull a few strings."

"In exchange for what?" Brae said playfully.

"A weekend furlough."

"Are you serious?"

"Very. I think a couple of days away from here would be good therapy."

"Okay. Agreed," Brae said enthusiastically.

"I want your help but only if it will take an hour or two of your time. No more."

"I think I could spare that," he said with a grin. "I'd be with my doctor, so what could happen to me?"

"There is one other thing."

"You'd rather I didn't mention this to anyone." Brae grinned.

"You're very perceptive."

"It's part of my job," Brae said as he rose. "You're not the only one who asks questions for a living, doctor. By the way, how long do I get on the outside?"

"From Friday night to Sunday evening," Jennifer replied.

Brae looked at her with a bemused expression. But after the door shut behind him, Jennifer felt the first pang of fear. What she had just done involved breaking a primary rule of her profession. She was not only beginning a completely unauthorized investigation into the practices of the institution that employed her but she was involving a patient as well. She had not only climbed out on a limb but was doing her best to saw it off behind her.

FOURTEEN

—◆◆◆—

When the bell rang at ten sharp on Saturday morning, Jennifer was just rising to the surface from a deeply satisfying sleep. The last two days of the week had buried her beneath an avalanche of work. Besides taking on two new patients, she was expected to prepare for a staff conference in which she had to critically evaluate the therapy and nursing staff. She had remained late at the clinic on both nights until she dragged her weary body home.

Now she stared at the clock as the buzzer continued insistently, thinking for a moment she was late for work. Then she remembered. She jumped out of bed and went to the intercom. "Who's there?" she shouted into it.

Answering static returned with the words, "Brae Haskill. We have a date, remember?"

"Can you wait a few minutes? I've got to get dressed."

"Sure. I'll be in the luncheonette on the corner."

Jennifer washed her face and showered, then tugged a comb through her hair and slipped into a pair of jeans and a cable-knit sweater. She pulled on heavy socks and hand-tooled cowboy boots, completing her outfit with a thigh-length suede jacket.

"Oh God, what you look like," she commented to the mirror as she scanned her puffy eyes. Her skin had the sallowness of a person who needed sleep.

She found Brae in the rear booth reading a newspaper with the remains of his breakfast spread out on the table in front

148

of him. He was wearing a turtleneck sweater beneath a well-cut sports jacket with deep side vents and, like her, a pair of often-washed close-fitting jeans. He had the rugged handsomeness that belonged on a cigarette ad, she realized. She had never looked at him that way before.

"What's the matter?" he said when she slid into the booth across from him.

"I can't face a poached egg before noon."

"Sorry," he said, piling the plates and handing them over to the counterman. "Can I get you anything?"

"Just coffee. Thanks."

Brae conveyed the order, while Jennifer began feeling the first real pangs of uneasiness.

"Why the worried look?" he said peering at her.

"First of all, this. Us here, together. I'm breaking about twelve million rules."

"It must be for a worthy cause."

"It is," she said seriously.

"You never said who the accident victim was. Could it be Dr. Freedman?"

Jennifer stared at him for a moment, wondering at his astuteness or her complete transparency. Then she nodded.

"Can I ask why you're interested?"

This time Jennifer shook her head. "I'd rather you didn't."

"Okay. No further questions."

"I'd appreciate it if you didn't ask any more. I just hope you don't mind giving up your time."

"I feel honored that you'd want to spend your time with a demented resident of a mental hospital."

"You're not demented!" Jennifer snapped. "That's not the kind of humor I appreciate."

"Then what am I?" he asked with pretended innocence.

"Someone who got himself into an emotional tangle he needed a little help getting out of."

"A lot of help," he said with a relaxed smile. "For which I am very grateful."

Jennifer felt her cheeks redden. She was saved from further embarrassment by the arrival of the coffee.

They drove downtown in Brae's Saab. Jennifer was surprised he even owned a car, living as he did in Manhattan. But Brae told her she would understand why once she began

taking the subway. Any inconvenience was worth not having
to ride in that grafitti-decorated purgatory.

Brae was quiet on the ride downtown, which allowed Jennifer to relax. The chances of her being seen with him were
small, she realized. Manhattan was vaster than she had ever
imagined. It was a place where even people who lived in the
same building seldom ever met.

The day was alternating between bright sunshine and
cloudiness, but the temperature made it an Indian summer
day. She had been told that autumn was the best season to be
in New York, but she had seen precious little of it outside the
walls of Montrose.

After parking in a nearby lot, Brae escorted Jennifer into
the confines of the new police headquarters with its grid of
windows that reminded Jennifer of the inside of an egg carton. He pinned on his gold badge before they went inside,
procured a visitor's pass, and began the entry into the bureaucratic maze with a sure grip on her arm.

Watching Brae operate was impressive. Jennifer liked the
ease with which he navigated his way through the various administrative channels. It reinforced the feeling she had that
the task was good therapy and a way of easing him back into
the mainstream of his life. She also found herself liking the
way he took charge of her, neatly reversing the roles they had
been performing these last few weeks. They were on his turf
now and the feeling took a little getting used to.

Jennifer had always gone out with interns or residents who
were closer to her own age. With Brae she felt a different sensation. There was no mistaking his discreet appreciation of
her as a woman. That had been there the first moment she
entered the luncheonette that morning and felt his eyes on
her. She made no move to discourage it. Still, it was not easy
to act natural while remembering that in spite of everything,
she was still his therapist.

The accident report arrived in the hands of a pudgy cigar-
smoking detective with a pistol clipped to his belt. Brae left
Jennifer in a cluttered office while he made a xerox copy,
then he escorted her out of the area after stopping to shake
several hands. Outside, she suddenly felt hungry and Brae
suggested they walk over to Chinatown.

Jennifer was eager to see a different part of the city that
was now her home. She had passed through the section once

as a tourist on an earlier visit but it was obvious that this time she was with an expert guide. Brae maneuvered her through the narrow streets, filled with colorful shops and markets featuring glazed ducks hanging from butchers hooks and a hundred other exotic delicacies.

The restaurant he took her to specialized in Hunan cuisine. An awning above the entrance was covered with Chinese characters. They climbed a flight of stairs to a huge dining room guarded by gilded dragons, where Chinese music blared and tables set for eight were filled with Oriental families eating from large platters with clicking chopsticks.

At Brae's request they were seated near the window, where they could see the teeming streets below. The crowd absorbed Jennifer's attention while Brae ordered for them. When the waiter stepped away, Jennifer turned to Brae. "It's fabulous," she said enthusiastically. "God, there are so many people."

"You should see it on Sunday. That's when Chinese from all over the area come to shop."

"I'd love to see that."

"We'll come again," he said as the waiter returned with soup and chopsticks and tiny spoons set on their own porcelain stands.

"I've never used these before," Jennifer said picking up the ivory implements.

"I'll show you. Watch."

Brae opened his hand and placed one stick between his thumb and ring finger. The other he rested on the end of the thumb and the index finger. Fascinated, Jennifer watched him manipulate the two sticks before he opened her hand and adjusted the chopsticks between her fingers. Jennifer tried picking up a boiled wonton but it slipped onto the table.

"Oh God. I can't," she cried.

"Keep trying. You'll get it. Once you master it you'll understand a principal difference between Eastern and Western culture."

"And that is?"

"We select our food in the kitchen and slice it up at the table. The Chinese do just the reverse. They cut it up in the kitchen and select it at the table. It's a subtlety not many Westerners appreciate."

"You sound like an expert."

"I used to work this area. I learned a lot here."

"Like?"

"Well, take personal relations for instance. Say you want a favor from me, so you come right out and ask. I say, what's in it for me? You let me know and expect me to decide."

"But not the Chinese."

"No. If I want a favor, I obligate you first by offering you something I know you want and would find impossible to refuse without insulting me. Since you must accept, you've obligated yourself. Now you've got to do what you know I want."

"But how do I know what you want?"

Brae's eyes fixed on hers. "There are plenty of ways I can let you know that."

Jennifer lowered her gaze, remembering that this was a doctor-patient relationship not a date.

"Do you think we can go over that accident report," she said quietly.

"Sure."

Brae reached into his pocket and put the xerox on the table between them.

The details of the report had been gleaned from the observations of the driver and two witnesses. Freedman was pronounced DOA at Bellevue of a broken neck.

"You don't look happy," Brae said when Jennifer was finished reading.

"I want to see the X rays. And talk to the witnesses. Can that be arranged?"

"I guess so. Why?"

"Freedman was an expert cyclist. I just want to make sure everything is on the up-and-up."

"Kosher is the word we use in this town."

The waiter put down their food and Jennifer found herself enjoying the unusual combinations. She was used to the modified Cantonese dishes served by most Chinese restaurants. This was special.

"Enjoying it?" Brae said at one point.

"Very much. I never realized Chinese food could be so varied."

There are as many tastes as there are provinces. Hunan, Canton, Szechwan—"

"Okay," Jennifer said laughing. "I believe you. I'd like to try them all."

Brae smiled and shrugged a why-not. Jennifer realized this was the first time she had really enjoyed herself since coming to New York. Ironically, it was with one of her patients and the shadowy presence of a dead psychiatrist.

The addresses given by the witnesses to the accident report took them to a quaint brownstone neighborhood in Brooklyn adjacent to Prospect Park. The numbers on the houses matched those on the report but there was no listing over the bells or in the telephone directory. The witnesses had stated their occupations as exchange students, but when Brae questioned several neighbors, they had no recollection of the names. Brae explained that foreign students often gave the police wrong addresses because they were fearful of being subpoenaed, something which might interfere with their ability to leave the country. This explanation did not satisfy Jennifer, but she said nothing until they traced the driver of the car to a two-family house on Staten Island.

The dark-skinned Italian woman who answered the door spoke with an accent. She shook her head when Brae asked if the name on the report was her husband's. She could not remember any accident. Her husband worked in New Jersey, she explained, which was why she found his presence in Central Park at that hour so puzzling. While Brae questioned her, Jennifer glimpsed a family portrait on top of the TV set. Pictured were a girl in a confirmation dress along with her mother and proudly smiling father, a swarthy Sicilian with a massive paunch.

Jennifer and Brae returned to Manhattan to question the cop who had filed the report, but finding Officer Washington was not easy. He was on scooter duty in Central Park, which meant he could be anywhere. Leaving the park precinct, they cruised along the roadway that snaked through the park in a patrol car, driven by a Latin cop with a handlebar mustache, who tried to locate the officer on his walkie-talkie.

"He ain't supposed to turn the thing off," the cop said apologetically.

Jennifer tried to imagine Freedman pedaling his bike in the early hours of the morning along the serpentine roadway. There were more than enough blind curves where a driver, trying to make time and beat the rush-hour traffic, would be unable to avoid hitting a cyclist, especially in the mist of early morning.

She began to feel jolts of panic. Suppose she was making a mistake, wasting valuable time she could use trying to perfect her research. Jennifer's stomach began doing flip-flops and she was about to tell Brae to forget it, when a burst of static came over the walkie-talkie, followed by a deep bass voice. "Washington, here. Keep your condom on. I'll be right there."

Five minutes later, the patrol car approached a beefy black cop in a leather jacket and helmet who had pulled his scooter onto the grass at the bend of a curve. "Sure I remember writing the report," he said when Brae had handed him a copy and they were all standing alongside the drive. "Didn't I dot all the *i*'s?"

Brae assured him that it was fine but that they wanted to know more about the accident.

"There's not that much to tell, except that it happened right about here."

"Isn't there anything else you remember, anything out of the ordinary?" Jennifer asked insistently.

Washington scratched his head. "Well, let's see. We get these accidents all the time. Bikes, skates, skateboards, you name it. People are pretty weird about the risks they take in traffic. Nothin' out of the ordinary though," he said with a shrug. "Unless you mean them witnesses and the driver all bein' Chinese."

It took almost fifty minutes to dig the bicycle out of the police property office in Little Italy. Jennifer and Brae spent the time sipping cappuccino in a gaudily decorated coffee house and staring at display cases filled with sumptuous pastries. Jennifer was aware of Brae's bemused expression every time she caught sight of it in the mirror that covered one wall. Her own face looked uptight. That's a switch, she thought. The patient is calm and the shrink is anxious.

"Are you feeling all right?" Brae had asked when they climbed back into the police car after speaking to Washington.

Jennifer had nodded but she was not all right. She could not shake the feeling of dread that was slowly enveloping her. *She was in the amphitheater again with Laura . . . only this*

time she herself was the patient, surrounded by the faces of
the staff . . . not human faces but grotesque Oriental masks
. . . like creatures out of a nightmare. . . .

She looked up from her reverie and faced an empty chair.
Brae had gone.

"He's on the phone," the counterman said when he noticed
her looking around.

"Thank you," she mumbled, feeling a strange shiver at
being suddenly alone.

A moment later, Brae sauntered back to the table. "They
just found the bike."

Freedman's Peugot was badly damaged. It had been struck
almost head-on and the frame was bent like the hump of a
camel. Paint scratches along one side indicated that the bike
had skidded sideways after the impact.

"Satisfied?" Brae asked after Jennifer completed her examination.

"I will be, once I see the X rays."

"Okay, let's get going."

Jennifer hesitated. "I've already wasted half of your day."

"For a dynamite shrink, you're not very perceptive outside
the office. I'm enjoying myself. Never stop a good thing while
it's going, okay?"

"Okay," she said, forcing a smile.

Bellevue presented another administrative tangle. While
Brae put pressure on the clerks, Jennifer dug out two aspirin
tablets from her bag to ease the constriction in her temples.
The hospital was newer than she'd imagined, considering its
history. A model in the lobby showed its development from
the first public health facility in the country to its present
colossal size. Jennifer knew its reputation as the finest
emergency service center in the city as well as its pioneering
work in mental health. But a nearly bankrupt city had
reduced the office staff, making their task more difficult. Brae,
however, knew how to chew on the clerks until he got what
he wanted. Within thirty minutes Freedman's X rays were
framed on a light board and were being scanned by a bearded
neurologist named Cornfeld.

They could see the area of trauma. The smashed vertebrae
were clearly pictured. The question Jennifer posed was how
were the injuries caused?

"Jesus, you mean he was thrown off a bike!" Cornfeld exclaimed when Brae related the details of the accident. "I thought he fell off a building or something."

"You're joking?" Jennifer said.

"Sure. But from the way the vertebrae are impacted he would have had to come down on something like the edge of a staircase to cause this kind of injury."

"Could landing on a curb have caused it?"

"If it were sharp enough or high enough."

Jennifer turned to Brae. Both had seen the curb in the park. It was low and not particularly sharp.

"What if he struck some part of the car?"

"Sure. If he was an acrobat. Look, you said the bike was struck in front. Figure it out. He'd have to fly up and over, performing almost a somersault in the air. When he landed he'd leave a pretty big dent in the car, especially with today's alloys."

Jennifer glanced at Brae. "There was no mention of a dent like that."

"I'll check with Washington," Brae said helpfully. "Be right back."

Brae went toward the phones while Jennifer continued studying the X rays. "Could he have fallen backward?"

Cornfeld looked dubious. "He'd have to sail straight back and come down on something protruding. Were there any rocks nearby, big sharp-edged rocks?"

"No. It was just a grassy area."

"The record shows no lacerations or skin injuries to his back and shoulders. There would have been some if he landed on the ground. Some scrapes, something."

Brae came back quickly. "I got the guy just as he was going off duty. He didn't recall any dents in the car. He remembered because he used the hood to write the report on."

"So you tell me what happened." Cornfeld said.

Jennifer wished she only could.

Any appetite Jennifer might have had deserted her by the time she and Brae left Bellevue and continued back uptown. Brae found a parking space and suggested a pizza and beer instead of a full-course dinner since lunch had been so filling. Jennifer agreed and they brought the meal up to her apartment. Jennifer found herself making excuses for its appearance, but Brae said, "It looks okay to me."

Brae opened the pizza carton and helped himself to a slice, but Jennifer refused.

"I guess I lost my appetite," she said.

"Funny, most cops get ravenous around a body. Even just the X rays of one."

"So do most interns," Jennifer remembered. She opened a beer and sipped it from the bottle while she waited for him to finish. Then she said, "Do you think he was murdered?"

Brae considered for a moment before answering. "I don't know. Even in this town there's usually a motive."

"I think there is one."

Jennifer hesitated, knowing how unwise it would be to say anything, especially at this stage, when she still knew so little. But she could not keep it to herself any longer.

"I think Dr. Freedman stumbled across something important enough to get killed for."

"Like what?"

"Unauthorized drug experiments on patients."

Brae did not look surprised. "I thought you doctors did that all the time."

Jennifer shook her head. "Not really. There's a certain amount, sure, but usually under the aegis of a government okay after a lot of lab work—years of it in fact. The investment is enormous, even before it's ever given to a human being. In this case I think it's being done without any okay and even before the lab work is all in. I think IPC is behind it in some way and certain doctors are going along for reasons I don't exactly know, but it could be anything from simple greed to advancing their reputations."

"How certain are you of all this?"

Jennifer took another sip from the bottle. "I think pretty certain, but I've got a lot of research to do before I prove anything."

"So you think so, but don't know so."

Jennifer nodded yes. "I haven't told anyone yet, except you."

"Maybe you shouldn't, until you're sure of your facts."

"I'm sure about one thing. Something strange is going on."

"Like what?" Brae questioned critically.

"Like four patients admitted with simple depressions who suddenly develop schizophrenia after they've been treated with these new medications."

"Isn't that pretty common in your line of work?"

"Not when the symptoms are almost identical."

"And the medication. Is that identical?"

"That's what I can't determine yet. I've got to get hold of their medical records first."

"What's holding you up?"

"Legal restrictions. Hospital rules. But also because information that should be available, isn't. I think something went wrong and they're trying to cover up."

"Paranoia, you said?" Brae commented with a hint of mischief in his eyes.

"No, the doctor isn't losing her mind. Not yet anyway. When I double-checked the computer I discovered that Dr. Freedman had begun working along the same lines before he got killed."

"Curiouser and curiouser."

"You think all of this is idiocy, don't you?" Jennifer said, in a sharper tone than she intended.

"Not really. But you'd have to prove a lot more before you'd get a police invesitation."

"With a major drug conglomerate financing much of what goes on at Montrose, isn't it possible that in exchange for its support certain doctors might be willing to experiment with medication before it's granted government certification? I mean the expenses involved in launching a new drug are tremendous. What if a drug company sees a way of cutting those costs by a little secret preliminary testing? Just to see if they're on the right track and the investment's really worth it. What does it matter if a few patients become permanently deranged and spend the rest of their lives living a waking nightmare? Think of all the money saved."

"Fine, but what kind of doctor would get involved in that kind of thing?"

"For a cop that's a pretty naive question. There are doctors and doctors. Some would do anything for money and the chance to get the backing of a multibillion-dollar company when they bring their drug to market."

"There would have to be lots of people involved, wouldn't there?"

"Maybe. But money can buy anything or anyone, can't it?"

"Sometimes yes, sometimes no," Brae said thoughtfully. "But you still need evidence. Hard evidence, to create any kind of linkage. What you're saying could also be coincidence."

"Even after what we found out today? IPC has a staff of Orientals they brought all the way from Taiwan just to protect Dr. Kessler's research. Do you think they'd take a chance on anything being uncovered that could jeopardize their operation?"

"Okay. Let's say I agree with all this. Dr. Freedman's death was pretty bizarre, but stranger things happen in this town every day."

"What about the phony witnesses and the driver giving a phony address?"

"You tell me. There's a lot of fear among foreigners here. Some are being spied on by their own governments. Others are here illegally, scared of being deported. Let's say the three of them were in the car together when they hit Freedman. They decide to invent a story. Two of them say they were witnesses, which immediately gets the driver off the hook. It was early. They could have hit and run but they didn't. They reported the accident. Giving phony addresses was a way of protecting themselves. I've seen it happen too many times. Especially in Chinatown."

"Don't tell me Dr. Freedman's head injury was accidental?"

"Unusual, sure. But I've seen weirder accidents. Any other conclusion is purely circumstantial."

"All right, what about the four women with identical symptoms?"

"What symptoms?"

Jennifer hesitated, wondering why she had involved Brae this far. Why she expected him to believe her she did not know. He was a cop after all. Had she been naive enough to think he would see the situation the same way she did, when all of his training demanded concrete evidence? But the terrifying image of horror imprinted on each woman's face made her feel the vividness of their agony. She could not dismiss their pain as mere coincidence. With her hands locked in front of her, Jennifer began to describe what she had seen. She included the drawings as well as her invasion of Dr. Kessler's center to see Leah. When she finished her account, Brae exhaled in amazement.

"You've got some set on you, doctor. I'll give you that."

"I had to go. Just to see for myself."

"I guess so. Now I see why you feel the way you do. Only
..." He paused.

"Only what?"

"Maybe you're overidentifying just a little. You really care
about your patients. That's not the norm in most hospitals
I've been involved with. Maybe it's not such a good idea,
considering how you have to protect youself emotionally.
Maybe it's because you're just starting out. But isn't it possible you're seeing a conspiracy where there is none."

"Now you're analyzing me," Jennifer said with a shake of
her head. "Hell, maybe I need it."

"Maybe you're just working too hard. You need a different
kind of distraction."

Jennifer was about to comment when she found herself
drawn into Brae's arms. The suddenness of the move took her
by surprise. His body was pressed against hers. The feeling of
his lips was electrifying. For an instant her instincts as a
woman battled her training. The doctor won.

"Please don't," she said, pushing him away. Brae released
her but remained close.

"Why not?" he asked softly.

"You know the answer to that," she said, raising her eyes
to meet his. "This was a mistake. It's completely my fault."

"No it isn't. I had something to do with it. You're a very
attractive woman, Dr. Westwood, even if you happen to be
my analyst."

"That's beside the point. I should know better. There are
rules to prevent this kind of thing from happening. I should
have followed them."

"I'm glad you didn't. I've enjoyed being with you today."

"But I feel I've used you."

"You know that isn't true."

"It's only natural for a patient to transfer certain emotional
feelings to his analyst. I took unfair advantage of that by letting my own feelings about this situation get the better of me.
I had no right to do that."

"Now look who's on a guilt trip," Brae said smiling.
"Look. I don't want my feelings for you to be reduced to a
chapter in a text book."

"It has to be, for both our sakes."

"I'm a big boy, doctor. This has nothing to do with our patient-therapist relationship and you know it as well as I do." Brae took a step toward her.

Jennifer felt her heart pounding. She shook her head as his arms closed around her again. "Don't," she whispered. But he tilted her chin up, searching her eyes. Jennifer's legs were trembling. The wanting was so strong it made her body shake. She felt his hardness against her belly and the sweet smell of his skin as he rubbed his cheek against hers. The roughness of his stubble made her shiver. One of his hands slid along the small of her back, pressing her even closer against him. She felt the pressure between her legs. Her nipples were hard. Her fingers gripped his strong arms. An intoxicating wave rose through her.

"No, stop!" With a sudden twisting motion she broke away. "I'd like you to leave now," she insisted. "Please!"

Brae did not move. Jennifer heard the sound of his breathing mingle with her own. They remained silent for a moment until he said, "Sure. You're the doctor."

Seconds later the door was shut behind him and she could hear the sound of his footsteps descending to the street. She went into the bedroom and threw herself across the bed, unable to stop shaking. Her eyes closed as the feelings he had aroused plummeted through her. She wondered just how she would explain to Dr. Boise that for the remainder of his stay, Brae would need a different therapist. And that she would have to be placed in isolation for her own protection. . . .

FIFTEEN

The week began with its usual churning pace. Jennifer was absorbed in a series of problems, involving the transfer of one of her patients to another floor following a weekend suicide attempt. The patient was anorexic and had wasted down to below fifty pounds, which required feeding by IV to keep her alive. Jennifer was attempting, by means of suggestion, to increase her intake of food, but beyond establishing a supportive relationship there was little she could do until the patient was out of danger.

Even with this problem Jennifer was still obsessed with the two factors in the forefront of her mind: the midweek conference for Carla DiMatteo and Dr. Freedman's computer readouts, which she believed were still in Dr. Boise's office.

On Monday afternoon, Jennifer made her first reconnaissance of Boise's territory. His office, which she had visited only once before, was located on the fourth floor. One of his three secretaries remained in the outer office at all times to cover the phones. His patients' files were kept in the inner office along with other administrative information. The floor was kept under tight security after hours because the main pharmacy was located at the other end. That meant she would have to chance getting inside during working hours. The problem was to make sure Dr. Boise did not return before she completed her search. She would have to arrange for a distraction to get him outside and keep him there. The answer to the problem came during her next to last session with

162

Jeffrey, who was scheduled to be discharged the following day.

Jennifer felt a personal sense of accomplishment over Jeffrey's recovery, though she was mindful of the dangers he was subject to once he left the protective environment of the hospital. Outpatient care had been arranged on a twice-weekly basis. The idea of seeing a new therapist was a fear Jeffrey expressed just before he left. Then he rose and took both her hands in his.

"I hate losing you, Dr. Westwood," he said, staring at her with his expressive eyes. "If I were straight, you'd be in grave danger."

Jennifer smiled at his remark. "I feel the same way, Jeffrey, but I expect two tickets to your next play."

"Two tickets? So there is someone. Why doctor, you're blushing."

When Jeffrey was gone, Jennifer returned to her desk and experienced a feeling of emptiness. She had looked forward to her sessions with Jeffrey, as difficult and dangerous as his stay had been for both of them. But the risk had been worthwhile. She realized that a therapist can get as attached to her patient as the patient to his therapist. It was a professional hazard she had not fully appreciated until that moment.

A glance at the clock informed her that Brae would be entering momentarily. Her brows knit at the thought. She knew she should have arranged for a new therapist, but she could not bring herself to do it. Brae's stay was coming to an end in several days. It was a period she would have to coast through. Besides, she needed his help, and that was perhaps the most important reason she offered to herself as a justification for continuing their relationship.

When he heard what she wanted, Brae was not as cooperative as she expected. Their first moments together had been the most trying, as Jennifer tried to reestablish them on a patient-therapist footing. Brae was cool and dispassionate, making brief and commonplace comments. Only the look in his eyes betrayed his feelings.

"Don't you want to hear about my weekend, doctor?" he said when they were halfway through the session.

Jennifer's stomach tensed. "There's something I want to ask you," she said ignoring the question. She found it difficult to look at him.

"That means you don't want to hear about my weekend."

"I think this is more important."

"You're having a problem forgetting me?" he asked, smiling.

Jennifer drew her eyes away. "I think I found a way to get my hands on those records."

"How?"

"Dr. Freedman never returned them to the computer library. Dr. Boise supervised the cleaning of his office. I think the records are still in his files."

"And you want me to break in and get them for you?"

"No. You wouldn't know what to look for. I can get inside his office, but I'll need someone to distract him down here long enough for me to make a thorough search."

"And the someone is yours truly."

Jennifer looked up. "Will you do it?"

"On one condition. That you let me see you once I'm out of here."

Jennifer clenched her lips. "You know how I have to answer that."

"Why does it have to be that way? I won't be your patient anymore."

"But you were. It isn't right for a lot of reasons."

"I'm not buying them. I'm going to make you an offer you can't refuse. I'll wait sixty days after I'm discharged before I call you. Would that be long enough to satisfy you that it's not just a temporary emotional thing, because you were my shrink?"

"I don't know."

"Why don't you admit that we're attracted to each other? It's got nothing to do with which end of the desk we're sitting on, so stop pretending it does. Or is it because I'm a cop?"

"Of course not!" Jennifer exclaimed. "That wouldn't make any difference."

"Then is it a deal?"

"All right," she conceded reluctantly. "But only on the condition that we have no contact once you're out of here, for sixty days."

"Promise."

"One more thing. I want you to tell him the department has found new evidence and is going to reopen the Freedman case. "I want to see how he reacts."

Brae sighed. "You don't give up easily, do ya, doctor?"

"As easily as you do."

Brae left the office after hearing her plan and agreeing to it. Jennifer glanced at the calendar. Sixty days was a long time. She wondered if she could wait that long. After Saturday night she might be the one who called first.

There was only one way Jennifer knew of getting Dr. Boise agitated enough to send for her. That was by radically altering her medication orders. Normally she brought them to the nurses' station at the end of the day, which would be too late for her purpose. So instead, she casually mentioned her intentions to Anne. Predictably, Anne relayed the information to Dr. Boise before noon. By the time Jennifer returned from lunch there was a note on her desk. Dr. Boise wanted to see her in his office as soon as she had seen her last patient.

"Okay, here we go," she said aloud, after Mr. Bradley closed the door behind him. She had already informed Brae of his role. She knew that Dr. Boise would have to rush downstairs to intercept her medication orders before they were filled. If Brae could keep him downstairs long enough she would have time to get inside Boise's office and search. Please, let it work, she prayed as the elevator took her up to the fourth floor.

All three secretaries were at their desks when she entered.

"Do you have an appointment, doctor?" she was asked by a florid-looking blond who wore glasses suspended from a chain that rested on her stupefyingly large bosom.

"Yes, at four," Jennifer answered, taking a seat outside Boise's office and placing the file she had brought on her knees. The clatter of typewriter noise was almost deafening. Jennifer leaned over and asked if she could wait inside where it was quieter, pointing to the work she had brought.

"Certainly, doctor," the secretary said, barely looking up from her machine.

Jennifer stood up and turned the knob. A moment later she was inside Dr. Boise's office, closing the door behind her.

Dr. Boise was livid. The medication orders in his hands were not just modifications but complete and radical alterations of every patient's medication on Jennifer's service.

"The woman is insane," he muttered under his breath.

Boise rose from Rita Kahn's desk and crossed to the pharmacy where he opened the drawer containing the week's medication orders and found Dr. Westwood's section. He removed the previous day's pink slips, laying them side by side with the new orders, and changed every one of Jennifer's dosages back to the previous day's level. When he was finished, he replaced the old orders and handed the altered forms to the medication nurse, then glanced around the station for someone to savage. But no eye met his. The staff was used to his rampages. Everything looked as if it was in order, so he turned to the room in general and said, "Could we do something about the condition of the lounge? It looks like a pigsty."

"Certainly, Dr. Boise," Rita said, with a fixed smile.

Her tone irritated him as usual but he had a better object upon which to vent his anger waiting upstairs in his office. Turning, he went out and started toward the elevator when he heard someone call his name.

Boise wheeled around and saw Brae Haskill approaching. Normally, Dr. Boise avoided direct contact with the patients unless they were presented at rounds. Even then he limited himself to a question or two. He was a strict believer in the theory that the patient spoke only to his therapist and the therapist spoke only to him. Possibly as a result, it was rumored that he himself spoke only to God.

Boise made a slight face, trying to sidestep but it was evident that he would have to speak to the man.

"Can I speak to you a moment," Brae said in a confidential tone.

"I'm afraid I can't stop right now, why don't you speak to Dr. Westwood about it."

"Because this concerns Dr. Westwood and this hospital." Brae said softly. "I think it's better if we spoke in private."

Boise felt a tremor of annoyance. Punctuality was a habit he tried to ingrain in his staff. If he stopped to speak to this patient he would be late for his appointment with Dr. Westwood. But the thought that a patient might be able to provide him with more ammunition against her made him open the empty dining room door and usher Brae inside.

After he closed the door behind him, Boise said, "All right, what were you going to tell me?"

Brae took his elbow and leaned closer. "We had creamed spinach again today."

Dr. Boise stared at him. "I don't understand."

"Creamed spinach today. Creamed corn yesterday. Creamed broccoli the day before. That's not a diet, that's a punishment."

"Well, I know the food could be more varied. Have you brought it up at the floor meeting?"

"Sure. And you know what happened?"

"I'm afraid not."

"Nothing happened, that's what happened. We're still getting creamed."

Boise glared at him suspiciously. "You got me in here to tell me something about Dr. Westwood and this hospital."

"I'm coming to that. When Dr. Westwood took over from Dr. Freedman I was hostile. Damned hostile. I liked Dr. Freedman."

"I'm sure you did."

"And he was killed so suddenly."

"Yes. I know." Boise said impatiently.

"It was difficult getting adjusted to Dr. Westwood, at first."

"Yes. I imagine it was." Boise waited for Brae to continue, staring at him with a puzzled expression. "Was that all you wanted to tell me?"

"No. I wanted to tell you the department is going to reopen the Freedman case."

Dr. Boise stared blankly at Brae. "Why?"

"There's new evidence. I wanted to give you advance warning."

"Advance warning?"

"So you can protect the hospital."

"Well, thank you. I'm sure I appreciate you telling me this. I'll convey what you said to the administrator. Now about Dr. Westwood. You said you were going to tell me something concerning her."

"Oh yes. I wanted to tell you that she's an even better therapist than Dr. Freedman was. All of her patients think so. She really seems to care."

Boise's face fell. "I see. Well then, that's very good news. Now if you will excuse me, I have an appointment." Boise unlocked the door and started out. But Brae still held his arm.

"I want you to know that I'll keep you posted on the progress of the investigation."

"Thank you. We'll appreciate it. I have to go."

Brae started to draw him back when a nurse passed. Boise called to her. "Phyllis, Mr. Haskill has some suggestions for the dietician. Would you make a note of them."

Before Brae could step out of the dining room, Boise had adroitly maneuvered himself out of his grasp and turned the nurse toward him. With an impatient step, Boise headed toward the elevator. Pressing the button yielded no results. He glanced at his watch and decided to take the stairs two steps at a time.

After entering Dr. Boise's office, Jennifer placed her folder on a chair that she had moved against the door as an obstacle against anyone suddenly barging in. She hoped it would provide enough of a distraction for her to close the file drawers. Instead of being nervous, Jennifer found herself extremely cool as she opened one drawer after another. The fear she had experienced on the way upstairs had disappeared. She felt rock calm as her fingers skimmed the dense mass of folders that was squeezed into every available space. I'd make a good thief, she thought. The only problem was where to find the loot.

Jennifer searched under each of the four women's last names but that yielded nothing. She tried to think like someone trying to hide a large clump of computer readouts but the drawers themselves were so full of computer material it became an impossible task. She could not possibly pull out all of them because they were so tightly jammed in. It would take more time to get them back than she could afford. The problems multiplied as soon as she glanced at the first pack she handled. Having no real idea of what the records looked like, she could not readily identify the material. Typically there was no label on the package. Each package would have to be carefully read to determine what it contained. And that could be done only by drawing the packet out, unfolding it, turning it sideways, and knowing what the code designations meant.

It was hopeless. Defeated, she pushed the last drawer she had opened back in place and stepped away from the files when it struck her. Why should Dr. Boise hide the files in the first place? Especially in his own office. Leaning down, Jennifer pulled open the drawer marked "F." There, behind a divider marked "Freedman" was a doubled-up wad of green-inked computer paper. Jennifer inhaled sharply and prayed. *Please God, let it be . . .*

It was.

They were all there. Patient records. Medication reports. Breakdowns of the admissions. CAT scans. EEGs. The works. Everything Freedman had ordered from the computer.

She barely had a moment's worth of exhilaration when panic returned. She had to get out of there with the material before Boise came barging in. With a shaking hand she carefully closed the drawer and rose. She placed the material in her file and closed the flap, pulling the chair out of the way and taking a seat on it just as the door opened and Dr. Boise strode in.

"Well, Dr. Westwood," he began, moving behind his desk. "I've just come from the nurses' station and—"

"I'm sorry Dr. Boise. I was here at four. It's now four-twenty. I've got a family conference scheduled in five minutes. I don't want to upset Anne's schedule. We'll just have to postpone this for another time."

Jennifer was out of the office before Boise could close his mouth.

SIXTEEN

Jennifer knew she should wait to examine the printouts in the safety of her apartment, but she could not repress the urge to scan them as soon as she locked the door to her office. Anne's conference with the parents of her anorexic patient seemed to drag on interminably, and although Jennifer knew how important it was to discover in depth the family's patterns of interaction in order to plan appropriate therapies, she couldn't help but feel impatient. The case was complicated by the extreme hostility between mother and daughter as well as the daughter's current state of regression.

When the conference finally ended, Jennifer rushed back to her office, locked the door, and spread the long green sheets of paper on top of her desk. The next two hours passed in a frenzy of concentration. What Jennifer read astonished her. Over the last twenty-four months more than two dozen patients who had been admitted to Montrose with a diagnosis of various forms of depression, developed schizoid tendencies after a short period of hospitalization. And none had prior histories of mental illness. Every one of them was eventually admitted to Dr. Kessler's research center.

For each patient the pattern seemed exactly the same. First the EEG showed an erratic reading, one that in no way cohered with the patient's condition upon admission and for all intents and purposes came out of the blue. Then the CAT scan revealed no significant brain trauma. Within two weeks of the scan each of the patients developed symptoms indicative of a schizophrenic condition.

Jennifer sat back. Her pulse rate was accelerated. She could feel the sensation in her temples. The knowledge that she was on to something enormous swept over her in tantalizing waves, provoking an almost unbearable excitement.

This was the kind of research she had only read about, the kind that produced notoriety for its investigators. Jennifer had a momentary daydream of becoming famous before it was washed away by a dark wave of trepidation. The implications were so frightening they made her heart beat even faster. An international drug conglomerate had destroyed the minds of its human guinea pigs and duped a world-renowned scientist like Dr. Kessler into treating what was left of the minds it destroyed. The stretch of roadway in Central Park swam into Jennifer's mind and the images of the three faceless Orientals. Jennifer realized just how frightened she was. *Oh Christ, Westwood, what hath thou wrought?*

Jennifer shuffled the papers once more trying to find a pattern in the kind of medication each patient had been given, but she could find none. The drugs listed were too varied and the forms themselves too complex to assimilate in a single reading. Besides, she realized, there was a very real possibility, if all the other facts cohered as she thought, that the medications actually given were hidden under other names. If this was the case, then she would need help to decipher which medications were actually administered. That could only be determined by backtracking through each medication log. She would need someone in the nurses' station. Rita's name immediately sprang to mind. But their relationship had not developed to the point where Jennifer could truly trust her. Besides, what if Rita's own negligence was a factor? Still, there was no one else she could approach. She would need Rita's help. She had to trust somebody.

Jennifer drew her bag over to the desk and started folding the readouts into three-page booklets to make them easier to conceal. She began working on the third set when she noticed that one of the names on the list had been marked with a felt-tipped pen. She turned the sheet around. The name underlined was Mary Ann Spreull. Jennifer remembered that she was the fashion model Dr. Freedman had treated. Beside her name was a pencil notation in Dr. Freedman's script. It read: VISITATION REFUSED. And next to it, circled in red ball-point, the words: URGENT BY 10/28.

Backtracking through the records, Jennifer discovered Mary Ann was one of the last new patients referred to Dr. Freedman before his death. But why did he circle her name? And what did "urgent" refer to? On impulse, Jennifer drew out the notations she had copied in Anne's office from Mary Ann's file. Freedman had ordered the computer material after Mary Ann had been admitted to the research center. It was evident that he had tried to visit her there and been refused. Jennifer looked at her desk calendar. October 28 was exactly ten days after Mary Ann's admission. With a shock Jennifer realized that was the very day Dr. Freedman had been killed.

What possible significance did that have, or was it merely a coincidence? What had Freedman learned that made the tenth day so important? Her mind jumped to the next possibility. Did the tenth day have any significance in any of the other cases? Backtracking feverishly, Jennifer calculated each of the women's admission dates. The only one for whom it became a factor was Laura. Today was the ninth day since Laura's admission to the research center.

Tomorrow was the tenth day.

With a certainty that was neither logic nor reason, Jennifer knew she must see Laura before the end of the following day. She had to get into the center again.

Jennifer's mind raced to find a strategy. What could she say to get the center to allow a visit on such short notice? She sat at her desk continuing to fold the printouts but nothing would come. When she finished folding them, she fitted them into her bag and then went to the window.

It was already dark outside. If she left now, she would lose an hour getting to her apartment. The center would close for the day, reducing her chances to zero. She had to find some excuse immediately.

"Jennifer Westwood, you idiot!" she cried aloud. It was so obvious she had to laugh. The one totally believable story used as an excuse by every student since time began. She dialed the center and waited.

The phone was picked up after three rings.

"Hello, My name is Mrs. Elizabeth Archer. My niece Laura is a patient at your hospital. Laura Archer."

"Yes. We have a patient by that name. What is this in reference to?"

"I would like to visit her."

"Certainly. When would you like to come?"

"I'm afraid it would have to be tomorrow."

There was a pause, then the operator said, "I'm sorry. We cannot grant a visitation on such short notice. We must have at least a week."

"I know and I'm sorry. But you see I'm entering the hospital for an operation the day after tomorrow. My doctor informed me of it today. It's something of an emergency."

"Well, perhaps when you get out."

Jennifer lowered her tone. "That's the problem. I may not recover. This would be my only chance to see Laura before I go in. I have no children of my own. She's the only niece I have."

"I see. Hold on please."

Jennifer sat back and waited. So faultless was the operator's accent that no one would have known she was Oriental. It was just another aspect of the seamless perfection with which IPC operated, a scrupulousness in handling of details that made it even more menacing in her mind. She felt jabs of fear. What was she doing?

"Mrs. Archer?"

The voice surprised Jennifer. She realized it was Dr. Kessler himself. A screw tightened inside.

"Yes," she replied, covering her voice with hoarseness.

"This is Dr. Kessler. Could you please explain the nature of your illness?"

"Certainly." Jennifer's mind groped for the medical course she was most familar with. "It's been diagnosed as atherosclerosis. My doctor explained it as hardening of the carotid artery to the brain."

"How old are you Mrs. Archer?"

"Fifty-six."

"I see. And what are your symptoms?"

"Well, I've been feeling drowsy. I get headaches. I can't concentrate very well."

"And you're going to receive an endarterectomy?"

"That's right, doctor."

"Well, this is actually highly irregular. You see a patient in Laura's condition is highly unpredictable. She is delusional and could even become violent. We try to spare the family the agony of such an experience by scheduling visits at long intervals and thoroughly preparing the patient."

"I understand, doctor. But I hope you appreciate my own situation."

"Of course." Jennifer waited for Dr. Kessler to continue. She could almost hear his breathing on the other end of the line.

"All right, Mrs. Archer. I think we could make an exception and allow you to see Laura tomorrow for a few minutes. But out of consideration for the extremely delicate condition of Laura's mind, you understand that the visit must be extremely short and unemotional."

"I understand that, doctor. You don't have to worry. I won't make a scene."

"Very well then. Would seven o'clock be all right?"

"That would be fine. And thank you, doctor. Thank you very much."

"Certainly. And good luck."

Jennifer waited for him to hang up before putting down the receiver. But instead of feeling joy at her success, she felt only numbing threads of anxiety as if she were skating on ice so thin that at any moment she could plunge through into oblivion.

SEVENTEEN

The printout material in Jennifer's bag felt as potent as a radioactive isotope. Any moment she expected alarms to go off and Dr. Boise to come running out after her shouting, "*Thief!*" But nothing like that happened. Jennifer negotiated the return passage home without incident.

She expected her nervousness to fade once she left the building and boarded the bus. Instead the opposite happened and she began to feel an even greater sense of anxiety as the bus chugged and rumbled to the tram. It was a feeling she could not exactly explain even to herself. Her first entry into the Forbidden City, as she privately termed Dr. Kessler's center, had been a kind of adventure, a last vestige of her school-girl rebelliousness coupled with a driving curiosity and the desire to convince herself that she could actually help Laura. This time she felt something else, something very akin to cold fear.

Perhaps it was because the stakes had increased so drastically. So much now rode on her investigation. If she succeeded, she would have the power to topple a Goliath. She was too frightened to consider what might happen if she failed.

The tram stop was crowded with commuters and Jennifer had to fight her way off. Instead of turning uptown toward home, she headed toward Third Avenue, where she shopped for the things she needed to transform herself into Laura's middle-aged aunt. The disguise would have to be more elabo-

rate than the first time. She could not risk the chance of
being recognized.

She found a drugstore near Lexington that sold theatrical
makeup and bought more than she needed. Time was too
short to return if she found she needed more. Her last disguise had been flamboyant; this time she would go the opposite route becoming bland and nondescript. But finding a
dowdy dress proved more difficult than she imagined, especially in her size. She solved the problem by remembering
a store over on Second Avenue that specialized in used and
antique clothing. The clerk was very helpful and Jennifer was
able to locate the style and even the color she wanted.

Carrying her shopping bags, Jennifer headed cross town.
She ate dinner in a health-food restaurant on First Avenue
before heading home. After spreading the printouts across the
dining-room table, she began comparing the medication codes
for each patient, searching for similarities. That was where
the difficulty began. Even after going through them twice, she
could not establish a coherent picture. The same medication
had been given to several of the patients but not to others.
Her mind struggled through the codes again and again. There
had to be a pattern—unless the medication reports had been
falsified. By midnight she had reached a dead end.

Jennifer realized she could not go further without backtracking through each medication log and perhaps even
through each physician's individual medication charges. Not
only was such a project vaster than she imagined, but she had
no real idea of just how to accomplish it. So much seemed to
depend on tomorrow and what she might discover, even
though she had no clear idea what she was even looking for.
But the notation URGENT that Dr. Freedman had scribbled in
the margin clicked on and off in her mind like a neon sign.

Jennifer undressed and showered. Naked, she stared at her
body in the full-length mirror she had nailed up on the
bathroom door. Her body was firm and sleek. She wondered
if she would allow Brae to make love to her after their sixty-
day waiting period was over. The thought made her nipples
erect but when she drew her fingers across them the delicious
sensation she expected failed to materialize. Her mind was
too distracted by thoughts of tomorrow. She could only think
of those other bodies equally young, equally ripe, that might

never know the pleasures of a man's hands or the feel of another body making love to their own again.

Jennifer slipped under the covers but she could not sleep. Her mind churned with the information in the printouts and the anticipation of what she might discover tomorrow. On impulse she sat up and turned on the light. She reached for the phone and started to dial her parents but a glance at the digital clock revealed that it was almost one. Her mother and father would be sleeping. She replaced the receiver, wishing she had someone she could call. But only Brae entered her thoughts. She wished he were already out of the hospital. Strange, she thought, the only person who knew what she was up to was a patient in the very hospital whose sanctity she was about to violate. She turned off the light and lay back on the pillows thinking about tomorrow . . . so much depended on tomorrow. . . .

Morning brought a different kind of torture. Instead of the hours flying by, the minute hand of her clock seemed to be weighted with lead. Jennifer's eyes opened an hour before she had to get up but sleep was no longer possible. She dressed and made herself breakfast, taking a last stab at the printouts in the hope that she had overlooked something and a pattern would emerge. But none did. The thought occurred to her that there might be something other than the medications that could be causing the disturbances. Beyond that her mind would not go.

She carefully packed her purchases in a large black tote bag and once more thought of calling her parents. But besides being too early, what could she possibly tell them? They would not really understand and her suspicions would only alarm them unnecessarily. No, she had to conduct this inquiry in as scientific manner as possible, without involving outsiders. Besides, her suspicions about Dr. Freedman's death were something the police would have to handle. She was a doctor, not a cop.

When she reached her office, Jennifer locked the door and stowed the tote bag in her closet. Then she checked her calendar. This was Jeffrey's last session. Her mind had been so preoccupied the hour had crept up on her unawares. Jennifer stared at her trembling fingers holding the page of the calendar and realized she was experiencing a case of nerves.

She even spilled a cup of coffee on her clinic coat and had to scrub the stain out at the sink. Fortunately, it washed clean. She realized Jeffrey was not her only concern today. She had to arrange for the admission of a new patient as well as finalizing Brae's departure two days from now.

Jeffrey's final session turned out to be the one bright spot in her day. He was excited and nervous but also more confident than she had ever seen him. Instead of the rush of words she expected, he placed a series of pages on her desk. They turned out to be the first scene of a new play. Reading it, Jennifer became aware of just how important her reaction would be to him. It threw all of her analyst's instincts into sharp conflict. Traditional technique made it imperative that she represent reality no matter how unpleasant. Yet she felt the need to offer a compliment, even encouragement. Fortunately, she did not have to decide. The scene was very good. The life he captured seemed to leap off the page.

"Well," he said when she put it down, "what's the verdict? Will the patient live or die?"

"The patient is wonderful," Jennifer said, watching Jeffrey's face light up. "It's marvelous, really. Quite marvelous."

"Coming from you, that's better than a good review in the *Times*."

"Not quite. But I think if the rest is as good, you won't have to worry about the *Times*."

"It didn't offend you? The language, I mean. Karl, the main character is a drag queen. I tried to make it as realistic as I could."

"You succeeded there." Jennifer said, smiling. "It had the feel of life."

"I'm glad," he said modestly. "This is our last session together."

Jennifer nodded. "How do you feel about leaving?"

"Funny, I guess. At the beginning I hated it here and couldn't wait to get out. I even tripped the light fantastic one Saturday night, if you remember."

"Oh, yes. I remember," Jennnifer said with a laugh. But she could all too vividly recall the fear she had felt that first night Jeffrey had decided to go AWOL. It was very similar to the fear she was feeling now.

"I won't say I'm not glad to be getting out," Jeffrey continued. "But in a way I'm sorry to be leaving. I guess you made me feel both exposed and protected. But the truth shall set ye free, isn't that so?"

"I think so."

"And you cared, Dr. Westwood. That was the most important thing I felt. I really believed you cared. Even with all the pain."

Jennifer was silent. How could she tell him that the pain she had caused when she took him off medication was a necessary evil. Only by trying to free himself of it would he truly get well. Perhaps that was where she had been most successful. Using the pain to produce insights into himself.

She became aware that he had placed another sheet of paper on the desk. "I wrote this for you," he said. "But read it when I'm gone, okay?"

"Okay," she agreed. "And the best of luck in everything, Jeffrey."

She rose and escorted him to the door.

"Can I kiss you?" he asked, in an almost boyish manner.

"Of course."

He pressed his lips to her cheek, then left the room with a quick motion, as if trying to cover his feelings.

Jennifer closed the door and returned to her desk. A strange feeling came over her. My first postpartum depression, she thought sadly. Or was she experiencing a feeling of hope? she wondered. Does every analyst feel this way when a patient performs a successful reentry? Giving birth to anything worthwhile produces pain. It mingled with her pleasure now.

A knock at the door startled her. "Come in," she called.

The door opened and Anne entered, leading a young woman into her office. "Dr. Westwood, this is Inga Robertson."

Jennifer realized this was her newest patient. Jennifer felt her carefully composed expression begin to disintegrate. The young woman was a carbon copy of Laura. Inga was younger, even prettier. But she had the same glazed look, the same air of disorientation. Seeing her brought back the feeling of fear, which flooded her mind with the implications of what she was about to do.

"Is everything all right, doctor?" Anne questioned.

"Oh yes. Perfectly all right. I was just distracted by something I have to do."

For an instant Jennifer was paralyzed by the feeling that

Anne *knew*. The sensation lasted only an instant but left her shaking. Recovering quickly, Jennifer said, "It's all right, Anne. You can leave Inga with me now."

"Certainly, doctor," Anne said, backing out of the office. "I'm working up a family history. I'll send you the results when I've finished."

Anne closed the door, leaving Jennifer alone with her new patient. The session became an anguish as the facts of the young woman's anxieties revealed themselves. They were the same fears of career failure that Laura had expressed and Jennifer herself felt so deeply. There was even a similar family pattern of critical father and protective mother. Jennifer felt her insides tighten as the session wound down. In only a few more hours she would be face-to-face with Laura and the horror of her ordeal.

Brae's session left her with a blank hour. He had been allowed to travel cross town for a session with his new outpatient therapist. Jennifer wanted to use the time to begin her investigation into the medication log. She left her office and headed toward the nurses' station. She was intercepted by Anne when she turned the corner of the corridor.

"Oh, Dr. Westwood, I was just coming to see you. Dr. Boise would like a word with you in my office."

"Why didn't he call?" Jennifer said with ill-concealed annoyance. Boise was the last person she wanted to see right now, especially when he was within sniffing distance of the nurses' station. It meant she would have to postpone her examination of the medication log.

"I don't know," Anne replied. "I suppose since I was going that way, he asked me to call you. I was just going to look in on Inga to make sure she's settling in okay."

"All right. I'll be right there," Jennifer said curtly. She continued down the hall, leaving Anne standing in the entrance to Inga's room. It was the same one Laura had occupied. That produced a strange shiver of premonition in Jennifer.

Dr. Boise was seated at Anne's desk, studying several patient records when Jennifer tapped at the door. Boise glanced up sharply.

"You wanted to see me?" Jennifer said.

"Yes. Please come in and shut the door."

Jennifer entered and did as he requested. She took a seat beside the desk, facing him.

"We never did get to have our talk," Boise said, swiveling toward her.

"What talk is that?" Jennifer said with mock innocence.

"Don't tell me you forgot I asked to see you yesterday?"

"Oh yes. I've just been so busy."

"Not busy enough to prevent you from doing some spontaneous research."

Jennifer felt a jolt of surprise. "What research?"

"Come come, Dr. Westwood. Don't tell me you forgot your little trip to the computer."

Jennifer glanced down at the desk. Xerox copies of her computer requests were on the desk in front of Boise. "I was curious about several patient histories."

"So I see. Exactly why, may I ask, considering they no longer are a part of your caseload?"

"I wanted to familiarize myself with Dr. Freedman's methods, as a sort of guide."

"Very commendable," Boise said with an unpleasant expression. "But why these patients? All of whom have been admitted to Dr. Kessler's center."

Jennifer felt perspiration begin running beneath her arms. It was beginning to feel like a third degree. "I was going to request others but these interested me."

"Really," he said archly. "You gave up rather easily on the others, didn't you? Why didn't you come to the administrator or even to me, as I am your supervisor and those are the rules? A copy of which you were given on your first day here. But be that as it may, let me come to the next point. Why did you suddenly change every patient's medication order without consulting me? Especially when you were specifically told not to."

Jennifer's stomach knotted. She knew she would have to face Dr. Boise sooner or later because of her little ploy to get him out of his office. But why now? She was in no mood to explain anything. Her mind was fixed on the moment several hours from now when she would enter the center.

"Don't you have anything to say?" Dr. Boise asked.

Jennifer shook her head. "No."

"That surprises me." Dr. Boise exhaled with a sigh. "Well, you had better think of something rather quickly, since I intend to bring you up on charges before the administrator."

The words made Jennifer jump. "What kind of charges?"

"Willful disobedience. Insubordination. Negligence and general incompetence."

"Incompetence!"

"Quite. One of the patients you took off medication and were about to discharge was so delusional he actually told me the Fredman case was about to be reopened. Naturally, I checked. The police, of course, confirmed it as nonsense."

"You are one hell of a son of a bitch, Dr. Boise. Has anyone ever told you that?"

"You just reminded me to add unprofessional conduct to the list," Boise said complacently.

Jennifer rose. "Do whatever makes you happy, doctor. We like to see all the inmates well-adjusted."

Jennifer left the office trembling. Instead of returning to her office, she made a detour to the elevator and went downstairs to the cafeteria. The cup of hot chocolate she sipped did nothing to help her condition. A shot of booze would have gone down a lot better, she thought.

"Hey, long time, stranger."

Jennifer looked up into Mark's smiling countenance. "Hi," she said, trying to return his smile but her face felt like wax.

"Thanks for inviting me, but I can't stay. And yes I will have a drink with you one night this week. Call you anytime, sure. Well, it's been terrific. Got to run."

Jennifer almost laughed at his antics as he pantomimed a clumsy dance between the tables on his way out of the cafeteria. She envied Mark for his determination to become a rich and successful practitioner no matter how many hoops he had to jump through. He would never have crossed Dr. Boise. Nor would he have questioned his patient's sudden schizoid reactions or the facts surrounding Dr. Freedman's death. No. Mark was a lot shrewder than she. Jennifer Westwood had decided to question authority and she was about to pay the piper, unless some miracle intervened.

In a way she felt glad that Dr. Boise had sealed off any possibility of retreat. The only way she could save herself now was by pointing the finger directly at Boise and through him at the illegal machinations of IPC.

"Do you mind if I join you?" Anne's voice rang out at her shoulder. Before Jennifer could answer, Anne had plumped herself down opposite her with a tray of coffee and an apple. The smile on her face was as artificial as her sugar substitute.

"Suit yourself," Jennifer said casually.

"I want to discuss Inga Robertson. I've been running down her family history, but I'm finding quite a bit of resistance."

Anne began a rapid-fire barrage of facts in her mechanical tone. Jennifer tried to look intelligent but her mind would not concentrate. The clock was edging closer to the moment when she would have to prepare. Once more, she rehearsed the steps she had outlined. She planned to use a downstairs rest room reserved for the handicapped to change in. She would smuggle her clothes out of the closet. Suddenly Jennifer froze.

Had Dr. Boise sent Anne to search her closet while he went over the charges with her? Had he discovered the computer printouts were missing? He would know that Jennifer had taken them. He would begin a search of her office. She had to get up there immediately.

"Please, excuse me," Jennifer said getting up.

"Dr. Westwood, are you all right?" Anne said, staring at her in astonishment.

"Yes, fine. Sorry."

Jennifer rushed away from the table, leaving her tray and threading her way between the tables. Only when the doors of the cafeteria swung shut behind her did she start to run.

Waves of anxiety pounded through her when she reached the elevator. Her throat felt constricted. Eyes darted toward her. Mouths were whispering. Terrified, Jennifer realized they all *knew*.

She rushed inside the elevator, turning to face the accusing glances. But no one was looking. The doors closed.

"Get a grip on yourself, Westwood!" she shouted. "You're getting paranoid."

She visualized the look on Anne's face when she had jumped up and almost laughed aloud at the memory. "Oh God, what am I doing? I'm scared shitless."

The doors opened and she headed back to her office. "Go slow," she whispered. Slow and steady.

Nothing had been disturbed. The closet was exactly the way she left it. Her tote bag rested on the bottom.

Jennifer sat down in her patient's chair and exhaled with relief. But her heart would not stop pounding. She needed something to calm her down but she shook her head at the notion. She did not want anything to distort her perceptions. She needed to be as alert as possible. The clock had ticked its way toward Four. Only two and a half hours to go . . .

EIGHTEEN

Utilizing the wide sink in the toilet for the handicapped, Jennifer was able to tint her hair with streaks of gray. Arranging the array of cosmetics in front of her, she applied pancake and blended it with various shades until her skin took on a pale and unhealthy-looking pallor; then she deepened her natural facial lines to give herself the appearance of age. Alum dried and cracked her lips. Then she arranged her hair, stepped back and looked in the mirror.

"Not bad," she said aloud. The careful blending of makeup had produced exactly the appearance she had hoped for. She looked somewhere in her late forties, gray-haired and obviously suffering from some form of illness. The drab shapeless dress added to the effect, along with dark stockings and plain black shoes. She also wore a raincoat to further hide her figure and adjusted her bra to lower her breasts. She decided against wearing dark glasses until she got inside the center. Then she opened a bottle of rubber cement and carefully covered her thumbprint, hoping enough would stick in the tiny grooves to make positive identification difficult.

After disposing of the rinse in the toilet, she dropped the bottle into the waste barrel, placed the other cosmetics in with it and unlocked the door.

She had waited until seven, when most visitors would be congregating in the lobby, before leaving the bathroom. The waiting area was filled with subdued conversation as the visi-

185

tors waited to go upstairs. Jennifer made her way through the
crowd with a tired and feeble step.

At the entrance she had just started through the revolving
door when she was almost run over by a group of young doctors on their supper break who brushed past her. One of
them bumped her shoulder and half turning, murmured, "Excuse me." Jennifer's heart jumped. The doctor was Mark Tobey.

Outside, it was already dark. The night had turned blus-
tery. November was only a few days away and the temperature was falling. I'm all ready for Halloween, she thought, as
she headed along the path toward the center, whose dome
was backlit by the surrounding floodlights.

Unlike the entrance of the main hospital with its constant
stream of people, the path to the research center was empty
and silent. Jennifer sucked deep on the cold night air and
continued toward the forbidding silhouette with a faltering
step.

At the entrance she stopped. Her heartbeat was irregular.
For a moment her courage failed her. Her legs felt like lead.
Panic rippled through her and she realized how crazy she had
been to come. They would recognize her instantly. But the
reaction lasted only a second. Her feet moved by themselves.
She had to go through with this, she realized. She could not
stop now.

"Yes, please?" the same receptionist she had seen before
asked, looking directly at her.

For a moment, Jennifer could not answer, waiting for the
woman to scream some accusation. But nothing happened.
The receptionist's face was blank of recognition.

"You have an appointment?"

"Yes . . . Yes I do." Jennifer faltered. Then she heard herself relate the purpose of her visit.

"Ah yes. Dr. Kessler authorized this himself. One moment
please."

Jennifer waited while the woman picked up the phone and
announced her presence. The woman nodded and replaced
the phone. On the desk before her was the fingerprint pad.

Jennifer allowed the woman to take her print. The tiny
window opened and Jennifer saw the reflection on the lens of
the camera behind it.

With a quick motion, she brought the handkerchief she had

balled in her fist to her face and began a carefully rehearsed fit of coughing. The window closed. The receptionist released her thumb and offered her a packaged cleanser.

"This way, please." The receptionist said, coming out from behind the counter to escort her toward the doors at the far end.

The doors opened automatically. A uniformed nurse waited to receive her. Not the same one, fortunately. Jennifer followed her along the same corridor to a different door of what was essentially the same room, identical in all respects to the first.

The nurse stood aside to allow her to enter and closed the door behind her. Jennifer was alone in the room. She could almost hear her heart thundering. Beads of sweat popped on her forehead.

The robotlike precision of the staff filled her with a sense of dread. None of them seemed human. She felt part of some science-fiction world operated by androids.

The door at the other end of the room opened and a young Chinese nurse entered, leading Laura into the room. Jennifer's breath caught in her throat. The woman entering resembled Laura the way a corpse worked on by an embalmer resembles a live human being. There was the same artificial perfection Jennifer had noticed with Leah. Her face was just as carefully made up. Laura's dark hair was fluffed, teased, and lacquered to form a perfect setting for her doll-like countenance. Her blue eyes had the same dull mannequin luster. When she sat beside the nurse on one of the facing couches, her hands lay her in her lap, reminding Jennifer of two dead pigeons.

"Sit please," the nurse said, after she closed the door.

Jennifer took her place opposite Laura, with her bag on her lap. "Laura, darling," she whispered. "Don't you know me? I'm your aunt Lizzie."

Laura looked at Jennifer. Something glimmered in her eyes, then went out like a fading light bulb.

"Laura, I wanted to see you before I went into the hospital. I'm going to have an operation." Jennifer leaned forward and took one of Laura's hands in hers. The nurse did not object. "Laura, I spoke to your mother, darling. She loves you. So does your dad. He wants to come and see you. He's disappointed that you're not getting better."

Jennifer thought she detected another glimmer, but she could not be sure. "Dr. Westwood also sent her regards. You remember her, don't you?"

Laura's lips fluttered slightly. But no sound emerged. Jennifer thought she noticed her chest rising and falling a little more rapidly.

"Dr. Westwood was so close to you, wasn't she, darling? You could tell her anything. She really liked you, Laura. She was your friend. Is there anything you'd like me to tell her?"

Jennifer sensed Laura wanted to commmunicate something. Her eyes began blinking rapidly. Jennifer leaned closer.

"Dr. Westwood is your friend, Laura. You can tell her anything you want to."

Laura's mouth opened. Her face lost its placid look. The muscles of her throat began quivering.

"Yes dear, go on."

"Please," the nurse said. "You must not excite her."

"I'm sorry. It's just that I've been ill. I'm going in for an operation tomorrow, you see . . . and . . ." Jennifer brought the handkerchief to her mouth. She began to spasm. Choking and coughing, she held out her hand. In her palm were two white pills.

"Water . . . please . . ."

The nurse looked confused. She half rose to bend over Jennifer.

"Water . . . I'm choking. . . ."

The nurse glanced at her, torn between helping and not leaving her patient.

"For God's sake. I can't breathe. . . ."

The nurse looked at Laura whose eyes had returned to blank stares. "One minute," she said, rushing outside and leaving the door half open.

Jennifer was on her feet instantly. She closed the door and placed her back against it. Then she reached over to turn Laura toward her.

"Laura, look at me. I'm Dr. Westwood. Talk to me Laura. Tell me what they've done to you."

Laura's eyes began blinking rapidly.

"Have they given you much pain, Laura? Try to tell me."

Laura's mouth opened and her lips began to tremble. But no sound emerged. Her eyes focused on Jennifer. She was trying to speak.

"I want to help you, Laura. Tell me what they've done to you?"

Laura's mouth closed. The blinking stopped. She was sinking back into catatonia.

Jennifer felt the knob turning against her back. The nurse had returned. With a desperate gesture, Jennifer reached inside her bag, drew out the picture Carla had drawn, and thrust it in front of Laura's face.

"What is this, Laura? What does this mean?"

Laura's eyes focused on the picture. For an instant she remained stock-still. Jennifer felt the knob turn the other way as the nurse tried to open the door, but she reached back to prevent it.

"Please, Laura. Tell me what this means. What are the snakes? Where do they come from?"

The scream that tore from Laura's throat froze her heart. Laura's eyes bulged with fright as she stared at the Gorgon's head. Her face began to contort in agony as her hands rose to her head and her hair came away in her fingers.

It took a startled instant for Jennifer to fully understand. Laura was wearing a wig made of her own hair. It slid away from her naked skull and Jennifer's own mouth widened with shock and horror. Laura's head was completely shaven.

Set into Laura's skull was a concentric ring of stainless-steel plugs, each the size of a quarter. They gleamed beneath the fluorescent lights like polished silver. In the center of each plug was a tiny female connection, open like a tunnel into her brain.

The door banged open behind Jennifer as the nurse shoved her way inside. Jennifer was thrown off balance, half across the couch. The nurse tossed away the paper cupful of water she was carrying and shouted something in Chinese. She rushed at Laura, trying to prevent her hands from touching the plugs set into her head.

Laura began biting and struggling violently. The nurse shouted again and again, trying to restrain Laura. Jennifer recovered her balance, realizing that the drawing had slipped beneath the nurse's feet. She bent to retrieve it, as the door opened and two orderlies barged into the room.

A hand fastened on Jennifer's arm. "Visit over. You come now!"

Jennifer tried to resist but the grip was too strong. She had just enough time to snatch up the drawing and slip it inside her bag before she was hustled out of the room. An instant later the door was slammed shut behind her.

"Visit over. You go!" the orderly shouted excitedly as he struggled to draw her back down the corridor. Almost before she realized it, Jennifer had been pulled through the waiting area past the startled face of the receptionist and through the double set of glass doors to the sidewalk outside.

She felt the wind whipping at her face; leaves blew up around her. But all she could see was the image of the scene she had just witnessed.

"Oh God, what have they done to her?" she said aloud.

Jennifer closed her eyes, shaking. The image of Laura's naked skull, with its set of steel plugs, permanently fixed itself in her mind. Then she began to run.

The phone rang in the large white-walled security chamber located in the first floor of the research center. The officer on duty answered it and was informed that the patient had been returned to her section.

The security officer, a lean amber-skinned Taiwanese with a severe mouth, pressed a button and cleared the circuit. That was when he noticed that the blue light signaling a computer warning had flashed on. The officer had been too preoccupied to notice it before, his attention riveted on the closed-circuit monitor that showed the patient being carried back to her area.

Now he touched a series of buttons and a picture of a fortyish woman with gray-streaked hair and her hand over her mouth was thrown up on monitor one. Beside it, on monitor two, was the picture of a flamboyant young woman in a green cape with red hair and sunglasses. The two women looked completely different but the letters flashed on the third monitor announced that their fingerprints were identical.

The officer snatched the phone beside him to his ear while his finger stabbed at the button marked EMERGENCY.

Jennifer realized she had run almost halfway to the tram in a blind panic. Her lungs felt like paper bags someone had blown up then set on fire. She slowed to a walk and began breathing through her mouth as she felt the first wave of exhaustion wash over her. It was the way she remembered feeling after her medical boards. Totally and completely drained.

In the distance she could see the lights of the tram stop. But as she approached, her mind whirled in utter and complete confusion. What had frightened her so? There had to be a plausible medical explanation for what she had seen. The work Dr. Kessler was doing in the center was experimental. What had been done to Laura was probably part of some new approach. Then why had Dr. Freedman marked URGENT on the record? What had he suspected?

Whatever Jennifer had expected to discover that evening was still a mystery. This was the tenth day, yet she still had no inkling of what would happen to Laura, or if indeed anything would happen at all. It was still one big muddle. With a discouraging shake of her head, she realized that all of her efforts had come down to nothing. Her big investigation was about to blow up in her face. She would be discharged from the hospital without coming any closer to finding support for her theory. She had only the look of terror in Laura's eyes to hold on to. And the fact of the three women's identical hallucinations. That had to mean something. But whatever it was, she knew she could no longer continue alone. She needed help. Only she had no idea where to get it.

That was when she heard footsteps behind her.

Jennifer half spun around. The blood was pounding so hard in her temples she would not have heard the sound at all but for the dry blanket of leaves that covered the path. It was impossible to walk anywhere without them crackling underfoot.

Two dark shapes moved quickly toward her beneath the trees. They came along the same path from the research center. It took another instant for Jennifer to realize they were both Oriental.

For a moment nothing connected. Then the image of the bicycle wheel came spinning into her consciousness. Jennifer turned and began sprinting toward the tram.

She passed one streetlight, then a second, before she darted a glance behind her. As she did so a steel wire seemed to slice through her heart. *The men had started to run.*

Panicked, Jennifer tore along the path. Ahead, the asphalt curved around toward the last bus stop. Beyond was a long stretch of dark road sloping up toward the tram. The searing

pain in her side told her she would never make it. *Oh God
... where's the bus?*

A few yards on she heard the familiar rumbling sound and
turned.

The bus was driving toward her around the bend, lit up
like a moving barn. Jennifer sped toward it with a final spurt
of energy, waving her arms and swinging her bag, hoping the
driver would see her in the darkness.

She reached the curve just as the bus careened by without
stopping. Jennifer knew how obstinate the drivers were about
picking passengers up only at designated stops. The stop was
still yards away. She would never make it.

The bus passed the stop then squealed to a halt.

The door opened and a passenger got out.

"Wait!" Jennifer shouted. "Please wait!"

The door wheezed closed. The engine snorted. Jennifer
wheeled around. The two figures were very close, sprinting
toward her out of the darkness.

The passenger, an older man in a tweed coat, banged on
the doors. The doors folded back open like angels' wings.

"C'mon honey. I gotta schedule you know," the driver
snapped impatiently.

Jennifer jumped in and the doors closed. The bus pulled
away in a cloud of noxious fumes. Through the smoke Jennifer could see the two men. The steel-hard dots of their eyes
imprinted themselves on her mind. One face was deeply
pitted with acne scars. The other's mouth curved like a sickle.

"Hey lady, you wanna put something in the box?"

Jennifer had forgotten to pay her fare. She fumbled in her
bag for the change. Then she seized a hand rail and tried to
calm her breathing.

"You'll get a heart attack runnin' like that," the driver exclaimed. "I've seen people drop dead tryin' to make the bus.
What the hell for? There's always another one."

The tram stop loomed ahead. Within seconds the bus had
jerked to a halt and the handful of passengers had disem-
barked. Jennifer jumped down first and ran up the ramp to
the change booth inside. She shoved a bill under the glass
while her eyes darted in all directions, searching for a transit
cop. But there was none.

"C'mon lady. It's pullin' out," a voice rasped behind her.

Jennifer scooped up her change and put her token in the

slot. Then she charged up the steps and into the tram itself, which was half filled with a group of teens, several of whom had roller skates slung over their shoulders.

Jennifer found a place in the rear where she could look down at the approach below. The two men had disappeared.

Pull out . . . please pull out, she prayed under her breath. But the doors remained wide open. Her eyes swept the area below. Where had they gone? Then she saw them, bounding up the stairs two steps at a time.

A bell clanged.

The doors hissed closed. A man in a black raincoat lunged through the opening just as they banged shut.

Both Orientals reached the platform but the barrier was locked against them.

The tram shook and began pulling out, rising quickly above the level of the island. Staring down, Jennifer watched the two men scurry back out of the station toward a black car whose lights swept the approach as it pulled up. Both men scrambled inside while the car was still moving. Jennifer watched the car make a full turn and speed away in the direction of the Roosevelt Island bridge.

The tram stopped dead.

Jennifer turned around. She could see the lights of the approaching tram coming from the Manhattan side. They would have to wait until it cleared the cable before proceeding.

Jennifer knew the black car would have to cross the bridge, then travel the length of a boulevard until it came to the Fifty-ninth Street Bridge. Rush hour was almost over. There would be few cars on the bridge to impede traffic. Jennifer knew the car had a better than even chance of crossing the bridge and reaching the tram stop located on the other side of Second Avenue, even before the tram made it across.

The second hand of her watch swept around with excruciating slowness.

Oh God . . . why aren't we moving?

Jennifer stared at the two points of light hanging suspended above the center of the river.

"This always happens when there's a high wind," one of the teens said disgustedly. One by one they sank to the floor. "Might as well sit down," another said. "We'll be here an hour."

The others laughed and one turned on the radio. Sounds of new-wave rock filled the interior.

Jennifer's insides were pounding harder than the music. Her makeup was beginning to run as a trickle of moisture streaked down her temple. A single thought pounded in her head. They had taken her picture. They knew what she looked like . . . or did they only know what her makeup looked like?

Jennifer dropped to her knees in a corner of the brightly lit interior. She pulled out her mirror and propped it on her lap. Using a bottle of cleanser and a packet of tissues she began wiping off the heavy pancake and thick mascara.

When she finished, a cheer erupted behind her. They had started to move.

"Go . . . go . . . go . . ." she whispered as she struggled to cleanse her face and remove the wrinkle lines from her neck. When she scanned her face in the mirror all evidence of Laura's sick aunt was gone. Only the gray streaks in her hair betrayed her. "Please let it be there," she prayed, as she searched through her bag. With a sigh of relief, her hand contacted the kerchief she usually kept in the bottom. She wound it securely around her head in a turban, which completely concealed her hair. All she had to worry about now were her clothes. They would still recognize those. With a determined gesture Jennifer started to undress.

The teens' chatter slowly faded as one by one they turned to watch Jennifer remove her clothing. She pushed the top of her dress off her shoulders and arms. With her back to the car she slipped back into the blue jersey she had worn during the day. She pulled her tweed skirt halfway up her legs and reaching underneath began removing the antique dress. Then she zipped up the skirt. She bundled the dress and raincoat into the tote bag, then pulled out her own jacket and slipped it on. She bent and changed her shoes.

She had just slipped them on when the tram began to slow for its sharp descent into Manhattan. Jennifer hurriedly transferred as much of the makeup from her tote bag as she could squeeze into her own handbag, finishing just as the tram was embraced by the metal arms of its berth.

Jennifer ducked out, a step behind the teenagers. KEEP NEW YORK CLEAN was lettered across the trash barrel which opened to receive the tote bag. Scooting to catch up, Jennifer reached the group of teenagers just as they passed through the exit and started down the metal stairs.

Jennifer gripped the rail and froze. The two Orientals were racing across the concrete plaza from the open door of the black car. With a determined step she started down.

The two men jostled past her, rushing up the stairs two steps at a time, carefully scanning the departing passengers.

Jennifer reached the bottom and turned toward Sixtieth Street, joining the swarm of pedestrians. She felt completely exposed, expecting claws to grab at her any second. But she did not turn around.

A cab had stopped to discharge two passengers in front of Cinema I. Jennifer raced for it, beating out an attache-case-carrying corporate type to the open door.

"Bitch!" the man shouted just as she slammed the door. The cab pulled into the stream of traffic. Jennifer gave the driver her address through chattering teeth.

"Are you serious! That's right around the block," the cabbie shouted back over his shoulder.

Jennifer pulled out several bills and stuffed them through the opening in the protective shield. The driver grabbed them without a word of thanks. Keys out, Jennifer rushed from the cab to the door of her apartment house and ran upstairs. Inside, she bolted the door and threw herself across the couch, bending double to ease the pain that circled her chest like a band of steel.

She stepped out of her jersey and skirt, threw off her bra and panties, and ran a shower, scrubbing the remains of the makeup away and the gray rinse out of her hair.

Wrapped in a bath sheet, Jennifer sat on the edge of her bed and blow-dried her hair. But her teeth still would not stop hammering.

The events of the last two hours replayed themselves over and over again in her mind. Why had they come after her? Did they think she was employed by some rival corporation, or was it even worse than that? Whatever the reasons, they had tried to stop her. Would she have wound up like Dr. Freedman, lying somewhere with a broken neck, or worse? Jennifer could almost visualize the headline and hear people clucking over the gory details, wondering how someone would be so stupid as to walk alone in such a dark place at night. A doctor no less!

Jennifer had outwitted them on the tram. But for how long? Her fingerprints were on file at the clinic. What if they were watching when she returned to work tomorrow morning, or was that no longer possible? Jennifer put down the drier and stared into space. In one evening her whole world had turned upside down.

Her first impulse was to call for help. But there was no one she could call. She knew almost nobody in New York. Who would possibly help her or even believe her?

The thought of what would happen next began to haunt her, especially when she realized that Dr. Boise had her computer requests. It would not be very difficult for them to make the connection. She had visited two of Dr. Freedman's patients. They would analyze both pictures. The resemblance would be seen. Bone structure could not be disguised. They would know it was she. Besides, all they had to do was check her fingerprints. The whole thing had been a farce. She had been insane to think it would work.

For the first time in her life, Jennifer truly felt the sense of her own insignificance. Blind ego had triggered her to believe she could take on a giant like IPC without help.

She lifted the receiver and dialed Montrose, asking for Mark's connection and immediately regretting it. She had no right to involve a casual acquaintance. She started to hang up but something made her wait out a full ten rings before she realized he had gone. The operator's voice came back on. "Dr. Tobey has left for the day. Would you like to try again tomorrow?"

"No, wait." Jennifer said. "Can you connect me with the patient phone on the second floor?"

"It is a little past visiting hours. Patient's can't receive calls past nine-thirty."

"Please try. This patient is being released."

"All right. One moment please."

Jennifer waited while the call was transferred, listening to the sound of her own heart pounding like a kettledrum.

The phone rang four times before it was picked up. "I'm sorry, patient's are not permitted to receive calls after nine-thirty." Jennifer realized, the speaker was Rita.

"Rita. It's Dr. Westwood."

"Oh." Rita sounded surprised. "Is everything all right? You sound a little out of breath."

"Yes . . . well no. Actually, I have kind of a problem."

"Is it anything I can help you with?"

"I think you could. Can we meet somewhere?"

"We could, only I'm doing a double shift tonight. Carol Mehan got the flu. I'll be on until midnight."

"I see." Jennifer felt her throat tighten. She had meant to call Brae but now she realized how foolish that impulse had been. Before she could invovle him she would need more evidence. Only Rita could help her now.

"Look," Rita said, "if it's that important we could talk over the phone. Things are slowing down here. I could call you back in a little while."

"All right. I'm at home. I'll wait for your call."

Rita hung up and Jennifer replaced the receiver. She slipped on her robe and went to the table where she tried going over the printouts again, but her mind would not function. It was still fixated on the two men who had chased her and the terrifying feeling of being so alone and vulnerable.

When the phone rang a half hour later, Jennifer snatched it to her ear. Rita was on the other end.

"I've got about fifteen minutes," she said rapidly.

"I want you to know how much I appreciate this," Jennifer said.

"No problem. We all need someone to talk to once in a while. Imagine me telling you that, doctor," she said with a laugh.

"This isn't exactly a personal problem, Rita. It concerns the hospital."

"Oh. In what way?" Rita said, sounding surprised.

"Rita. What I'm about to tell you will sound a little strange. But I want you to bear with me until I finish, okay?"

"Sure. Go ahead."

It took Jennifer a full ten minutes to outline the scope of the situation. She mentioned her own suspicions, the drawing she had found of the Gorgon's head, then the identical ones drawn by Leah and Carla. Then she told Rita about Dr. Freedman's research and the computer readouts detailing over two dozen schizoid reactions.

"But how do you know there is any connection?" Rita said in an incredulous tone.

"Because I've seen the reaction myself."

"But how could you? No one from the clinic is allowed into Dr. Kessler's facility without a special invitation."

"I got a special invitation. I sent it to myself."

Jennifer briefly described both visits, omitting what happened afterward. She did not want to alarm Rita.

"This is incredible," Rita said when she was finished. "You must have some idea of the cause."

"I think it's a form of medication being used experimentally. Without the proper testing permits."

"You mean without any government authorization?"

"That's right. I think certain doctors may be prescribing unauthorized drugs."

"Dr. Boise?"

"I don't know," Jennifer said.

"But you said the readouts didn't show a pattern."

"Not that I can read. That's why I need your help. I think some of the medication charges may have been falsified before they were fed into the computer. The only way we would know for sure is if someone backtracked through the medication log to find the discrepancies. You'd have to check each medication charge against the drug log to find out what was actually compounded. I'd need you to xerox a log so I could compare it."

"But we don't even know the name of the drug."

"We don't have to. All we need to find are the discrepancies between what was actually given and what was reported as given."

"Suppose some of the nurses were involved. They could have entered false information, couldn't they?"

Jennifer realized she had not thought of that. "Yes. I suppose so. But I don't know where else to begin. There's got to be some discrepancy somewhere. Will you help me find it?"

There was a pause that turned into an agony before Rita said, "Okay, doctor. Give me the patients' names and I'll check the book."

"Rita you're wonderful!" Jennifer exclaimed.

"I only hope I can help."

Jennifer gathered up the printouts and read the list of names.

"Okay," Rita said when she was finished. "I'll get started right away. Where will you be if I find anything?"

"Right here."

Jennifer hung up, feeling a sense of relief. She was no longer alone. Now she had someone she could confide in, someone who did not think her story was some kind of crack-pot theory. But the point Rita made haunted her. She had overlooked the obvious, thinking only a single doctor like Boise was involved. There could have been others, nurses as well as doctors. Medication logs could be falsified as easily as the medication charges were.

Jennifer began to feel even more desperate. If the lead evaporated, then where was she? Trying to prove a conspir-acy without a shred of evidence. *Oh shit,* why had she gotten herself involved in the first place.

As the minute hand crawled by, Jennifer realized how im-possible it was for her to remain inside. She should have gone back to the hospital to help Rita but she was too frightened. She was also too nervous to remain inside the apartment. But where could she go?

She tossed off her robe and tore open a drawer. Within minutes she was dressed in jeans, boots, and a jacket. She carefully refolded the printouts and stuffed them into her handbag. Then she let herself out and locked the door. She could call Rita from an outside phone.

The night air was sharp against her cheeks. Jennifer started toward the corner, realizing she had no clear place in mind. Instead, she walked to the nearby bar she had gone to with Mark the night they had pub-crawled.

The bar was far from crowded. A few regulars joked with the bartender who served Jennifer a beer. She took the glass and moved to a stool at the end of the bar where she had a clear view of her house across the street.

The street itself was dark but there was enough light to see anyone going in and out the front door. Jennifer checked the clock and decided not to call Rita until eleven. She had to give the head nurse time to attend to her own duties.

Time passed slowly. Jennifer tried to focus on the color TV above the bar, which showed two Latin welterweights try-ing to pound each other into oblivion. Occasionally one of the younger regulars darted a glance in her direction but no one came over except the bartender to refill her glass and of-fer a bowl of roasted peanuts. Nibbling them, Jennifer real-ized she had forgotten to eat that day. She suddenly felt ravenous and devoured the entire bowl.

The street outside settled into its normal pace. By ten o'clock the half dozen or so double-parked cars found spots or their drivers drove away in disgust. By ten-thirty there was only an occasional passerby and the usual number of dog walkers.

At ten to eleven Jennifer asked the bartender for change. She was about to get off the stool and head for the phone when a movement outside caught her attention.

A black car crawled to a stop in front of her house.

Jennifer made out the shapes of the men inside. There were three of them. Jennifer caught her breath and leaned back against the window frame making it nearly impossible for her to be seen.

The car remained stationary for several minutes. The men inside seemed to be discussing something. But she could not see their faces until another vehicle turned into the street and slowly approached the black car. Light flashed across the windows. One of the men inside turned his head. The skin of his swarthy face was pockmarked with acne scars.

Jennifer's insides turned to ice. She was unable to move, focused on every movement of the men outside as if they had been projected in slow motion on some giant screen. *They knew who she was. . . .*

The second car glided to a stop. Jennifer was so absorbed it took another instant for her to realize it was the police. An officer gestured and the driver of the black car started up and moved away.

"Another beer, hon?" the bartender asked. His voice jolted Jennifer out of her stupor.

"No thanks," she said, placing a bill on the bar. Then she slid off the stool and headed for the phone in the rear, pursued by a low wolf whistle and the patrons' lewd laughter. Suddenly changing her mind, Jennifer spun around and started outside.

She went quickly to the opposite corner. A cab pulled toward her when she raised her hand. She jumped in and gave the number of Frank Richie's precinct.

"You in some kind of trouble?" the driver called back over his shoulder.

"No," Jennifer answered in an unnatural voice. The driver was young and wanted to flirt, but Jennifer ignored his backward glances, concentrating on trying to control the turmoil raging inside.

How had they found her so quickly?

She tried to find an answer, then dismissed the thought from her mind. None of that mattered now. All that mattered was for Rita to secure the evidence Jennifer needed. Holding on to that gave her a kind of focus and kept her from dissolving into panic.

Frank's precinct was housed in an aging building with narrow barred windows and green lights bracketing the main entrance. Police cars were angle-parked all along the block. Jennifer had never been inside a police station but when she entered she realized it had the same stale atmosphere as a hospital emergency room.

A powerfully built black sergeant interrupted a harangue about pro football long enough to point out the detectives' room. Inside, she was confronted with a grouping of empty desks and a round-shouldered man with a pudgy face chewing a wad of bubble gum, which he clacked into little explosions. He informed Jennifer that Frank was not on duty that evening.

"Can I call him at home?"

"No you cannot call him at home," the detective said, scratching his armpit.

"Then can I leave a message?"

"Yes, you can leave a message."

The detective provided a pad and ballpoint. Jennifer scrawled a note, then started to leave. She picked up the pen again, scratched out her number at the hospital, and wrote that she would call him tomorrow.

"Please see that he gets it," she said as she handed the note to the officer.

"He'll get it," the cop said firmly.

Jennifer found a public phone in the entrance and dialed the nurses' station.

Rita answered, saying, "It's okay, it's me." Then her voice dropped to a whisper. "You were right. Something is wrong. I tried to call you."

"I was out." Jennifer said, feeling an immense jolt of relief at Rita's words. "That's the first piece of good news I've had in a week."

"I made copies of the log," Rita whispered. "Where can we meet?"

"I don't know."

"I can come to your place when I'm off duty."

"No, don't." Jennifer said abruptly. "Look, there's something I left out when I spoke to you before. After I left the research center tonight, I was followed."

"Oh my God."

"The men who followed me showed up at my place about an hour ago. All of them were Chinese."

Jennifer heard Rita's sharp intake of breath. "We could meet at my place."

"Where is it?"

"On the West Side, in the seventies."

Jennifer jotted the address on the edge of the printouts. Then she said, "Okay. I'll see you there at, say, twelve-thirty. Okay?"

"Yes. That sounds fine. Where are you now?"

"Out and around," Jennifer said, hoping she sounded confident. She didn't want to spook Rita before she had the log in her possession. "See you then."

Jennifer hung up and stepped outside, standing aside to allow two uniformed officers to escort a badly bruised man in handcuffs up the stairs. She hurried to the corner and waited for a cab. The streets were seedier than she had first imagined. Several young men swaggered by menacingly. Jennifer darted anxious glances back toward the precinct until she realized the young men were actually rough trade for older men who were cruising slowly by in their cars.

After ten minutes of frustration, a cab finally pulled over. Jennifer gave the driver Rita's address, then realized she would be too early. She remembered Mark mentioning a bar on Broadway, close enough for her to walk over to Rita's when the time came.

Driving uptown, Jennifer felt a sense of relief. Rita was more than a straw to clutch at. She had become a professional ally. Rita's information would provide her with the proof she needed to convince Frank Richie and hopefully his superiors. Frank was the protection she needed. Her association with Montrose had ended that evening. Jennifer realized with regret. She would most likely have to find someplace to hide while the legal investigation went forward. She thought of returning home, then dismissed the notion. It would be the logical place for them to look for her. She must avoid logic and make random choices from now on. But first she would have to warn her parents and inform them just what kind of hot water their daughter had gotten herself into.

The cab let her off on Broadway in front of the saloon. It turned out to be a pleasant-looking restaurant full of plants and wood. The maitre d' asked her if she wanted a table but Jennifer realized she was a little short of money. She would have to go to the bank tomorrow and withdraw everything she had deposited. She went to the bar instead and ordered a glass of white wine, which she nursed with one eye on the clock.

Several attractive midforties' types approached her in the next half hour. But Jennifer merely smiled politely and told them she was waiting for someone. It never rains but it pours, she mused regretfully.

At twelve-fifteen, she left the restaurant and stood outside, debating whether to call a cab or walk the two blocks toward the park. It was hard to classify this neighborhood. Jennifer knew its reputation as a dumping ground for mental patients. She also knew many of the blocks had been renovated and were sites for expensive co-ops. Besides it was just cold enough to keep the vultures off the streets. She waited another five minutes but no cab put in an appearance. She decided to walk.

The cross streets were silent and deserted. Jennifer traversed one brightly lit block filled with newly refurbished brownstones. The next block became its opposite, filthy and run-down. The jutting staircases of each brownstone presented a shadowy menace where someone could hide. Jennifer realized she had been stupid to have come on foot. She felt tremors of fear returning. A cat shot from beneath a car, scaring her half to death before it disappeared between two garbage cans. From a half-lit window a dark face peered down, hostile and menacing.

Jennifer reached the corner of Amsterdam and hurried across. Garbage swirled in the wind. She passed a cavernous school yard covered with broken bottles and pieces of discarded clothing. She heard her own breathing echo in the stillness. She could see Central Park dead ahead, dark and more than a little frightening, and considered everything she had ever heard about never venturing in there at night. The trees were shorn of their leaves and presented a filigree of shifting forms as the wind picked up.

Jennifer's heart began galloping as she slipped past the dark mouth of a gutted building. A dim light illuminated the numbers on the houses. Jennifer located Rita's address and stepped into a small rectangle separated from the sidewalk by a rusty metal railing. Rita's name was listed beneath one of the bells but when Jennifer rang there was no answer. She rang again. Still no response. She checked her watch and began to feel uneasy.

It was 12:35. Rita would have gone off duty at midnight. Thirty-five minutes was cutting it a little tight, especially if Rita had to wait for a bus or if the next shift was a little late. Jennifer felt a little annoyed at herself. She should have waited at the bar for Rita to return and called first. Fear had prompted her actions. She had to resist it from now on. She pressed the bell again, then decided against waiting. It would only increase the chances of being victimized on the street, but she dreaded the thought of having to retrace her steps through the ugly streets she had just come through.

Headlights loomed toward her, coming slowly down the one-way street. For a moment, she thought it might be Rita's cab and started toward it when she realized it was an amublance. Jennifer stopped in her tracks.

Two men were in front dressed in white. Both of them were Oriental. When it passed beneath the street light she saw the lettering on the side. MONTROSE CLINIC.

Jennifer turned and began to run. She headed away from the ambulance in the direction of Central Park West, the wide boulevard that bordered the park.

She heard the squeal of tires as the ambulance accelerated. Garbage cans were clustered on the curb ahead. With a sideways motion Jennifer kicked one can after the other, sending them rolling into the gutter. The ambulance jerked to a halt as the cans spewed refuse into the street.

Jennifer sprinted straight toward the corner. She had no clear idea of where she was going. This part of New York was alien territory to her. Her mind whirled in panic. Should she turn right or left? The decision was made for her.

A dark figure turned around the corner ahead. Jennifer's

heart leaped at the promise of help. Then the light of the streetlamp on the corner revealed his deeply pitted face.

Without changing pace, Jennifer darted between two parked cars, crossing diagonally toward the opposite corner. She was three car lengths away when she heard a shout and a figure sprang around the edge of the building toward her. Jennifer gasped when she saw his hard sickle-shaped mouth.

She skidded to a halt. She felt suddenly very calm, as if she had entered the eye of a hurricane. Everything became very clear and precise. The two men were rushing toward her from both sides. The ambulance maneuvered around the cans behind her. There was no escape. She was trapped.

"What the hell is going on here?"

The voice exploded out of the darkness, accompanied by the rapid barking of a dog.

Jennifer twisted her head. A savage-looking Doberman, poised for attack at the end of a thick leather leash with bared fangs, was held in check by a shaggily bearded man in a raincoat who had just stepped out of his brownstone.

The pockmarked man skidded to a halt, backpedaling away from the snarling animal.

Jennifer charged toward the man, oblivious to the dog snarling at her approach.

"Sit, Major!" the dog's owner commanded. "I said sit!" Reluctantly, the Doberman obeyed.

"I need some help," Jennifer managed to say through heaving lungs.

"What's going on?" the man asked with suspicious eyes.

"These men were coming at me." She edged closer. The dog bared its yellow teeth but did not move.

"Shit. Let them try it," the man said testily.

Jennifer watched both Orientals slink away silently and withdraw around both corners.

"We can go inside and call the cops," the man said.

"Thanks. But it's all right. I just want a cab."

"Are you sure?"

"Yes. Please. I'll be okay. I just need a cab."

"Okay, lady, this way."

The man started toward Central Park West. "Don't worry, Major won't bother you," he said, noticing Jennifer's obvious nervousness.

"It's not a great idea to be alone out here at this time of night."

"I know. I was supposed to meet someone but she hasn't shown up yet."

"You should call each other first. People get killed around here."

"I know. I was stupid."

Jennifer darted a glance up and down the wide boulevard. She did not see the two men. She and the man waited but few cars passed and none of them were vacant cabs.

"I'm sorry. I'm keeping you."

"No sweat," the man said. "I've got to walk Major anyway. Say, maybe these guys could give you a lift."

Jennifer swiveled in the direction he pointed and stared at the ambulance which had pulled alongside. She jerked back as the window was rolled down, eyes wide with terror.

"No please!" she cried as the man walked forward. "I'd rather wait for a cab."

The man stepped over to the window and said, "Would you two guys mind—"

He never finished the sentence. The driver raised a pistol fixed with the long barrel of a silencer, and as Jennifer watched in horror he pulled the trigger.

Jennifer's ears filled with a whooshing sound. The man grabbed for his chest, then fell forward onto his knees, releasing the leash.

The Doberman leaped through the open window, fastening his fangs on the arm of the man wielding the weapon. The man screamed as the dog tore sideways. The gun slipped out of his hands as blood spurted across the windshield. The dog had torn open an artery.

Jennifer watched the door on the driver's side spring open and the driver jump out, his eyes fastened on her like steel dots. She swung her handbag and the man ducked. It gave her the instant she needed to spring by.

She started down the avenue when she saw a shape dart from between parked cars. Someone shouted and she turned her head. The second man had also concealed himself halfway down the block and was racing toward her. There was only one direction she could take, directly into the park ahead.

A stone wall lined the border of the park. Benches were set

against it. Jennifer reached the sidewalk, sprang onto the bench without breaking stride, and propelled herself over the wall.

She came down on a steeply angled slope that sent her crashing toward the bridle path below. She landed on her knees in soft earth that smelled of manure. Regaining her footing, she ran headlong into the trees ahead.

She heard the shouts of all three men and the savage barking of the dog, mingled with the cries of the wounded man. Ahead, lamps lined the pathways. Beyond the path was a rolling meadow shiny with yellow moonlight.

Jennifer skirted along the side of the path, using the trees and bushes as cover. She had no real idea where she was heading but knew if she kept straight on she would eventually reach Fifth Avenue on the other side of the park. Hotels lined the park and expensive apartment houses with round-the-clock doormen. She could find shelter there. Beyond that she could not think. She must cross the park and get away. The thought jackhammered in her brain.

Pain cleaved her side and burned her kneecaps where she had skinned them coming downslope. Her mind reeled with a single thought as she ran. *She was in the same park where Dr. Freedman had been killed. . . .*

Ahead, a row of boulders rose like open shelves. She reached them and began climbing. Near the top she pressed herself against the black stone and gulped air. Glancing around she saw the screen of dark trees she had just come through. She caught a glimpse of white and realized it had to be the ambulance driver. The other two men were harder to spot but she could hear the scrambling sounds of their movements as they searched for her.

She climbed around the rocks and edged herself down on the other side. A path pointed to a dark stand of trees. Jennifer sprinted toward them, remembering that the park was divided into a series of open spaces and patches of woods. It was possible for her to step off into the trees and become invisible until morning. But she was too terrified to stop.

The path led past the trees and up a hill over long uneven steps. She crested the narrow rise and followed the path down over a bridge that spanned a rivulet of swiftly running water. She thought of getting off the path but the ground was covered with a thick layer of dry leaves, which would give away her movements.

She emerged on a wide avenue heading toward the serpentine roadway on which car traffic was permitted. It was brightly lit with streetlamps. Avoiding it, Jennifer struck off across the uneven ground toward the mouth of an underpass. Reaching it, she drew to a stop within the darkness of the tunnel. Her breathing echoed in the stillness. The tunnel smelled of urine and decaying food. Something scurried away almost under her feet. It sent a shiver of revulsion along her spine until she realized it was only a squirrel.

She came out at the other end of the tunnel onto a path sheltered with willows and lit by old-fashioned lamps that gave off dim light. Crouching to keep her back level with the tops of the benches, Jennifer reached the high shoulder of a hill. She slowed to a walk and recovered her breath. She was passing what she realized was the dark silhouette of a skating rink. When she reached it, she paused.

From the crest of the knoll she could see the outline of buildings along Fifth Avenue across a wide meadow. She was very close now. The path descended toward the open area, bordered on one side by a thick line of trees. Jennifer decided to chance it in the open. She left the shelter of the rink and started down the other side of the slope. Then she saw the boys.

There were six or seven of them wheeling toward her on bikes along a path that bisected the meadow. Streetlamps haloed their bushy Afro hairdo's and muscular teenage bodies. Jennifer increased her pace, praying for some outside chance that they had not seen her.

"Hey pussy!" a voice called to her. "Hold on. We wanna rap with you."

Jennifer started running as quickly as she could. But two of the boys detatched themselves from the others and seemed to float across the ground on their racing bikes in an attempt to cut her off, front and rear.

"Don't worry, little pussy. We ain't gonna hurt you . . . much."

Jennifer heard a chorus of lewd laughter and realized she was cut off. Terror speared through her; she felt like a trapped animal.

Thick brush ran alongside the path on the side away from

the oncoming boys. Without changing pace, she turned and
ran headlong into the bushes. She fought her way through the
brittle, stinging branches that clawed at her skin and face, finally coming to an abrupt halt on the edge of a retaining
wall fifteen feet above the surface of the sunken roadway that
bisected the park.

"Get your asses in there and get the cunt before she makes
it outta here!" the same voice shouted behind her.

Without hesitating, Jennifer knelt, gripping the rough stone
edge of the wall, and allowed her body to hang a moment before she dropped to the sidewalk below.

She crashed down along the wall, tearing skin and flesh as
she fell. She landed on her heels before tumbling backward
onto the asphalt roadway.

Pain tore through her back and side, but she scrambled to
her feet again. The road curved up a gentle slope out of the
park. Fifth Avenue was just beyond. Limping painfully, Jennifer propelled herself on, aware of the shouts of the boys on
the wall above.

"Jump down. Get her ass!"

Jennifer broke into a run, crying out in agony each time
her foot struck the ground. She had to reach the avenue
ahead. She had to. . . .

The curve swept her onto Fifth toward a traffic light. She
saw the lights of the buildings ahead. Doormen were on duty.
Someone would help her—had to help her.

She heard the slap of sneakers on the roadway behind her.
Oh God, please, don't let them . . .

She reached the corner and stumbled. Headlights zoomed
toward her. She raised her arms in front of her face. Tires
screeched to a halt. She glimpsed the yellow of a cab.
Through bursting lungs, she cried, "Help me!"

The cab sped by, turning into a side street. Jennifer forced
herself to rise. Glancing around, she saw the boys' dark
shapes hesitate, waiting for the traffic to pass.

Lights shot toward her down the avenue. Jennifer stumbled
forward into the street. Pain seared her side. Her palms were
bleeding. Her chest felt on fire. But she could not stop. Waving her arms, she hurled herself at the oncoming traffic.

A horn blared. Her legs gave way. Jennifer tumbled backward into the gutter.

A door opened. Feet ran toward her. Someone grabbed her

around the shoulders. With an effort Jennifer sat up. The features of the man who held her was Chinese.

"No—you bastard!"

With a scream Jennifer shoved her elbow into his chest, tearing herself out of his grasp. She saw a canopy a few yards away. She struggled to her knees. She had to reach it.

Lights blinded her. She felt a terrible force rush toward her, then over her. Something solid struck her in the side and she flew headlong. She felt the impact of landing as if she belly-flopped into a swimming pool. She tried to cry out but her mouth would not open. Light and darkness blended together in waves. Her ear filled with a hollow sound like oncoming surf. She heard the sound of voices that filled her ear like singing.

"She threw herself in front of the car. Someone call a cop."

"I already did. I got a phone in the cab. I saw her running out of the park before. I almost hit her myself. Then I dropped my fare and doubled back. Here are the cops. Do you believe it?"

A strange face peered down at her, going in and out of focus like a fun-house mirror. She glimpsed a blue uniform and could almost make out the number of the silver badge.

"It's okay. An ambulance is on the way. You're gonna be all right."

Hands reached down to lift her. The pain came from all directions now. Jennifer closed her eyes and bit hard, trying not to cry out. The pain did not matter. Nothing mattered. She was safe. They could not reach her now.

Darkness rose like a climbing wave scooping her up. She did not resist. The police were here. She was safe. She allowed herself to slide into the void.

Jennifer was wheeled to the rear of the ambulance by the two white-clad attendants. They lifted her up and slid the stretcher inside, then closed the rear door, printed with large maroon letters.

MONTROSE CLINIC

NINETEEN

She was falling through a gleaming metal tunnel toward a tiny circle of light. Her body whirled in weightless suspension as if she were floating in a pool of water. Only she was dropping rapidly, unable to halt the spiral of motion that dragged her down in an ever-narrowing space. A scream flew back from her lips like the ribbon tail of a kite. She fell faster . . . the light spun toward her . . . she was falling through. . . .

Jennifer's eyes opened.

She was moving along a corridor. Rectangles of bright light blipped past her vision like compact clouds. She was being wheeled on a hospital gurney. Straps held her body from falling off. Everything passed before her through a pleasant haze, like opening her eyes after a nap on a summer day. She felt as if she were on some kind of high, but without the negative sensations of paranoia. She was calm, almost joyous. Bubbles of laughter seemed ready to burst from her lips.

Doors opened in front of her. The corridor bent like a soft elbow, then straightened out again. Where was she going? She started to turn her head but there was pain when she did that and she stopped. She heard herself moan. The sound filled a cartoon bubble above her head.

"It's all right, Jennifer," a voice reassured her. "Just don't move. You've had a slight concussion, that's all. We're going to take some pictures of your head."

The nurse sounded gentle, almost familiar. But the words

seemed to jumble as she heard them, like cars colliding with
each other at the entrance to a too-narrow tunnel. She had a
concussion . . . but she had been hit in the side, hadn't she?
Why did they want to take pictures of her head?

Her mind obligingly replayed the picture of her accident.
She saw the headlights, heard the screech of tires and felt the
impact. She had fallen sideways onto her side and shoulder.
Nothing had struck her skull. She remembered being thankful
for that just before she lost consciousness. They were making
a mistake. She had to tell them.

Jennifer tried to open her mouth but her tongue felt like
an enormous sleeping cat. It would not move, even when she
willed it to. She wanted to laugh because it was so ludicrous.
Her tongue was a large sleeping cat. . . .

Her eyes opened.

She must have drifted off. They were stopped now. The
gurney was in front of a doorway. Jennifer could hear
muffled voices, floating somewhere above her. The speech
sounded like different instruments. She heard a woman's
voice that sounded like a violin, then a man's that sounded
like a cello. Letters floated across the metal door. They
moved in one direction, then another. Jennifer felt annoyed
that they would not remain still long enough for her to read
them. But being angry made them stop.

CAT SCAN. AUTHORIZED PERSONNEL ONLY

Now she understood. They were going to take pictures of
her brain. But she did not want them to. That was not where
it hurt. She no longer felt like laughing. Darkness opened like
a pit in front of her, fitted like two sheets into which she
could slip.

Jennifer fought the desire to lose consciousness. The angles
around her lost their softness. Objects no longer floated. She
felt more awake, more anxious.

There was a buzz and the doors in front of her opened.
The gurney began moving again. Jennifer saw the glass window of the technicians' chamber pass in front of her, then the
stainless-steel face of the scan itself, shimmering with fluorescent highlights. In its center was the cup for her head.
She knew there was nothing to be afraid of. They were only
going to take a picture.

But they were not stopping at the scan. They wheeled past

it along another corridor to a second set of doors. These opened to face a long passageway made of curving glass. Jennifer could see the sky through the glass. It was dark and full of stars. *Where were they taking her?*

Elongated shapes kept pace alongside, reflected in the glass. She stared at them for a time until she realized they were shapes of people she knew. The nurse wheeling her was Rita Kahn. Walking a step behind her was a man with a shock of white hair that matched the color of his clinic coat.

The man was Dr. Kessler.

A scream twisted through her like a locomotive going out of control. But no sounds emerged from her lips. Jennifer twisted from side to side trying to get free. But she could not move. *Please God, don't let them take me in there.* . . .

The gurney stopped.

Jennifer heard Rita murmur something, then she saw the face of Dr. Kessler leaning toward her.

"Don't worry, Dr. Westwood. Everything will be all right. You're where you belong now."

Glass doors slid open. The gurney rolled forward. People moved around her dressed in blue uniforms. Their faces were expressionless and efficient-looking. Jennifer knew she had been wheeled into the research center. *They had her now and she would never get out . . . never . . .*

Jennifer watched Rita step aside. With a smile, Rita gently brushed the hair away from Jennifer's face. Then she turned and walked back through the doors, which closed behind her silently. Only Dr. Kessler remained. Jennifer could feel the weight of his hand on her shoulder.

Jennifer was wheeled through a sterile entrance chamber toward another set of matching doors.

When she looked up she saw a single strip of light running down the center of the ceiling. Jennifer could hear the soft shuffle of crepe soles on the linoleum floor.

Another door opened and Jennifer was rolled into a different kind of chamber. The gurney halted. She was in a kind of preparatory area with walls but no ceiling. Above it was darkness although Jennifer could make out lights like distant stars. Technicians and nurses surrounded her, moving with practiced precision.

The straps were removed. Jennifer was transferred to a dif-

ferent kind of wheeled table whose end was raised so she
could sit up. She tried to move but restraints were fastened to
her wrists and ankles.

"Don't excite yourself, doctor," she heard Dr. Kessler say.
"The drug you've been given makes it impossible for you to
move your limbs. Relax, let my staff do their work."

Kessler slipped away, leaving Jennifer to focus on what
was being done to her. An IV rack was wheeled into place
and various needles injected into her veins. A pressure bandage was wrapped around her arm. Another nurse exposed
her breasts, allowing a male physician to press a stethoscope
to her flesh. Her reflexes were tested with a triangular hammer, while an oscilloscope was wheeled into position nearby
and the leads attached to record her heartbeat.

Another nurse approached with a razor and lather. Jennifer
struggled, afraid that her head was going to be shaved, but
only a tiny portion of hair was actually removed before the
nurse moved away.

Jennifer was left alone for a moment, allowing her mind to
focus on the space beyond.

She was beneath a large domed ceiling, enclosed in an atmosphere that was neither night or day. Light emanated from
seamless strips of fluorescent tubes, creating a moonscape of
light and shadow. Jennifer found it difficult to discern the rest
of the objects around her until the table was pushed forward.
Then she stared around her with startled eyes.

Running completely around the room like a bicycle wheel
turned on its side, was a circular tube of glass. The tube was
raised above the level of the floor on stainless-steel supports.
Where each support joined the next there was a rib of steel,
which circled the tube and divided it into room-size compartments.

As Jennifer's eyes became accustomed to the gloom she
had a full view of the people inside each compartment. They
were all dressed in identical blue hospital gowns. Each person's head had been shaved, making it difficult to tell them
apart. Each skull was fitted with the same set of stainless-steel
plugs she had seen in Laura's. The scene resembled an enormous hive, whose inhabitants were in various stages of activity. Some lay on their beds asleep or resting. Others stared
listlessly into space. Some lay on tables identical to the one

Jennifer had been strapped to and were twisting against the restraints. Their faces were imprinted with the same look of horror that had transfigured Laura's when Jennifer had shown her Carla's drawing. Eyes bulged. Mouths opened in endless screams that sent a chill of terror spearing through her.

A motor whirred nearby and Jennifer turned. A ramp was moving toward her. When it was in place the table began to move. Jennifer was wheeled up along the ramp toward a platform that was located in the exact center of the circular tube. Lights were switched on.

That was when Jennifer saw the Gorgon.

Now she understood the imagery in each woman's drawing. A machine was suspended over the circular platform. It resembled a steel bowl turned upside down. Coils of black rubber hung in snakelike loops that were twisted like a nest of serpents. At the end of each coil there was a set of gleaming needles, each curved like a fang.

Jennifer counted twelve hoses. One for each of the twelve implants set in each woman's skull. Now Jennifer understood why each hallucination matched the others. In the minds of each of the deranged women the coils of tubing became vipers, the needles turned into hissing fangs that seemed to be growing out of their own heads, which became giant Medusa skulls of living serpents. That was why each of the women had tried to tear away the snakes growing out of her head. The image drove them even further into madness.

Jolts of panic raced through her. This was no mythical image. This was real and it was happening to her.

But why?

The table stopped when it was directly beneath the cupola. Above her, Jennifer made out what appeared to be a drill-like apparatus, protruding from the center like the tentacle of an enormous octopus. She watched it descend toward her with mechanical precision until it was only a foot above her head.

Hands began fixing an apparatus around her head that Jennifer could not make out. It seemed to be a padded helmet that pressed against her cheeks and chin, locking her head firmly in position beneath the drill.

She tried to move, to cry out, but the restraints held her

too firmly. Her body was controlled by the drug. Only her mind was completely alert.

"Don't fret, doctor. You won't feel any pain," Dr. Kessler said against her ear. She watched him come into focus in front of her. He had changed from his white coat to a green surgical gown and pants. A cap fitted snugly over his head and a mask hung around his neck.

"I know all of this seems a bit confusing. But I'll explain everything in a moment. I think I owe you that."

As he spoke, Kessler began to adjust a series of mechanisms Jennifer could not see. Her range of vision was tightly restricted by the helmet. She could only see what was directly in front of her. Just to her right she could make out a console on which was the outline of a human head and a series of multicolored calibrations. With a shock, Jennifer realized she was looking at a fluoroscope of her own skull.

Kessler reached up and adjusted the apparatus around her head, making minor adjustments between the machinery and what he saw on the screen. He began speaking as he worked with all the casualness of a dentist about to fill a cavity.

"You see, doctor, anyone visiting here would be somewhat startled by the appearance of our patients, until they understood that each metal implant is capable of stimulating a different section of the brain. By attaching these hose connections you see above you, various regions of the cerebral cortex can be manipulated as never before. The promise of such treatment offers revolutionary breakthroughs in the treatment of schizophrenia. That is if we were actually using it in the treatment of schizophrenia, which as you have so cleverly deduced, we are not."

Kessler paused to study the configuration on the console, then returned to Jennifer and made another adjustment.

"Oh, of course, the machine is actually capable of creating such stimulation and we use it for that purpose when we have to give a demonstration. But naturally, that is not its real purpose, which is something entirely different. But that is something you could not have guessed." Kessler stepped back. "Ah perfect."

He seemed satisfied with the adjustment and stepped back to face her. "No doctor, clever as you are, you could not have deduced the real purpose for which the machine was built. You stumbled onto the truth through the back door, thinking certain unauthorized medications were causing mildly disturbed patients to experience schizoid delusions. That is not quite correct. Our patients' delusions begin with a visit here."

Kessler assumed an apologetic expression.

"So you see, you were on the right track but were looking for the wrong cause. You would have been better served if you had tried to trace the course of my own research. Nitholin was only the first stage in the development of a drug to completely alter the structure of the human mind. What I discovered while perfecting it was the presence of an undiscovered enzyme, an enzyme that exists exclusively in the cerebrospinal fluid of the female brain. We men are not so fortunate. Our systems do not produce it in nearly adequate amounts. So you see, you belong to an exclusive sisterhood. From the fluid extracted from your brain a new drug will be created. One that will completely alter habit formations and the conditioned responses that lie at the root of all human behavior. You see the implications, of course. Nitholin proved we could create a susceptibility in the human mind greater than that of hypnosis. Even better, we were able to get the subject to alter his behavior in direct opposition to already established behavior patterns. A remarkable breakthrough, don't you agree? But only the beginning of what lay ahead." Kessler turned and said something that Jennifer could not make out to one of his technicians. Then he faced her again.

"The enzyme I have extracted from these patients you see around you provides the serum base for a dosage far more concentrated than Nitholin. My research is still primitive but surprisingly effective, somewhat like the early stages in the development of electricity, when its discoverers knew its potential but were not exactly certain how to control it. My new drug will create complete susceptibility in the brain, preparing the ground for total mind control. You are, of course, familiar with the experiments Pavlov conducted with his famous canines. Imagine if you could transfer the same kind of results to the human consciousness. All Pavlov had to do was ring a bell to get them to exhibit behavior as if real food were present. My line of research indicates we can accomplish just that. By using my drug as a reinforcing agent, we can control various levels of human performance. You can of course see the implications."

The technician returned and Kessler turned away, stepping out of Jennifer's line of vision. What Kessler had just told her numbed her mind. She could not focus on the implications of his research, only on the terrible reality around her. The women locked in the compartments of his glass tube were a herd of human cattle being milked for the fluids of their brains.

Kessler returned to face her once again.

"Oh, I understand just what is going on in your mind, doctor. You see me as a sadist. A monster keeping these two dozen or so female patients in perpetual bondage. But consider a moment. Weigh their loss against the millions who will benefit. Think of the rapid degeneration of our society. The conditioning of centuries responsible for civilization, a conditioning that taught reverence for God, obedience to the Ten Commandments, respect for governmental authority and the moral law of religion, is no longer operational. All the old forms are falling away. The family degenerates beneath the pounding of easy divorce laws, with all its attendant disorganization and chaos for the individual and the children of broken homes. Government has become anarchy. Morality turns into sexual promiscuity. We have become victims of random violence and crime. Our society seems unable to protect itself from the enemies within. It has taken a more authoritarian regime to see the real dangers and do something about them.

"The degeneration has been far more shocking to those in the East where traditional values are almost holy. They are witnessing the erosion of discipline more rapid than our own, a discipline that has held their societies together for thousands of years. Witness China, Japan, India. The vast majority of human life on our planet resides there. These societies have seen the danger. They understand that drastic means are called for to save their civilizations from going under. A vaccine is needed for this, just as it was needed to stop the scourges of small pox and polio. That is why IPC, which is actually funded by several governments in the East, both Communist and non-Communist, has poured millions into my research. They stand ready to reap the rewards of my breakthrough. Once we can produce a serum in large enough quantities, we can completely reverse the effects of this degeneration. The millions, no, billions of its people will lock step once more, instead of scattering in a thousand different directions. Society will be uniform, precise, and obedient."

Kessler stared at her. Jennifer could see the complete conviction stamped in his eyes.

"Of course, until I can produce the serum artificially, a portion of society, like these women around you, will have to undergo the unpleasant side effects that accompany the cure to any disease. So far we have not been able to counterbalance the effects on the brain produced by such a sudden loss of essential fluid. As you have seen a certain amount of personality disorganization results, creating a condition very much like schizophrenia. The chemical imbalance causes the conscious mind to loose control and allows all the demons of the unconscious to flood the mind: All the primordial fears, anxieties, and dreads of our prehistoric past return to capture the brain and envelop it in a state of permanent nightmare." A technician stepped to Dr. Kessler's side with a nod. Kessler nodded in reply and turned back to Jennifer.

"We are ready, doctor. In a few moments the device above you will penetrate your skull and remove a small amount of fluid from the area of the motor speech centers, causing you to appear delusional. During this time a suitable diagnosis of schizophrenia will be obtained as well as your family's permission for you to be admitted to the center. A few days later the implants will be fitted, and within ten days your condition will be more or less permanent. It is regrettable. You would have made a first-class psychiatrist. However, at least your body will provide a contribution to medicine, which is why I refused to allow the security team to terminate your life."

Kessler stepped away. Jennifer heard the whir of a motor. She tried to struggle but she was completely paralyzed.

"Don't worry, doctor. I promise, you will feel no pain."

Jennifer felt a slight pressure on the top of her head. She smelled something burning as if someone had struck a match. Then the darkness fell. Terror welled up, drawing her into its whirlpool.

Through the mist she saw the head of the Gorgon alive with hissing vipers.

The scream began within the deepest recesses of her mind, spreading out into the darkness around her like streams of lava.

But the horror had only begun. . . .

TWENTY

Brae's last morning at Montrose quickly became an anticlimax. There was little fanfare to mark the end of his stay. Easing him out of the hospital was accomplished with a minimum of disturbance to the other patients. There was an inventory he had to make of his possessions after his valuables were returned. Then he carefully folded his clothes and packed them in his suitcase along with his personal items.

Almost no one seemed to notice his leaving. Brae had made few acquaintances besides the man he had been asked to room with. He supposed there was some therapeutic motivation for having them room together but never figured out what it was. The man was undergoing electroconvulsive therapy, he was too withdrawn to provide invigorating company. The nursing staff had been pleasant enough and several nurses and orderlies stopped by to wish him well. But Brae's main interest was seeing Jennifer for their last session.

He had missed his appointment with her the day before when he had traveled cross town for his first outpatient visit with Dr. Arbus, the therapist the hospital had found for him. The doctor was in his middle fifties, a kindly-looking and talkative man, quite unlike the picture of a silent and aloof being Brae had formed in advance.

Dr. Arbus had devoted a good part of his practice to veterans and cops suffering from their respective forms of battle fatigue. His manner put Brae at ease almost immediately and made it possible for the two men to establish a pretty good rapport. Brae realized he had Jennifer to thank for that. She had broken through to him and he had been more accessible ever since. The person he had been when he entered Montrose seemed like a stranger, part of some evil dream.

After Brae packed his bags, he impatiently puffed on a cigarette and repeatedly checked his watch, waiting while the minutes crawled by and it was time for his meeting with Jennifer. It was not going to be easy, he realized. There were sixty days to wade through before he could see her again, as he had promised.

Crazy world, he thought with a smile. Here he was involved with his own shrink, an idea that only a month ago would have seemed complete madness to him. As insane as it was to think that Brae Haskill would have needed a shrink in the first place, to think he had then proceeded to fall in love with one was too much to believe.

His mind picked over the facts of his recent past, especially his relationship with Mercedes. Strange how he could think about her now without straightjacketing himself with guilt. Even more important was an understanding of the dark tunnels of his own complicated inner workings. Paradoxically, the breakdown had actually concealed a blessing. It had become the means of seeing behind the surface into the deepest parts of himself. There had been a flaw in him he had failed to recognize. His mending would provide greater strength for the most dangerous travel of all, the journey within.

Brae paused for a moment, turning something over in his mind. No, he could not see Jennifer before the time they had agreed upon. That would mean giving in to an even greater weakness. Besides, there was wisdom in what she had made him promise. It was possible that his feelings for her were only temporary. But he did not think so. He had experienced too much in life to believe that. Jennifer was a prize worth possessing.

His watch finally offered relief. Brae stubbed out his cigarette and headed down the hall toward Jennifer's office. He had composed something witty to say about her mysterious investigation but the remark remained glued to his throat when he opened the door and faced Dr. Boise, who was seated behind her desk.

"Please come in, Mr. Haskill," Boise said, offering an artificial smile.

Brae entered and took his usual place. "Where's Dr. Westwood?" he asked with a frown.

"I'm sorry, she won't be able to be with us today. She's not feeling very well, so I thought we would spend a little time together discussing your feelings about leaving."

Brae experienced a sinking feeling of disappointment during the next forty minutes as the session dragged on. He took a few stabs at finding out what was wrong with Jennifer but Dr. Boise skillfully parried his questions, stating merely that it was some minor ailment. But Brae felt uneasy at this response. Jennifer had never missed a day. He wondered if it was something more serious than Dr. Boise was letting on, but he allowed the feeling of irritation at not seeing her to pass. He did not want to compromise her by allowing Boise to think there was anything personal in the question.

When the session finally reached its conclusion, Dr. Boise stood up and shook Brae's hand. Not a bad guy, Brae thought, when he returned to his room to pick up his bags. But he was as suited to being a psychiatrist as Brae was to becoming a transvestite.

Frank was waiting in the lounge with a self-conscious smile.

"Jeez," he said, slapping Brae's back, and jerking his head toward the nurses' station. "How do I get in here?"

"Just go inside and tell them you're Adolf Hitler."

Frank made a face and picked up one of Brae's bags. Brae took the other and they headed for the elevator.

Downstairs, Brae stopped near the phones. "I want to make a quick call, okay?"

"Christ, the guy's not outta here two minutes and he's already hustling some chick."

Brae went to the phone and, pulling out his notebook, found Jennifer's number. "What the hell," he said aloud letting the dime drop. The sixty days starts after the phone call. That was only fair after being deprived of seeing her that morning. He let the phone ring ten times before he hung up. "Sick, my ass," he muttered. "She's probably out shopping."

Frank stared at him suspiciously. "They let you outta here and you're talkin' to yourself? Maybe you'd better check back in."

Frank's car was waiting outside and they loaded the bags inside. The day was bright with sunshine. As they drove away from Montrose Brae realized how good he was starting to feel. Frank seemed to sense it too. He turned to Brae and said, "Hey, you know you're lookin' good."

"I feel good," Brae answered, scanning the expanse of river ahead. The usual oily slime was covered with dancing highlights of color like an Impressionist painting.

"Why shouldn't you look good?" Frank continued in the same joking tone. "With the doc you had, I'd be dancin' too."

Brae turned toward him with a puzzled expression. "What do you mean?"

"Hey pal, don't bullshit me. She's some little piece."

"How do you know what she looks like?"

"Oh shit. Now I did it. I guess I wasn't supposed to say nothin'."

"You mean you met her?"

"Yeah. She contacted me after you were inside about a week."

"You told her about Mercedes?" Brae asked pointedly.

"I thought it might help. It seemed to be the only way of reaching you."

Brae reached over and touched Frank's arm. "Don't sweat it, Frank. You did right. It may be the reason I'm sitting here right now."

"You're sure?" Frank said guiltily.

"Positive."

"You know what I liked about her. She was feisty as hell. She really gave a goddamn. Not like most of them."

Brae nodded, feeling a sudden sense of gloom. Sixty days was going to be a long, long time. Maybe he was taking too much for granted. She was a doctor and he was a cop. Not the likeliest combination. She had probably agreed to see him only to humor him along. Christ, he was a fool to think it could turn out to be something more.

"I'll tell you what else though," Frank continued. "She didn't stop just because you were nearly comin' out. That's what I really liked."

"What do you mean?" Brae asked.

"She came down to the precinct the night before last. Would you believe it? Late too. I was off duty so she left a note."

"What kind of note? Let me see it."

"Hold on. Don't freak out on me. I got it here someplace."

Frank switched hands on the wheel and began searching through his pockets. "Here is is."

Brae took the crumpled piece of paper. On it were the words, "I need to see you. Urgent." She had written down her number at the hospital, then crossed it out and wrote instead, "I'll call you tomorrow."

"What did she say when she called?" Brae demanded.

"That's just it. She didn't. I guess she was too busy."

Brae glanced at the note again. A knot of worry appeared in his forehead. Why had she said "urgent." He had not undergone a crisis during the last few days.

"Pull over," he ordered. "I want to use the phone."

Frank drew the car over to a phone on the corner. Brae got out and dialed. Again, he allowed it to ring ten times. But there was still no answer. Where was she? he wondered.

Frank helped Brae upstairs with his bags. The apartment looked the same. The maid he used twice a month had been in. Everything was clean and orderly. The furniture even smelled of polish.

Brae spent the next few hours with Frank. They had dinner and a few drinks which Brae had to forgo because of his medication. Jennifer did not pick up when he tried at five, nor at seven. He fell asleep and woke up at one-thirty. He was tempted to call then but decided against it. His mind became filled with all kinds of strange ideas, most of which he dismissed as pure idiocy. Especially when he remembered the Saturday they had spent together and how amused he had been at Jennifer's suspicions. His smile turned into a frown when he realized she might be out with someone.

But why not? She's beautiful and she's human. She entitled, isn't she? *No—she damned well wasn't.* Not when he was so crazy about her.

Shaking off his irritation, Brae took a pill he had been given but still found it difficult to sleep. He had the next few weeks off duty, during which time he was scheduled to visit Dr. Arbus three times a week. At sixty bucks a shot he was supposed to be getting a bargain. He was in the wrong business, he realized. Luckily the PBA contract with the city paid for psychiatric care, or he would have gone broke paying for the sessions.

The pill finally took effect and Brae fell into a deep dreamless sleep. He awoke at eleven. Shaving and exercize kept him busy until noon when he left the apartment and ate a leisurely brunch at a local bistro. When he was finished with his dessert, he put down the paper he was reading and called Jennifer. There was still no answer at her apartment and he realized she had probably returned to work. He hung up and started back to his table. Sixty days was sixty days. No. Fifty-nine, if you counted yesterday. So he would cheat a little. But he had decided to be a good boy and wait it out. Then he paused. Since when had he ever been a good little boy.

He shoved a dime back into the phone and dialed the clinic, wondering if they would put him through.

"Dr. Westwood, please," he said when the operator answered.

"One moment please." There was a click as he was put on hold. Brae had to put another dime in before the operator came back on. "I'm sorry. Dr. Westwood is presently on a leave of absence."

Brae was not sure he heard correctly. "A what?"

"A leave of absence."

"That's impossible. When did this happen?"

"I wouldn't know, sir. Would you like me to connect you with personnel?"

"Thank you," Brae said, waiting while his mind churned with confusion.

A few minutes later a female voice announced, "Personel."

"I'm calling about Dr. Westwood. I've been told she's on a leave of absence."

"That's right, sir. For medical reasons. It was granted yesterday."

"I don't understand. What's wrong with her?"

"I can't disclose that information, sir. Are you family?"

"No. I'm not."

"I'm sorry. You'll have to call the director of personnel. He is out at the moment."

Brae hung up. Tracing Jennifer's parents was a simple matter of calling Washington, D.C. information. Only when he dialed their number no one answered. Brae spent the next hour tormented with questions. What could have happened that would cause Jennifer to take a medical leave and where the hell was she?

After trying Jennifer's parents' home again and again, he still received no answer. Remaining inside became impossible especially after he called the hospital again. He was told by the director of personnel that he could not disclose any information except to a relative who would have to appear at his office in person.

Brae left his apartment and took a cab uptown. He wandered around near Third Avenue, entered Bloomingdale's, scoured the men's department, then emerged and crossed over to Second. Jennifer's apartment was only a block away. He tried not to feel anxious, but no matter how hard he worked to squelch them the needles of anticipation would not disappear.

Brae glanced up at Jennifer's building before going into the small vestibule and pressing her bell. He did not expect a response and got none.

Jennifer's parents were still out when he tried them again. He returned to his own apartment and made some calls. Then he dialed the precinct and got hold of the detective who had taken Jennifer's message. His name was Savage.

"Sure, I remember," Savage said with a chuckle. "Who wouldn't? She was some little looker."

"What was she acting like? Did she seem sick, scared, or what?"

"No. She was in control. She wanted me to call Frank but I told her I couldn't, so she left a message. Other than that, she seemed okay."

"Anything else?"

"Yeah. I saw her make a phone call in the lobby. Then she split."

"Okay, Savage. Much obliged."

Brae called the Washington number again. After receiving no answer he called the information operator and, using her parents' address, attempted to get the phone numbers of the houses on either side. One phone was unlisted. But he got the operator to give him the other number. With fingers crossed fingers, he dialed and waited. A woman picked up.

"Hello," Brae said. "I'm a friend of the Westwoods. I've been trying to get hold of them but no one answers. I'm a little worried."

"They're not home right now. Who did you say you were?"

"My name is Brae Haskill. I'm calling from New York. I wanted to speak to the Westwoods about their daughter. I'm a friend of hers."

"Oh, I see." The woman's tone changed to the register used to convey bad news. "Yes. We've heard Jennifer was ill. Mr. and Mrs. Westwood left for New York yesterday."

"Could you tell me where they're staying?"

"Certainly. They're staying at a hotel on the East Side. The Carlyle."

Brae thanked the woman and hung up. He rang the hotel but the Westwoods were not in their room. He pulled on a sweater and a tweed jacket and left his apartment. Traffic was heavy. It took almost twenty minutes for him to cross the park from the West Side. He used the house phone but no one responded. Then he went to the desk. The clerk answered his inquiry by saying the Westwoods had just returned and gone into the bar.

Brae did not have to inquire again. The dark-haired woman in a smart two-piece outfit looked more like Jennifer's sister than her mother. Her husband was a well-built executive type with graying temples.

Brae walked over to their booth and leaned over. "Mr. and Mrs. Westwood?"

The couple looked up. Brae could detect the strain and lack of sleep in their faces.

"Yes," Mr. Westwood answered.

"My name is Brae Haskill. I know your daughter. May I sit down."

"Certainly."

Brae took a seat on the other side of Jennifer's mother. She said, "You say you're a friend of Jennifer's? From the hospital?"

"That's right."

"Are you a doctor?"

"No. But your daughter and I worked together."

"I see," she continued. "Then you know what's happened."

"No. I'm afraid I don't. I've been calling Jennifer at the hospital but I was told she was on a medical leave. I called your house because I thought she was there. A neighbor told me you were here. I'd like to know just what's going on."

Jennifer's mother glanced over at her husband. He shook

is head and bit back the emotion it was costing him to peak. "We got a call yesterday morning—or was it the day before? I can't remember. Anyway, it was from the hospital. They said Jenny had . . . had tried to kill herself."

"Kill herself?" Brae uttered in surprise. "Who told you that?"

"The head of service. A Dr. Boise. Do you know him?"

"Yes. I know him."

"You seem surprised." Mrs. Westwood said.

"I am surprised."

"Then Jenny wasn't acting strange or anything."

"Who told you that?" Brae questioned.

"Dr. Boise said she was under a strain, being new and all. And having to take over from that other doctor who was killed. He said she was overworked."

Brae was silent. None of this made any sense. "Where is she now?"

"At the clinic. As a staff member she's entitled to special care."

"Thank you," Brae said, starting to rise.

"Wait a moment, please," Mr. Westwood said. "Could you tell us anything about Jenny's actions before this?"

"Mr. Westwood, as far as I could see, your daughter was handling the pressure pretty damned well. I should know; I put plenty of it on her."

"I don't understand."

"Mr. Westwood, I was one of your daughter's patients."

Brae shared a cab to the hospital with the Westwoods, hoping he would be allowed to see Jennifer. He caught the look that passed between them as they drove. It expressed concern for who he was and why his interest went beyond the normal patient-doctor relationship. But Brae remained tight-lipped and they did not question him further.

At Montrose they were informed that visitation had been denied. Dr. Boise appeared to inform them that Jennifer was experiencing delusional episodes and had to be physically restrained. Her parents took the news calmly until Boise walked away, then Brae could see the effect it was having on them. Jennifer's father put a protective arm around his wife but his own face was ashen. His lips trembled and Brae could see how close he was to tears.

Dr. Boise seemed surprised to see Brae, but he did not as'
why he had come. Brae did not like his manner. It seeme
practiced and artificial. The concern in his eyes was unreal.

"It just doesn't seem possible that something like this coul
happen to Jenny. She was always so rock solid," Jennifer's fa
ther said on the ride back to Manhattan. Brae merel'
shrugged. He had seen too many inexplicable tragedies. Hor
rors that sprang out of nowhere to destroy the illusion o
life's predictability. His job had taught him that nothing wa
safe. Not even his sanity.

He did not express it to them but he knew something wa
wrong. All his cop instincts were aroused. He felt as if h
had swallowed something it was impossible to digest.

Just before they arrived back at the hotel, Brae leaned ove
and faced Mr. Westwood. "I never asked you how they saic
Jennifer tried to kill herself."

"Oh yes. I'm sorry. I didn't mention it. They said she trie
to throw herself in front of a car."

Brae's forehead notched quizzically. "Where did this hap
pen?"

"Over on Fifth Avenue, somewhere near here. Just as she
was coming out of Central Park."

If a siren had been included as part of Brae's anatomy it
would have gone off. The feeling propelled him cross town
like a fire truck. But when he got to the park precinct he discovered no report of the accident had been recorded since the
jurisdiction belonged to the precinct adjacent to the park.
Cursing the red tape, Brae walked the five blocks to the mid-
eighties, where the detective on duty found the report faster
than Brae expected.

As usual the description was accurate as far as it went. But
there had been an eyewitness, one Morris Kohn, a taxi driver.
Otherwise it was pretty clear cut, except for a single factor.
The ambulance that responded to the call came from Montrose, not from one of the city's own hospitals. Brae found
that puzzling. The city was divided into special catchment
areas. The obvious hospital to respond to the emergency was
over on First Avenue, which was where an ambulance would
have been dispatched from. Why had Montrose responded,
especially to an emergency call?

Finding the cop who had handled the call was easy. Getting him to remember anything significant was more difficult. He had arrived on the scene and discovered Jennifer sprawled on the street. An ambulance had appeared before he even made the call. But that was explained by the taxi driver, who told the cop he had called his dispatcher who had phoned the hospital. Brae thanked the cop and left the precinct.

He was probably reading too much into it. The driver most likely dug into her bag and found her ID. Then he must have called Montrose. It made perfect sense. A cabbie would know how long the usual wait was for a city ambulance.

Morris Kohn was out cruising somewhere in midtown when he got the call from his dispatcher, who put Brae on the mike.

"Sure I remember," the cabbie said after Brae explained why he was calling. "Who could forget a beautiful girl like that."

"Mr. Kohn, one question. How did you happen to call Montrose?"

"Montrose? You mean the loony bin over on Roosevelt Island?"

"That's right. The woman you helped was a psychiatrist there."

"No kiddin? I didn't even know."

"You mean you didn't find her ID?"

"What ID? All I did was tell the dispatcher to dial 911. With all due respect officer, you can die in this city waiting for a cop or an ambulance. But this girl was lucky. The ambulance arrived before my guy even made the call."

"Before he made the call?"

"Yeah. In this town that's a bigger miracle than gettin' the Dodgers to come back to Brooklyn."

"Mr. Kohn. Is there anything else you remember? Anything out of the ordinary?"

"Nothin' . . . unless you count the two guys who got out of the ambulance," he said with a chuckle. "They were both a coupla a Chinese characters. And neither one of 'em knew how to speak English."

Brae knew he had to calm himself down and take a deliberate step backward. He returned to his apartment and spent the rest of the evening trying to chart a course through the jumble of information he now possessed.

Jennifer's suspicions about Dr. Freedman now took on a different coloration. There had to be more to it than mere coincidence. Both incidents had taken place in the park. Had Jennifer stumbled across something dangerous enough to be almost killed for? But Brae knew she had nothing definite to go on. Her theory was only a surmise, unless . . . With a sudden movement, Brae grabbed his jacket and tore out of the house.

Jennifer's apartment house was a toy. The pretense at security it made would not have prevented some ten-year-old burglars he had arrested. He picked the locks to the outside door in less than two minutes and let himself in. He received his first surprise when he turned the knob to her apartment. The door was unlocked. The second came when he switched on the lights. The apartment had been ransacked. Someone had gone through it with surgical precision. Drawers had been pulled open and their contents neatly stacked. Closets were gaping open. Clothes had been piled everywhere. Even the back of the TV had been opened.

Brae took a seat in the kitchen and lit a cigarette. In a strange way he felt a sense of satisfaction when he viewed the wreckage around him. It confirmed his suspicions and tied everything he was feeling with a ribbon of credibility. Jennifer had asked him to delay Dr. Boise so she could get hold of the information she was seeking from his office. He had to assume she succeeded. What else would have prompted the search? He ruled out the idea of a burglary. The timing was too improbable; besides, nothing had been taken. Everything of value was still inside. No, someone had turned her apartment upside down because they believed she possessed something incriminating, something she had almost been killed for. But why had they allowed her to live? The answer that came back caused his stomach to sicken. Was she being used in the same drug experiments she suspected the other women had been involved in?

There was another reason. It would not look particularly wholesome if two doctors in the same hospital, on the same service, had been killed within less than a month of each other. This way no one's suspicions would be aroused. They would feel safe, whoever they were. Brae wanted that feeling to continue.

Telling Frank about his suspicions became another ordeal.

His partner faced him with a sour expression of disbelief when they met the following morning for breakfast in an East Side deli Brae knew Frank liked.

"So what do you think?" Brae said after he concluded his presentation.

"You want to know what I think?" Frank said over his pastrami sandwich. "I think it's you who's having delusions."

"You mean none of this adds up?"

"I'm trying to tell you, go slow. You went through a pretty rough time. What are you trying to do to yourself?"

"Frank, look, it doesn't work that way. A breakdown isn't like having the flu or getting over an operation and having to take it easy. I got myself wound up over Mercedes. Now I'm unwound."

"You call this unwound? Fine. You're unwound."

"Frank, I'm fine." Brae insisted.

"But you're still seeing a shrink."

"Sure. There are lots of things I've still got to find out about myself. But that has nothing to do with Jennifer. Why can't you understand that?"

Frank looked at him skeptically. "Jennifer, huh? Nice. Very nice. What were you two doin' on that couch?"

"Cut the bullshit, Frank! This is for real. This girl is in a mess she can't get herself out of. Someone inside that hospital is screwing around with her mind. Don't you understand that?"

"I think something is fucking around with yours. Is that straight enough for you—or maybe I should lead a SWAT team in a full-scale assault on this Dr. Kessler's research center, drag the girl out, and call a press conference. I'll tell 'em the girl who's crazy isn't crazy, it's the doctor who's crazy."

In a low tone Brae said, "Maybe someone will have to do just that." Then he stared at Frank with a neutral expression. "Thanks for the trust, partner."

Frank leaned across the table, placing his hand on Brae's arm. "That's wrong and you know it. Because I'm your partner I'm telling you to go slow. Lay off this crap. Take care of yourself first. And don't do nothin' you'll regret later."

Brae took a deep breath and tried to smile. "Sure, Frank. I read you. Don't worry I'm not going bananas again."

Frank nodded but the worry in his eyes expressed a different opinion.

After parting with Frank, Brae walked back to his appointment with Dr. Arbus. Most of the session was devoted to exploring Brae's childhood, which relieved him of having to spill what was really absorbing his mind.

When Brae left the analyst's office he took the bus cross town and entered the Carlyle, where he contacted Jennifer's parents on the house phone. They had spent the morning at the hospital in a special session with Dr. Boise and Dr. Kessler. In a tremulous tone, Jennifer's father told Brae they had given their permission for Jennifer to enter Dr. Kessler's research center.

Brae's insides tightened, remembering Jennifer's fears for the women who had been admitted there. He paused and decided against informing Jennifer's parents of his suspicions. They were too disturbed. Besides how could he tell them their daughter might be the victim of the very people they had entrusted with her care? And coming from a recently released mental patient, the information might carry less than full weight.

Leaving the hotel, Brae felt the first real bite of fear. Jennifer's confinement drew a band of tension around his chest. He suddenly became flooded with the same fear Jennifer had expressed, about the interval between the time the patient first showed delusive symptoms and the moment when the symptoms became permanent. If the same drugs were being used on her, then how much time had actually been lost? He could no longer delay. If he was going to do anything, it had to be now.

TWENTY-ONE

Brae made half a dozen circuits around the research center before he took a seat on the low stone wall bordering the river. He lit up and scanned the fence that surrounded the building. Spotlights were situated every few yards. The fence itself was wired so that any weight, no matter how insignificant, would trigger an alarm. Closed-circuit cameras scanned the area from concealed locations beneath the molded concrete ring that edged the dome. The exit doors were sealed tight and anyone trying to gain entrance through the front had to pass through a double set of glass doors into an enclosed lobby. There was a service entrance, but that too was carefully protected.

Brae considered the possibility of the glass-enclosed walkway, but that also seemed impossible. That was when he noticed the green garbage truck pull up to the gate.

The driver leaned out and spoke into an intercom fixed on a pipe in front of the gates. A buzzer sounded and the gates opened electronically. The truck started down a ramp beneath the building.

Brae moved quickly, taking up a position beside the fence that enabled him to observe the truck's progress. The ramp led down to a concrete driveway beneath the center's main level. The truck's hydraulic system lowered an empty disposal container to the ground. Then the driver got out and began climbing a metal ladder to a catwalk that bridged the three

waste containers positioned beneath the building and connected to it by three metal chutes.

Brae realized the chutes were actually three metal tubes
that funneled down beneath the center to feed the disposal
units. It was a distinctive feature; he had never seen a setup
quite like this one before. The sanitation truck could drive
into position below the main level and all the driver had to
do was disconnect a full container and replace it with an
empty one by merely unlocking one of the chutes.

It seemed fairly obvious that the waste system formed a
kind of bowels within the building, funneling garbage down
through the chutes to the disposal containers underneath.
Brae could see that the tubes were wide enough for a man to
crawl through. All he had to do now was to confirm the en-
gineering fact, and if his guess was correct, he had just found
a way inside.

Frank Richie was worried. And he was a man who did not
like to worry. But the claw that gripped his chest like an attack of heartburn could not be ignored. His conversation with
Brae had circulated in his mind for the last twenty-four
hours, bringing alternating waves of concern and guilt. Brae
had wanted his trust and he had responded like a prick, giving advice instead of understanding.

Frank had tried calling Brae to make amends but the
phone had not been answered. As the hours passed, Frank
felt more and more irritation. *Where the hell was he?* Out
gallivanting, screwing some broad most likely. But even as he
thought it, Frank knew he was wrong. Brae's words came
back to haunt him again and again.

Someone will have to do just that. . . .

Just what? Break in to the hospital and . . . and then?
Frank's mind refused to churn out the possibilities. Brae knew
better, reason informed him. Brae was the best and the
brightest. He would never act out of some rash misbelief. But
Brae had just been discharged from a loony bin. Frank
remembered the pretty doctor's words about his medication.
Once they had you hooked on that you were capable of anything.

Frank fidgeted in his swivel chair in the detective's room.
Then he went out to the coffee machine, remembered how
lousy it usually was, and crossed the street to the coffee shop

that serviced the precinct. He plopped down some change while he made some meaningless chatter with the counterman. Then he picked up his container and a danish. He was two steps through the door when the counterman shouted that they had just gotten the evening papers. Frank shook his head. He had enough on his mind without the rest of the cockeyed world burning its usual holes in his brain. But habit won out and he could not resist a quick glance at the headlines.

The words struck his mind with the force of a bazooka.

MONTROSE . . . KESSLER . . . NITHOLIN . . .

The ice-cold claw vised his heart. *"Oh Jesus . . ."* he whispered. What if Brae . . . ? But the thought was never completed. He dodged across the street toward the gray-walled police station at full speed. He had to move fast, as much for the safety of the hospital and its personnel as his unbalanced partner. Frank could no longer ignore his instincts. He knew exactly what Brae was about to do.

The stench within the waste container was almost more than Brae could stand, even with nose plugs. The container had been hosed down and was still dripping when he broke into the private sanitation hauler's lot and secreted himself inside. But the stink would not wash away. It had seeped into the texture of the metal itself.

Brae cursed repeatedly as the truck slammed its way over the no-man's-land of potholes most city streets had become. He made the trip crouched in a corner, seated on the equipment he had purloined from the Police Property Office, with his arms braced against the walls.

Brae was dressed in dark gray coveralls over which he had strapped a special climbing harness. A battery pack was concealed in a small knapsack on his back. Its terminals connected to wires that had been strung along his arms and ended at his wrists where they were fastened by tape to his skin. When he was ready, he would connect the terminals to the electro-magnetic disks he would use to raise himself along the center's metal chutes.

The idea had not been his. It belonged to an ingenious gang of gem thieves who had used the magnetic gadget to gain entry through the ventilating system of an office building from which they stole over a million dollars in uncut diamonds. One of the gang members had been a junkie and it was through exploiting his compulsive needs that Brae had been able to crack the case. The gang members had pleaded guilty to lesser counts and their equipment, no longer needed as evidence, had been sealed in the vaults of the property office where Brae had resurrected it.

The truck jolted to a stop and Brae braced himself. He had no idea how long it would normally take for the truck to drive from the lot to the center. A stop meant either a traffic light or a stop sign or just stalled traffic. Brae did not expect the sharp downward turn when the truck started up again. He tumbled off his perch and rolled to the other end of the container before the truck leveled off beneath the research center itself.

Brae moved quickly. He picked up the disks and connected them to the wires on his wrists. Then he turned the current on. He placed the disks against the roof and felt the powerful tug as metal joined metal. Then he drew himself up as close to the roof as possible, so he would not be seen by the driver when he opened the specially fitted hatch and connected it to the chute descending from the hospital.

A series of bone-shattering jolts kept Brae informed of their progress. First the hydraulic lifted the container off the truck and dropped it to the concrete driveway. Then it was wheeled into place beneath one of the chutes. Brae heard the clatter of work shoes on metal as the driver climbed to the catwalk and opened the hatch. Brae held his breath, curled up as far in the corner as possible. His arms strained to hold the rest of him as close to the roof as he could.

The driver seemed to take an age adjusting the chute and fitting it into the hatch. Brae was not prepared for a small avalanche of waste that shot into the container when the protective grating covering the chute was opened. All of it was from the kitchen and Brae realized his climb would be less than pleasant. The hatch was finally fitted around the chute but Brae waited until the driver scampered back down the ladder before he lowered himself to the floor. Checking his watch, he realized he still had several more hours before nightfall.

Brae had decided to wait until evening before making his ascent. No matter how watchful its security normally was, all institutions followed similar patterns, and Brae had been on enough stakeouts to come to believe in this maxim. Night brought a slowing down of all activity. It was the one chance he had of not being seen in the corridors when he finally emerged from the disposal system.

He would have preferred getting the building's plans, but there had been no time for that. Besides, he had a feeling that the architect's plans on file downtown, would have been changed in the final days of construction especially since security was such a factor. Accurate plans provided easy access for thieves, a fact security people were well aware of. They would have made enough subtle changes to render inaccurate any plan already available. He would just have to take his chances and pray.

The next few hours were among the most unpleasant in his life. Boredom came with the territory in a stakeout, but this time he had to deal with the continuous downpour of swill, which soon filled the bottom of the container to the level of his knees. Along with the unbearable odor and the physical discomfort came an even greater mental worry. What if he were already too late? What if Jennifer's mind had been turned into the permanent nightmare she most feared? He tried to fight the image but it had already poisoned his mind. He had to repeatedly restrain himself from moving before he had planned. The burning in the pit of his stomach would not go away. If they had hurt her in any way, damaged her mind so that she was no longer the woman he knew, then the automatic he carried in his coverall pocket would be the means of his revenge. What he had once fantasized about Mercedes' killers would now become a reality.

Brae had discarded the pills he had been supplied with when he left Montrose. Now he cursed himself for not bringing them. As the hours passed, the level of his own anxiety began to rise. Sweat poured off his body, less from the heat inside the container than the waves of stress that rocked him. The ordeal he had just come through had weakened him and suddenly he could feel just how much. Now he began to doubt his ability to face the ordeal to come. *Move, you bastard*, he screamed inside. But time remained still. Every minute became a torture, every hour a special ordeal, until he leaned his head back and slipped into a dark and fitful slumber.

He awoke in a choking collar of his own sweat. It was pitch-black inside the container. Reaching into the outside pocket of his coveralls he fished out a penlight and aimed it at his watch. It was after eleven. He had missed his mark by one hour. It was time to move.

Brae got up and positioned himself beneath the chute, which opened above him like some monstrous mouth. For an instant he froze, listening to his own rapid breathing. He felt the same kind of fear that confronted him each time he had to face a locked door behind which some freak might be waiting with a drawn gun.

Okay . . . up you go.

Each magnetic plate had been fitted with an on-off switch that operated with the pressure of his thumb. It had been well engineered. Brae raised the disks above his head and slid them into the chute. He pressed the switch and felt the instant pull of metal wedding metal. It worked. He pulled himself up and began to climb.

It was nowhere near as easy as he had imagined. Slime coated the chute, making the magnets slip. Luckily, the chute was just wide enough to allow him to wedge his back against one side and his feet against the other while he doubled up his knees and shimmied up. He managed to reach the kitchen level in less than five minutes. The hatch had been locked. Brae prayed the other waste doors had been left open as they were in other hospitals or he would have to cut his way through with the acetylene torch he carried in his knapsack.

He flashed the light over his head. Above he could see where the main chute branched out in several directions. He heard the scrape of metal and doused the light. A door slammed shut and a shower of wet cotton rained down. That meant the hatches were open. So far so good. Brae sucked in and began climbing again, pausing at the main junction before deciding to take the left-hand route. He squeezed himself into the smaller chute and struggled to place one disk over the other and haul himself up.

The going was slower and more arduous because of the narrow space. Sweat rolled down and blinded him. He felt that the tunnel would close in on him but fought the claustrophobia and continued toward a tiny crack of light above.

He reached it and gently pushed the hatch open. He could see the ceiling of the corridor overhead. That bothered him.

He was hoping the hatches would be inside closets as they were in other hospitals. Now he had to pray no one came along the corridor while he hoisted himself out.

He twisted around until he could ease himself out backward. Pushing with the back of his head, he edged the hatch open all the way. Fortunately it was large enough to accommodate his shoulders. Lifting his head slightly, he was able to see the corridor in both directions. He had come out in some kind of administrative area. A row of doors faced him on both sides, with the usual set of double doors at either end. The doors had no windows which meant he would have to take a chance no one came through while he was emerging.

All right pal . . . it's now or never. . . .

Brae tensed and raised his arms over his head, using the wall above as leverage to draw the rest of his body out of the chute. The process became an agony. Brae had to wriggle out far enough to turn around. With the cutting edge of the hatch in his guts, he struggled to reach the floor with his hands and tumbled out of the swivel door.

The corridor was silent except for the electrical hum of the ventilating system. Brae raised himself and gently closed the hatch above his head. Then he rose and moved stealthily toward one end, hugging the walls as closely as he could. He slid the disks into the knapsack and opened the zipper of his coverall pocket. Reaching inside, he eased off the safety on the weapon but did not draw it.

He reached the double doors and carefully eased them open just wide enough to see through. The area beyond looked identical and as deserted. Brae continued through the doors and crossed the corridor toward a turning. Ten yards beyond the angle he saw another set of doors. When he reached them he realized they were locked.

Using a burglar pick he teased the tumblers open, tensing against the possibility of an alarm. But none went off.

Brae squeezed through the door and froze. He had entered an immense space, shrouded in semidarkness. Light cut through the gloom from several sources above. A row of metal arches faced him, supporting what looked like an elevated subway train made of a continuous tube of tinted glass. Brae darted beneath the supports and glanced around.

The tube continued in a circle beneath a huge dome. What he first took to be separate cars were actually chambers in which he could see figures moving. A ramp connected the tube to a circular platform in the center on which he made out a strange-looking contrivance from which hoses dangled like vines. Brae realized the ramp was motorized and could connect each of the chambers to the center platform mechanically. At the moment, the ramp was positioned opposite the large plate-glass window of a nurses' station. Brae made out several figures in blue uniforms moving back and forth. Beside the station was another set of double doors that seemed the only other way out of the area.

Brae began moving toward it when he saw the woman.

She stood revealed in the glow of light like something from another galaxy. Her head was completely shaved. But that was not what startled him. With a shock he realized that her skull had been fitted with metal disks, each the size of a quarter. Imprinted on her face was a look of horror that made him recoil. Her eyes bulged hypnotically, fixed on the machine in the center of the floor, while her fingers twisted around the flesh of her skull trying to pull imaginary strands away from her face. Brae stared at the gleaming injectors at the end of each rubber hose, remembering what Jennifer had told him. Then he understood.

"My God," he hissed, feeling his gorge rise in outrage. His heart began pumping hard, as the woman's face became Jennifer's. But it was not Jennifer . . . yet she was here. *She had become their victim.*

Frenzied, Brae moved from one support to the other, scanning the face in each of the chambers. On each he saw the stamp of a living nightmare. The horror of their ordeal resounded inside him with increasing force. *Where was she . . . what had they done to her. . . ?*

Only when he returned to the set of doors behind the supports did Brae realize Jennifer was not there. Then where was she?

Brae recrossed the area until he stood in the shadows beneath the ramp below the nurses' station. He used the metal ladder to climb to the main level and crawled on his hands and knees to the edge of the wide plate-glass window and peered inside. Three nurses were working at different tasks. All of them were Oriental. A large chart covered one wall. Brae could make out the list of names he assumed were the names of the patients housed in the glass compartments. On the last line he saw Jennifer's name.

Leaning back, Brae forced air into his congested lungs, trying to clear his head of the turmoil of aroused emotions. *All right, think!* Jennifer's name was on the list, which meant she was already housed in one of the compartments or was about to be. The latter seemed more plausible when he glanced inside again. He noticed there were no notations beside her name, as was the case with the others. Only a printed label too far away to read.

Obviously she was housed somewhere else in the center. But where? That was when he remembered the wheeled cart containing each patient's record. They had one in Montrose. They would have one here. Craning his neck, he darted a glance inside. The records' cart was positioned in the center of the station. Each record was contained in a metal binding with the patient's name lettered on a band of adhesive tape along the spine. Jennifer's was on the bottom.

Brae knew he had to get inside. The book would tell him where she was. But first he had to get the nurses out. Desperate, he shot a glance around. For the first time he noticed the small circular platform that ran around the inside of the glass tube fenced by a slender metal rail. The rail had regular openings in front of the door to each compartment.

Brae glanced back inside the station. The women were preoccupied with their tasks. Crouching, he darted across the ramp and began making a circuit of the ring. As he passed each cubicle he turned the handle and opened each glass door. Recrossing the ramp, he flattened himself beside the double doors alongside the nurses' station and waited. It did not take long.

One of the nurses put away a sheaf of papers and glanced outside. Brae could see the shock register on her face as she saw patient after patient moving through the open doors and begin wandering along the platform outside their compartments.

Two nurses burst through the doors immediately. The third grabbed a red telephone and began shouting into it. She slammed down the phone and raced after the other two. When she charged through the double doors, Brae ducked behind her and slipped inside.

Dropping below the level of the window, he reached the

wheeled table and drew it back behind a desk. He pulled out
Jennifer's book and opened it. But it was blank. None of the
pages had been written in. Brae felt a tiny surge of fear.
What if they . . . ? He did not have time to complete the
thought. His eye had moved to the label on the wall. Beside
Jennifer's name were the words STAGE I SURGERY. And a notation listing the date and time. Ten P.M. Checking his watch
Brae realized the date was today. Surgery had begun over an
hour ago.

Fighting the waves of panic traveling through him, Brae
scrambled toward the door. He heard the rush of footsteps as
orderlies and nurses charged by into the dome. Peering
through the windows, he could see that several of the patients
had become violent and were struggling with the nurses in the
narrow space of the platform.

Brae waited a moment before slipping back through the
door into the corridor outside. An elevator faced him. The
light above it signaled it was moving to his floor. In seconds
it would open, trapping him.

He glanced around desperately and saw a triangular red
light over a door in the center of the corridor. It had to be a
fire exit. Brae crossed the hall in two steps and seized the
handle. Opening it, he faced a fire stairs. He hesitated only a
moment, then closed the door behind him and charged down.
He had to reach the operating room, but where was it?
Think! He was on the dome level. The operating room had to
be on one of the two floors below. Brae ruled out the first
floor. At the second level he reached for the handle and
pulled open the door. The latch clicked and a beeping sound
filled the stairwell. He had set off an alarm.

Brae barreled into the corridor, drawing the .45 from his
pocket.

The corridor went on endlessly, past the locked doors of
various hospital departments. His heart pounded. His vision
blurred.

Where was it? It had to be here. He had to reach it before
. . . Then he saw the closed-circuit cameras above each set
of double doors. They had already discovered his presence.
The beeping filled his brain like a pulse.

He raced past a room marked RECOVERY. Then a room
filled with X-ray equipment. Beside it was a window opening

on a view of metal sinks. A sign faced him on the next set of double doors. OPERATING SECTION—NO ADMITTANCE.

Brae burst between them.

A red light flashed above a metal door. Brae kicked it open and propelled himself inside.

A figure in a green surgical gown turned toward him, trying to block his entrance. Brae lowered his shoulder. He felt bone crunch against flesh before he sent the man toppling.

The figures beside the operating table looked up. Brae could see surprise in their eyes. Then he saw Jennifer.

She was lying on the operating table, surrounded by the surgical team. Her eyes were closed. A rubber mask was about to be fitted over her face. Her head had been completely shaven and the skin marked with some kind of ink. Brae could see the indications for each of the metal plugs. They were about to transform her into one of the zombies on the floor above.

"Don't touch her," Brae warned. His voice was a shout and a command.

Confused glances passed between the team. One of them stepped foward.

"Who are you?" he demanded without removing his mask. "How dare you come barging in here?"

"I'm a cop, doctor, so step away from the table, nice and easy."

The doctor stepped backward. "You're interrupting a crucial operation that may save this woman's life."

"Shut up, you son of a bitch!" Brae spat. "I know exactly what's going on here."

The doctor pulled his mask away from his face and Brae recognized Dr. Kessler. All the others in the room were Oriental.

"Please let me explain. My name is Dr. Kessler."

"I know who you are. I want you to get her off that table."

"That's impossible. She's unable to move."

"Can she hear us?"

"Yes. But you must understand—"

"Shut up." Brae commanded, taking a step closer to the table and waving the others away. He was holding the weapon in both hands straight in front of him with elbows locked.

"Jennifer, listen. It's Brae. Hang in there. I'm getting you out of this."

He caught the glimmer of metal out of the corner of his eye an instant before pain jolted through him. Wheeling, he fired point-blank. The green-clad Oriental flew backward, crashing into the anesthetic console.

A scalpel was sticking out of his arm. Brae pulled it out and sent it clattering across the floor.

"You're hurt," Kessler said. "Let me help you." He started to take a step closer. Brae spun around, pointing the gun at his chest. "Don't fucking move."

"But you're bleeding."

"You should be used to a little blood by now, doctor. Now get that table over here." Brae motioned toward the gurney positioned against the rear wall of the operating theater.

Kessler moved toward it. His eyes were filled with fear. "What are you going to do?"

"I'm not going to do anything." Brae snapped. "You're going to get Jenny onto that table. Now!"

Kessler's eyes darted toward the team. He motioned with his hands and two nurses stepped to the side of the operating table while Kessler himself drew the wheeled gurney over. Gloved hands slid Jennifer from one table to the other. Then the nurses stepped away.

"We're going to take a little stroll. All three of us."

Kessler's eyes widened. "You don't know what you're saying. You'll never get out of here. Don't you hear the alarm? They already know you're here."

"That's all right, Doc. I've got you to protect me." Brae turned to the others. "On your faces," he ordered.

"Do as he says," Kessler commanded. "These are skilled surgeons. Don't shoot."

The team dropped facedown to the floor, with their hands stretched in front of them.

Brae crossed the floor and shoved Kessler against the table. He kicked the brake on the wheels. "Now push."

Kessler grabbed the end of the gurney and shoved from behind as Brae guided it toward the doors.

He pushed it open slowly and darted against the opposite wall. The alarm was still screaming. But the corridor was empty. Brae assumed security was still preoccupied with the women upstairs.

"Okay, out," he commanded.

With Kessler pushing from the rear, Brae drew the gurney through the door and toward the bank of elevators. He glanced back at Jennifer. Her face was immobile but her eyes were open.

"It's going to be okay," he whispered. "We'll make it."

"You don't know what you're doing," Kessler said forcefully. "This woman is schizophrenic. Only my treatment can prevent her from permanent insanity."

"Bullshit! She's this way because you made her this way. Save your speeches."

"You don't understand. You're jeopardizing years of research."

Brae glanced up. A light was approaching the second floor. Brae took a step back and jammed the .45 into the small of Kessler's back.

The elevator doors opened. Two security men stepped out. They saw Kessler and stopped.

"Let us pass," Kessler said. "This man is armed. He's already shot one doctor."

The security men stepped aside.

"On your knees, assholes," Brae ordered.

The security men knelt, facing the wall.

"Okay. Inside."

Kessler pushed and the table rolled into the elevator. Brae shoved Kessler in and pressed "one." The doors closed and the elevator began its descent. Seconds later it stopped.

"They've cut the power." Kessler said.

"So I see."

"You'll never get out of here." Kessler's voice sounded desperate.

"Maybe."

Brae stepped over to the control panel and shrugged off his knapsack. From the side compartment he extracted a screwdriver and began unscrewing the panel. Blood from the scalpel wound began covering his hand as he worked. The pain had deadened, probably from the shock. That was an asset Brae was thankful for.

"You've got to listen to me," Kessler pleaded. "You'll never get out of here alive. Too much is at stake. Millions have been invested in my research."

"We're getting out of here, doctor. You're my insurance policy. You're their investment."

"You don't understand these people," Kessler said harshly. "They can't allow their position to be endangered. The repercussions would be devastating. They'll kill us first."

Brae dropped the panel to the floor and reached inside. He found the mechanism he was looking for and they began a gravity descent.

"I'm begging you to reconsider. You said you're a policeman. Think about this. If you leave now I will personally guarantee your freedom. I'll go outside with you. You can name your price."

"Do you really believe that crap, doctor?"

"I'm giving you my word." Kessler's face was red. His eyes were bulging. "Dr. Westwood made the mistake of prying into something much too dangerous for her to know. I kept her alive. In here she'll be safe. I don't know what your relationship is, but you'll get over it. You'll have enough money to do whatever you want. Go wherever you choose."

"Do you think your people would ever allow that?"

"Yes. Because you don't know anything."

"How do you know I don't?"

"Because I know what she knew. Save yourself! Let me call them," Kessler said reaching for the phone.

"Put it down, doctor." Brae said evenly. He raised his weapon. Kessler dropped his arm.

"You've doomed us. You fool. You stupid fool. You don't even know what you're doing. How much of the future you're affecting."

"If it's anything like the horror you've created under that dome of yours, then the future deserves to die right here."

Kessler put down the phone and the elevator jerked to a stop.

Brae pushed Kessler face forward against the wall, then he bent over Jennifer. "I'm going to get you out of this, now."

Jennifer began blinking her eyes. Brae could see she was responding. She understood.

"I know you understand. No matter what happens, you won't be like the others," Brae whispered.

Brae slid his arm around her and gently eased her off the table and onto the floor, drawing up her legs so she was placed as protectively as possible in the corner beside the door.

"I love you," he said softly.

Brae rose and reached inside the panel. He turned off the lights.

"What are you doing?" Kessler cried in a terrified voice.

"Shut up," Brae said, stepping to Kessler's side. The doctor's panic was almost visible. Brae could feel his tension building unbearably. Brae knew the kind of desperation Kessler felt, hurtling him toward a final loss of control. But before the doctor could act, Brae snapped the door release and jerked Kessler down. Brae crouched behind him, extending the gun over Kessler's shoulder.

"What are you doing?" Kessler cried. "You can't open the doors, they'll kill us!"

"Not when they see you." Brae whispered through clenched teeth.

"You don't know what you're saying. You don't understand!"

The doors slowly opened.

They faced the main lobby. Three security men stood in front of the double doors, watching the area outside. They had not expected the elevator to move.

"Don't shoot!" Kessler shouted.

The security men wheeled around, reaching for their weapons. Brae recorded the startled looks on their faces before he fired.

One guard flew backward, taken off his feet by the force of the shell. The second guard clutched his chest and crashed across the gleaming counter.

Before Brae could stop him, Kessler knocked his arm aside and rushed toward the doors. "Don't shoot! I'm Dr. Kessler!"

The third guard's arm wavered. Brae could see the fear and confusion in the man's face, caught between his orders to kill Brae and his desire not to harm Kessler.

Brae shifted toward cover against the corner edge of the elevator, his gun arm extended.

The guard fired. The bullet pinged against the metal above Brae's head.

Kessler waved his arms frantically, his body blocking Brae's field of fire.

"Don't shoot!" Kessler screamed.

The guard panicked, firing point-blank. The first shell caught Kessler in the temple directly above his right eye. The second drilled his cheek.

Kessler tumbled headlong. His legs crumpled beneath him as the momentum hurled his heavy body into the startled security man.

Brae fired twice. The guard fell sideways, striking the polished floor with his head. His weapon clattered across the gleaming expanse of marble.

Scrambling across the floor, Brae reached the doors and turned. The closed-circuit camera faced him above the counter. Brae cupped his wrist, aimed, and blew the lens to pieces.

Brae tried the doors but they were locked. He knew he had only seconds to search for the keys before the area would be filled with security. But none of the dead guards whose pockets he searched had a set.

He sprinted back to the open doors of the elevator. Jamming the .45 back into his coverall pocket, he eased the gurney out and positioned it in front of the first set of glass doors. Leaning back with his feet off the floor he shoved as hard as he could, propelling the heavy cart toward the doors.

The glass splintered but did not shatter. Brae pulled the table back and shot it forward again. This time large chunks of glass fell to the floor. Now the second set of doors faced him. But the entrance was too narrow for the gurney. In desperation, Brae aimed and fired the rest of the clip. The plate glass filled with spiderwebs but failed to shatter.

An electric buzzer sounded.

Brae skidded back to the elevator, ejecting the spent clip as he ran and shoving a new one into the handle.

He knelt beside the elevator doors and waited. His chest was pumping furiously. His temples hammered with the knowledge that they would never get through the second set of doors. Their only chance would be to hold them off until morning.

Brae knew it was a vain hope. They could come at him from both sides through the double doors at each end of the waiting area. A single shell ricocheting off the inside of the elevator could be as fatal as a direct hit.

They were finished. It was only moments before they would rush him. Brae heard the sound of shuffling behind the doors. He watched one set begin to open before he fired two blind rounds. Then he ducked inside and slid his hand inside the panel. The elevator doors closed.

Brae dropped to his knees beside Jennifer. He turned her head to face him. "Sorry about not waiting those sixty days. I guess I just got impatient. You don't have to laugh. I'll do that for both of us. Anyway the nice thing about this is you can't say no."

He leaned closer and kissed her. He could feel a slight response. When he pulled back, he saw that her eyes were wide open.

The sound of gunfire penetrated through the door like muffled explosions. Brae scrambled to his knees and pressed his ear to the door.

"Nice little trap we're in," he muttered, moving back so that his body shielded hers. He raised his weapon and waited. In the darkness he might be able to get off a few shots before they zeroed in on where he was.

He felt his heart beat, quieter than before. He felt strangely calm. He traced his finger across her face. When it reached her lips, he felt them move and he smiled. He leaned over and kissed her again. The tremor of response was all he would ever need.

"Listen, you goddamn hardheaded son of a bitch. Don't shoot. I'm going to open the door." The voice was muffled but it was still recognizable.

It belonged to Frank Richie.

"Frank?" Brae uttered incredulously.

"I'm tellin' ya. Don't shoot!"

Someone pounded on the door. Brae knew they were trying to hit the emergency release. He heard a catch unlock and the door parted a few inches.

"It's Frank, you goddamn schmuck! Don't fire."

Hands clutched the edge of the doors and slowly eased them back. Light streamed inside. Brae saw Frank's scowling face and the faces of the men behind them, dressed in SWAT gear.

"What's going on out there?" Brae asked. "Barnum and Bailey in town?"

The lobby was strewn with the carnage of battle. Plate glass was scattered everywhere. Brae saw other bodies but none of them were cops.

"Are you okay?" Frank said, kneeling beside him.

"I was until I saw your face."

"Yeah, you're okay," Frank commented dryly. "Where's the doctor?" he asked, peering inside. "Oh, there she is." He turned and shouted behind him. "Hey! She's in here!"

"What are you doing here?" Brae asked.

But before Frank could answer, two men in hospital whites rushed into the elevator and knelt beside Jennifer.

Frank helped Brae to his feet and drew him outside.

"Hey. You're bleeding."

"It's not too bad," Brae said, suddenly feeling dizzy. Before he could fall, hands helped him into a wheelchair. He must have blacked out for a moment, because when he opened his eyes he found a doctor beside him, wrapping a bandage around his arm, and Jennifer back on the gurney being looked after by an ambulance team.

"You want to tell me about this?" Frank asked.

"First, is she all right?"

"The docs say she's been given some kind of anesthetic. But otherwise she looks okay. We'll know better when they take some tests. We're runnin' both of you over to New York Hospital."

"What are you doing here?" Brae asked.

"I been here since this afternoon, tryin' to keep some crazy cop from doin' somethin' he'd regret. After four hours the captain thought *I* was crazy. Then we heard the shooting and tried to talk our way in. They turned us down, which was all the invitation we needed."

"I don't get it," Brae said groggily. "How did you know I was here?"

"I didn't. But I couldn't take the chance. Here." Frank reached into the pocket of his raincoat and pulled out a folded newspaper which he thrust into Brae's lap.

Brae's eyes blurred. It took a moment to focus.

First he saw a large photo of Dr. Kessler. Above it in bold headline type were the words: NEW YORK DOCTOR WINS NOBEL PRIZE FOR WORK WITH NEW DRUG.

Brae leaned his head back and stared at the ceiling. He had a feeling he was about to begin writing a great many detailed reports. It looked like his vacation had just come to an end.